ALSO BY
SUE CHAMBLIN FREDERICK

The Juan Castillo Spy Series

The Unwilling Spy

Madame Delafloté, Impeccable Spy

The Ivy Log Series

Grandma Takes A Lover

The Boardinghouse—Return To Ivy Log

EverSweet

Visit the author at:

www.suechamblinfrederick.com

The Front Porch Sisters

The Front Porch Sisters

A Novel

SUE CHAMBLIN FREDERICK

ACKNOWLEDGMENTS

A small town in the south is like a goldmine. Full of shiny nuggets of laughter, love and friendship, Pinetta, Florida, sits at the top of Florida, in the rolling hills of Madison County. I discovered Pinetta was painted by some very colorful brushes while interviewing the fine folks who live there.

My heartfelt thanks to Mary Nell Washington Goff, a most delightful Pinetta native who remembered 1956 like it was yesterday. Dale Gibson, a farmer, whose knowledge you'll find throughout the book. Bill, Sam, and Mike Washington, brothers who provided much humor on almost every page. Sandra Chamblin, a woman who lives and breathes her Pinetta roots as proudly as anyone I know.

CHAPTER ONE

She had no idea why most everyone thought she was a hard woman. There had been times when she'd look in the mirror searching for a clue of some kind, a sign that said *watch out for this woman, she will kick your ass.* It didn't matter how long she stared at her image; she saw nothing that was slap-you-in-the-face, unmistakable, rock-hard meanness. Perhaps, when she wasn't looking, a sign had been taped to her back that said, 'Beware: Hard Woman.'

Then, one day, she figured it out. It was a simple thing, right there in front of her, sitting on the opposite end of the almost endless front porch. Delicate and pretty. Not one single flaw that she could see. All softness, nothing hard to be found, except maybe the black bible she held in her hands. Her sister Jewell. It was obvious she'd never hold a candle to her. Stand the two sisters side by side and there it was, just as obvious as warts on a nose. And that was their life together: hard and soft, tough and tender.

When stars appear in the night sky high above the fields of Madison County, the starlight seems to fall the brightest along the Withlacoochee River, then across the Bellville road before settling quietly on the rooftop of the Donnelly's grand house and its magnificent front porch.

No one could really remember precisely when it all began: the importance of the porch. It was as though its roots were entrenched before the birth of time; the porch façade of faded white boards seeming to wear an expression that fell somewhere between slumber and the prick of a thorn, reminding one of the memories that had been created there, under its sloping roof and where jasmine twisted wildly around the white columns.

There was no doubt that the porch was the soul of the rambling house, its heartbeat lasting at least until the Rapture or maybe even beyond. The porch heard and knew everything; tears, cussing and maybe even lovemaking in the cypress swing with the creaky chain.

The porch ran east and west, all fifty feet of it shaded by hundred-year-old oak trees that promised cool afternoons during the furnace heat of a Pinetta summer. The distance between the two ends of the porch might as well have been to the moon and back— each end separate from the other and divided by the differences of the two Donnelly sisters.

In its heyday, the long porch, studded with rockers like jewels on a crown and swings built from pond cypress, sagged with the onslaught of Sunday afternoon visitors who drank iced tea and ate Edith Donnelly's famous buttered rum pound cake. The women, frilly church hats flopping on their heads, chatted non-stop about the canning of tomatoes and green beans, while the men leaned on the porch railing and smoked their cigars or chewed tobacco, all the while worried if it would rain on their newly-planted tobacco fields.

But, that was then, and the echoes of those times lingered quietly in the nearby Mt. Horeb cemetery, where folks from as far back as 1700 lay in their final resting place, not far from the dark waters of the Withlacoochee.

"Well, I do believe we've got company." Jewell Donnelly leaned forward in her freshly painted Adirondack chair, a chair surrounded by her daily life, a life broken up into piles of lovely books, dainty teacups and the distinction of being one of Madison County's most beautiful women. "I can't imagine who it is."

From the other end of the porch, nestled in a swing made by her grandfather and still in her faded pajamas, Essie Donnelly glanced up from her book. "Well, hell, Jewell. It's DooRay. Who else do we know with one arm and a goat pulling a cart?"

Jewell frowned. "Mama won't like that cussing, Essie."

"Mama can't hear a thing, Jewell. I told you that—she's resting over at the cemetery. Has been for over fifteen years."

The lane was about a hundred yards long from the house to the Bellville road. Made of rich dirt, some clay and a little sand, it was a straight, grassless path to one of the most elegant homes in the tiny town of Pinetta, Florida. Essie squinted and watched DooRay shamble down the lane, the goat following, pulling an empty cart. DooRay reached the edge of the yard and Essie moved to the railing, looking down at the entourage that had arrived just at the top of noon.

"DooRay, where're you going?" She eyed the goat harnessed to the cart and the rooster that sat on top of the goat's back, squatted like it was laying an egg, its pair of bright red, fleshy wattles dangling as if they were small testicles.

"Hey, Miss Essie. Miss Jewell." DooRay pulled the hat from his head and fanned himself. "I reckon I'm going on over to Clyattville."

"Clyattville? That's over eight miles. Mighty long way with those bare feet. How come you're not riding in your cart?"

DooRay grinned and looked behind him at his goat. "Murphy's mad at me right now. He won't pull me nowhere."

"How can Murphy be mad at you, DooRay?" Essie studied the white goat, the long lashes on the dark eyes silently sweeping every time it blinked.

DooRay hung his head. "Guess you hadn't heard, Miss Essie. Lightening done hit my house yesterday evenin' and burned it up into a pile of black ashes. Murphy got singed a little bit. Wasn't nothing I could do it happened so fast."

"Oh, my, DooRay. I'm so sorry. That why you're going over to Clyattville?"

Murphy stuck out his long tongue and bleated softly. DooRay scratched the top of the goat's head. "I sure am. Looks like DooRay gone live with Uncle Mustard a while."

"Uncle Mustard? Mustard Aikens? Why, I know him." Essie hurried down the brick steps into the yard, her bare feet crunching dried oak leaves. "Biggest thief there ever was. Worked for daddy one summer and stole everything he could get his hands on. Daddy shooed him off the place and told him to never come back. He's a mean rascal, DooRay. I can't believe he's your uncle, and you're gonna live with him."

3

DooRay scuffed his bare foot through the dirt and nodded. "Gots to do that, Miss Essie."

"Oh, no, you don't, DooRay. The old tack room at the side of the barn is a perfect place for you. There are a few spiders in it, but we'll clean them out. It's dry and got a door and window. There's an outhouse only a few yards away down by the tobacco barns." Essie shook her finger at DooRay. "Now, let me get a broom for you…" She stopped and looked at the one-armed DooRay. Essie's voice softened. "Gosh, DooRay. I'm sorry. I guess you can't really sweep, can you?"

DooRay threw his head back, his laughter bouncing up into the branches of the oak tree above him. "Oh, Miss Essie, DooRay can do just about anything. Why does you think I go barefooted all the time?" The skinny black man lifted his leg, pulling his foot level with his chest. "See this? This here is my missin' arm. This foot can do anything my hand can do. Why I can even put a worm on a hook with these long toes."

Essie grinned at the black man and watched as he returned his foot to the ground. "Say, DooRay. Just how did you lose your arm? You never told me, and I've known you since we were kids."

"Oh, that's a story from a long time ago, Miss Essie. A sad story. You don't need to hear no sad story." DooRay was a black man who was not whole yet deserved dignity no matter how poor or damaged the shell in which he lived. It was evident to anyone who knew him that his dignity had been polished by a lifetime of humility.

Essie's eyes held DooRay's face. It was a kind face, smooth and licorice black, his eyes even darker, eyes with wiry eyelashes that were as thick as sheep's wool. "You're right, DooRay."

Essie walked to the edge of the lane and pointed toward the open field. "It's the biggest barn—the one over there. You'll see the tack room on the north side. You pull anything out of there you need to and put it into the barn. I'll check on you later and bring you some iced tea and a sandwich."

"Yes, mam, Miss Essie." DooRay placed his hat on his head and pulled on Murphy's reins. "Let's go, Murphy. We got us a new home." The rooster squawked and dug its feet into Murphy's back, his wings flapping loudly.

When DooRay was only a few feet away, Essie hollered. "DooRay, that rooster isn't going to get into my flower beds, is he?

"Oh, no. Killer don't bother no flowers."

"Killer? Your rooster's name is Killer?"

"That's right, Miss Essie. He do likes to kill snakes. If they's a snake within a mile a this here place, my Killer will find it."

Essie stared a long time at the rooster, then at the goat, then at DooRay. The cart was empty; everything DooRay owned had burned in the fire.

CHAPTER TWO

E ssie, it's 12:00 o'clock." Jewell settled in her chair and closed her eyes. She hummed and waited for the radio program she had listened to every day for years.

"Noon?" At the other end of the long porch, Essie turned on the radio, already tuned to the a.m. station out of Madison. The Gospel Hour with Brother Wilbur and Sister Gladys had already begun. Soul stirring gospel music, sweet as honey, filled the air like a cool breeze. Jewell's worn bible lay in her lap, open and ready for the day's scriptures. The word of God drifted from the plastic radio and for a few moments pushed the devil clear back to Lon Terry's hog pens.

Essie had slipped off her pajamas and dressed in a pair of jeans and one of her daddy's old shirts. She nestled in the porch swing and opened *Peyton Place*. Hardly a moment had passed when she heard a car turn off the Bellville road and move slowly down the lane.

"Damn! That's the preacher's car." She glanced over at Jewell. "Don't you say anything, Jewell. I'll handle this." Essie turned down the radio and walked to the edge of the porch. She crossed her arms over her chest, eyeing the moving car, and waited.

The preacher—Reverend Denslow Grimes—drove a black Cadillac, the front grille heavy with chrome, the back fenders finned like a fish. The walled tires gleamed virgin white as they slowly rolled toward the large two-story Donnelly house. The preacher required a new car every year, the tithes of his parishioners paying for the indulgences of a man who felt entitled. After all, he was a man of God.

He parked near the front porch, and Essie could see his red hair through the car's window. Below the red hair was a thin face that ended in a chicken neck. Reverend Grimes opened the car door and stepped out.

"Well, good morning, Sister Essie. Sister Jewell. It's a lovely morning, isn't it?" He ran a hand over the top of his thinning hair and smiled. "Haven't seen you girls for a while."

Essie said nothing. Jewell smiled and nodded. The preacher took a step forward, a bible in his hands. "You haven't been to church for a few months now. God doesn't like His children to miss church." His perpetual grin pushed his cheeks up and slitted his eyes. In her head, Essie called him Preacher Slick. That's what he was—slick. She didn't care if he had a bible in his hands or not.

"Oh, Jewell and I haven't been missing church."

The pale, freckled face sobered. "That right?" His voice caught.

"That's right. Haven't missed a Sunday." Essie smiled an easy smile and rocked on her feet.

"What church is that?"

"Oh, over in Clyattville. Why, those folks over there take me and Jewell to Thomasville to eat at The Farmer's Market every Sunday after church. We ride the church bus and sing the whole way."

The preacher's eyes opened wider. Again, "That right?"

Essie snickered to herself. "Hmmm. Best lemon meringue pie I ever ate." She saw Pastor Grimes stiffen, his face flush.

"There's no reason to change churches, Essie." The preacher's words came out in a huff.

Essie shrunk back. "Oh? Maybe Eloise shoulda thought twice about moving Jewell to another Sunday school class."

The preacher looked away and mumbled. "Eloise was only doing the best thing for Jewell."

"The best thing for Jewell?" Essie stomped down the steps. "Here's the reason Eloise moved Jewell to another class—she wanted

7

to make sure her class won the monthly bible verse contest and got a free barbecue dinner in Madison."

Hands on her hips, Essie took a breath. "Jewell knows her bible verses better than anyone in the entire church. Just because she's slow doesn't mean she doesn't know them. Those folks in the other class are forty years older than Jewell." Essie glanced up at Jewell, then back at Reverend Grimes. "Eloise took her out of a class where all her friends were. She should be ashamed."

Pastor Grimes backed up a step. "Eloise thought Jewell would be... more comfortable in the senior class."

"Senior class? Jewell's only thirty-five years old—that's a long way from being a senior, wouldn't you say?"

"Well, now, Essie, you have to admit Jewell is a little... little more than slow." The condescending smile on the reverend's face spread wide.

Essie reached out and slapped the bible out of the pastor's thin, freckled hand. "You get outta this yard. Right now!"

The preacher leaned over and picked up his bible. His bony fingers brushed off the dirt while he leveled his eyes at Essie. The angelic smile had disappeared. "What about your tithes? Your mama and daddy were founders of the church. Before they died, they committed their monthly tithes through you and Jewell."

"Oh, now I get it. It's not about me and Jewell coming to church. It's about the money." Essie stretched out the word m o n e y as she looked over at the brand new, shiny Cadillac, then back to the expensive suit and tie, the manicured hands. "Well, well, preacher. You and Eloise make a fine pair. The preacher's wife controls the parishioners, and the preacher controls the money. I don't care if mama and daddy promised you the moon, you won't get it as long as I'm alive."

Essie huffed back up the steps and onto the porch. When she turned around, the preacher lifted his bible and slapped it with his left hand. "You are not the Christian woman you would have everyone think you are, Essie Donnelly. Eloise won't like any of this—you'll be hearing from her."

Essie stared at the bible a long time, then up to the preacher's narrow eyes. A sly grin eased over her face. "Did I mention that the Clyattville church deacons come pick us up for church if it's raining? Walk to the door with umbrellas for us?"

The pastor flung open the Cadillac's front door and slid across the leather seat. Essie noticed his face was the same color as his thinning red hair. She watched him swing the car around and head down the lane. He swerved right onto the Bellville road, kicking up dirt. The man of God may have had his face in the scriptures, but he committed deeds under some twisted interpretation of the Bible. He had hung onto God's words like a wooden plank floating in a deep ocean, yet his actions were as foul as a barrel of rotten apples.

From the other end of the porch, Jewell pressed a napkin to her lips, and her lovely green eyes turned to Essie, questioning. "Essie, I do not recall ever attending a church in Clyattville, nor eating at a restaurant in Thomasville."

Essie grinned wide at her sister. "Me, neither, Jewell. Me, neither."

CHAPTER THREE

Her radio program over, Jewell yawned. "I'm tired. I think I'll go up and nap for a while."

Essie closed her book. "What about lunch?"

"I'm not very hungry." Jewell stood from her chair and smoothed her skirt. Only five foot three, she was frail, tender like a rose petal. But, she'd always been thin. Her twice-a-year doctor visits to Tallahassee revealed nothing new: her near drowning had diminished her ability to remember some things from the past as well as infused in her a child-like behavior that betrayed the appearance of normality.

In conversation, Jewell was personable, though not analytical nor questioning. Some days her demeanor was totally ordinary; no signs of anxiety or concern for her surroundings. Other days, her mind left and her unpredictability became prevalent.

"Okay. I'll read awhile, then go out and help DooRay."

Essie removed her shoes and leaned back into the swing. *Peyton Place* had lured her into a scandalous world outside Pinetta, Florida. *Hallelujah!* The novel's characters were fiction, but they were real to Essie. In the midst of reading the story, she discovered she was a sexual being—she was not a plain farm girl from Madison County who loaded watermelons all her life.

She almost got away. Small suitcase in hand, she had arrived at the Greyhound station in Madison. She'd left her mama and daddy, her sister and the three-hundred-acre farm where she'd been born and raised. She sat on the bus an hour before its departure time and dreamed of a place far away from tobacco fields. Almost asleep in the back of the bus, she had heard someone call her name. "Essie! Essie! Come quick! Your mama's done had a heart attack."

"Mama? Mama had a heart attack?" She jumped up from her seat. "Can you take me to the hospital?"

"Hospital? No, girl. She's at the funeral home. Git off this bus right now."

Years later, she still had the bus ticket; her small suitcase lay under her bed, nothing removed. Time had stood still.

She had wanted her life to be like music, a music composed by heart and soul. Yet, she felt she had failed. Either that or she had not asked for the life she wanted in plain enough words.

On the farm, she lived her life hemmed in by fence posts and cornfields, a maize that allowed no escape, even down the long, winding Bellville road. Her dreams had gone to pieces like raindrops hitting cotton candy and left her empty. Sometimes she wished she were the rock on the end of a slingshot that would hurtle her into the Universe, then drop her across the ocean in some exotic place where there was not one damn cornstalk.

Essie heard the creak of the front-screened door. Jewell, her face distraught, had returned to the porch, wringing her hands, her shoulders slumped.

Irritated, Essie closed her book. "What's wrong, Jewell? Can't sleep?"

"There's a naked man in my bed." She hurried to her chair.

Essie sat up from the swing. "A naked man? Who is it?"

Jewell floundered and squeezed her hands. "How do I know? All I saw was his… his derrière," she replied, with a primness learned at a finishing school in Switzerland.

Essie nodded and watched Jewell's nervous hands tie knots in the sash of her dress. "I'm sure he's gone by now. Go on back up the stairs and get some rest."

Jewell hesitated. "I've never seen a naked man before."

"Me, neither. Now, go on."

Jewell reluctantly opened the screened door and disappeared. Essie listened to her steps on the stairs and leaned back into the swing. She would mention Jewell's hallucinations to Dr. Anderson on their next visit to Tallahassee.

She opened *Peyton Place* and smoothed the page. After one paragraph, the screen door opened again. Jewell stood motionless, her head dipped to her chest.

"Still there?" Essie asked.

Jewell licked her lips and nodded.

"Okay. I'll go up and ask him to leave so you can get some rest. Sit down—I'll be right back." Essie went into the kitchen and opened the refrigerator, took out some bologna and cheese. The tea pitcher was half empty, so she placed tea bags into a tin pan on the stove. When she came back out on the porch, Jewell hadn't moved. "He's gone, Jewell. Go on up."

Jewell obediently left her chair and climbed the stairs. Essie returned to the kitchen and began making sandwiches for DooRay when she heard footsteps coming down the stairs. She turned and saw Jewell shaking her head. "Still there?" she asked.

"Yes, and he rolled over and… and…. exposed himself."

"Oh, my." Essie closed the jars of mayonnaise and mustard and put them back in the refrigerator, wiping her hands on the dishtowel. "I'll be back." Frustrated, she took the stairs two at a time and left Jewell at the base of the stairs watching her.

On the landing, Jewell's room was on the right, across the hall from Essie's. Even in daylight, the landing was dim, its pine floors the color of old butterscotch. Their mother and father's room was at the opposite end of the hall where, even after their deaths, it remained pretty much the same. Essie kept their windows open, and a breeze swept down the hallway, through the landing and out the open windows in the other bedrooms. The faint fragrance of oleander and the soft light seemed reminiscent of a funeral home.

Essie stepped into the doorway of Jewell's room. Jewell's vision had not been a hallucination: stretched out on the bed, one bare foot touching the foot board and the top of his head pressed against the headboard, was an obviously tall man. And he was, indeed, naked. He lay on his stomach, his arms wrapped around Jewell's embroidered pillow, one knee pulled up toward his chest. The skin to his belt line was the color of the Withlacoochee, filtered through sunlight.

The butt that had so offended Jewell gleamed as white and smooth as the meringue on Edith Donnelly's lemon pies. For an instant, the newly discovered sexual being in Essie wanted to reach out and rub her hand across the loveliness of the stranger's perfect skin.

A pile of clothes was scattered on the floor beside the bed. Prison clothes—the kind the road crews wore. Essie stepped back into the hallway and looked down the stairs. Jewell was motionless, staring at Essie. Essie placed her finger over her lips to shush her.

"Don't go." Behind her, Essie heard soft words, almost pleading. She leaned against the wall outside the door and waited. Again, "I know you're there." Gentle words, unassuming, almost humble.

Essie faltered. Her legs jerked; she wanted to run down the stairs, call the prison farm and tell them another prisoner had escaped the Madison County road gang. But, the farm girl

who had worked in the fields all her life felt herself grow a little taller, a little meaner, her mouth puckering into a hateful sneer. "I would advise you to get your naked ass outta my sister's bed and get the hell out of here."

A quiet snicker from the bedroom. "I'd be glad to do that—just give me some clean clothes and I'll be gone."

"Really? Just like that? Oh, no. Not before I call Uncle Lester and tell him one of his inmates is hiding in my house."

"Inmate? Hiding? You tell Lester to come and get me and take me into Madison."

"You've got a lot of nerve. Who do you think you are?"

"Oh, you know me." There was laughter in his words. "And I know you." Essie heard the bed creak. If she peeked around the doorway, would he still be in bed? Or, would she see a tall, lean naked man standing in the middle of Jewell's yellow and white bedroom?

"You know me?"

Quiet laughter drifted through the doorway and into the landing. "I remember you riding the homecoming float back in '41—right there on the ball field."

Essie huffed. "You have a piss-poor memory. That was Jewell!"

A belligerent few seconds passed. "You had on a yellow dress, strapless. A pink corsage on your wrist. You were beautiful."

Yellow dress. Beautiful. Jewell was the beautiful one. Mama had sent her to a finishing school in Switzerland when she was seventeen, where she would acquire social graces, as well as a cosmopolitan aura not found anywhere in Madison County.

"Listen here, I don't know who you are, but I know one thing—

13

you're running away from the county work farm, and you've got five minutes to leave this house."

Essie stomped downstairs, each step matched with a well-chosen curse. She pushed Jewell aside and picked up the telephone. "Put me through to Uncle Lester."

A gravelly voice came through the line. "Lester Terry."

"Uncle Lester, you got another one of your prisoners over here. This is the third time this spring and—"

"It's Sam Washington, isn't it?"

"Hell, if I know, Uncle Lester. I don't care if it's the King of England—just come over and get him off my farm."

"That boy! He just had one more day of his 30-day sentence, and he would have been on his way. Dang it!" Essie could hear Lester groan. "Your mama wouldn't want you cussing like that, Essie."

"Oh, shit, Uncle Lester. I'm not the one who went to Europe to become a lady—it was Jewell. Now, get over here or I'm gonna get daddy's shotgun."

"Oh, no. Don't do that, Essie. I'll be there in ten minutes. Just have him stand out on the Bellville road."

"Don't be late." Essie slammed down the phone. *Sam Washington*— the Washington boy who went off to college and became a fancy lawyer. What was he doing on a prison work detail? She flew back up the stairs and eased to the doorway, not stepping inside the bedroom, but lingering against the wall, her fingers itching for the shotgun.

"Uncle Lester said to be out at the road in ten minutes." Her voice was a snarl.

The room was quiet. From outside the window, DooRay's voice carried high into the oak limbs. *I've got a home in glory land that outshines the sun. Do, Lord. Oh, do Lord. Oh, do remember me.* From the hallway, Essie raised her voice. "Well, you got five minutes now."

"Five minutes? Well, get me some clothes to put on—I'm not wearing that prison garb another minute. Either that or I'll walk out to the road buck naked."

"Fine with me. Parade yourself up and down the Bellville road till the cows come home."

Essie heard the bed creak, footsteps across the wooden floor. She backed down the hall, hardly breathing, and watched the doorway to Jewell's bedroom. "You got one more minute," she called, her voice shrill.

Sam Washington's lean body filled the doorway. The embroidered pillowcase—yellow daisies intertwined with pink phlox on a white background—covered him. A grinning Sam Washington casually walked down the hall—no, he didn't walk—he strutted—toward the stairs. He passed Essie without looking at her. She saw his eyes were the color of a blue jay's feather; so blue they should have been glued to the sapphire and ruby encrusted crown of a king. His shoulders were broad and muscled. As he walked away from her, there was the white butt, rounded and firm. "Bet you're lookin' at my butt," he said.

She was. Again, she realized she was a sexual being. "I'm gonna burn those damn prison clothes."

"Burn 'em," he said and walked down the stairs and out the front screen door. Essie ran to the front window of her mama and daddy's room and hollered through the screen. "You leave that pillow case on the mailbox!"

Not turning around, Sam Washington raised his hand in a wave. At that moment, Lester Terry, the superintendent of the county work farm, skidded to a halt at the end of the lane. Sam slid into the county car, and Essie could see Lester's arms waving in anger. The yellow pillowcase hung from the mailbox, a breeze flipping up the ends as if saying goodbye to the fancy lawyer from Madison.

CHAPTER FOUR

While Jewell napped, Essie carried a sandwich and iced tea to DooRay. As she walked across the yard, she heard him singing *Oh Cloudy Day*. His voice could knock finches from the sky, the words drifting through the air like butterflies in love.

The tack room, swept and somewhat organized, lay in a quiet memory. Harnesses for the horses and mules were arranged all along the walls, dormant for years—ever since Hubert Donnelly had died and the fields leased to Emmett Gaston for his peanut, corn and tobacco crops.

"You'll do just fine here, DooRay. And, I'll tell you, I'm not half as mean as Mustard Aikens."

DooRay laughed between bites of his sandwich. "That's good, Miss Essie. Yes, sir. Me, Killer and Murphy will do jus' fine out here."

"Yes, you will. You come on up to the house after a while, and we'll find you some of daddy's clothes. He wasn't as tall as you, but they'll fit. Got a bed in the barn. We'll have to put it together, but that'll be easy."

"I sure do appreciate this here place, Miss Essie. DooRay will do all he can to help you and Miss Jewell." The dark eyes shone bright, his smile came easily. "I'll catch us some fish, too. I didn't know you was so close to Grassy Pond."

DooRay stilled and seemed to study the soft white bread of his sandwich. "Miss Essie, I cooked me a buzzard one time. Stewed it with

16

some collards. It weren't too tasty, but it sure did keep my belly from shrinkin' up." He looked up at her. "This sho' is a good sandwich."

Essie smiled as her eyes traveled to the rafters. "See those old cane poles up there, DooRay? They'll catch you all the fish you can eat. I reckon those poles are fifty years old."

DooRay craned his neck and looked up. "Well, I do declare. I'll find me some hooks and head to the pond late this afternoon. I bet the bream are bitin'. Why, we'll have some fried fish for supper."

Essie tried not to look at the place where DooRay's arm had been. She couldn't imagine how he'd put a worm on a hook. She glanced at his bare feet and the toes that were used as fingers. She looked up and saw DooRay was watching her, knew what she was thinking.

With a smile, he said. "Those worms just shrivel up when they sees them big toes coming at them. They seem relieved when I slide them on a hook." His laughter was deep and rich. "Got to find some worms." he said. "They is some old rotten boards over by the tobacco barns. I bet they's some big old fat red worms under them."

Essie looked through the tack room door and eyed Murphy, unharnessed and nibbling on weeds. Killer had scratched out a hole in the dirt and fluffed his feathers as he rested only a few feet from the goat. "Murphy still mad at you, DooRay?"

DooRay grinned. "Naw. I had a long talk with him a while ago. I done told him we has a new home, and he can wander all over the place if he wants to." He pointed to a washtub under an oak tree. Clean, fresh water dribbled from the edges. "They gots good water, too."

The smells in the tack room were familiar but from long ago. Essie found herself drifting away, away to hot summers and watermelons and tobacco. Corn grew in rows a mile long, with tassels that seemed to play music in the winds that blew from the west—winds from Tallahassee, Georgia and, probably, from as far away as Alabama and Texas.

The horses and mules, whose long-empty harnesses hung in a peculiar sadness, were long gone, faded away like her mama and daddy. Things never stayed the same except maybe the dirt, the winding Withlacoochee and the hundred-year-old oaks that swept their limbs over the land and whispered secrets that only the night owls understood.

"You go get your worms, DooRay, and I'll wash up the cooker." Essie stood and picked up the tea pitcher and sandwich plate.

"Yes, mam. I'll look under them boards, then I figure I'll just get some soapy water and find a shady spot somewhere and start diggin'." He squinted at Essie. "You got some soap?"

"Sure do. Come on up to the house. There's some on the back porch by the washing machine." A small ache entered Essie's heart. Had DooRay had two hands, he would have taken life and squeezed everything he could out of it. But, a one-armed man could only pound out a life. It was, however, his large brick-like fist that harbored a simple, fundamental principle that ensured his place in the world would be filled with love and kindness. He would live his whole life by it.

Essie left the tack room, the goat, the rooster and the one-armed black man. Her steps were purposeful; she would call Uncle Lester and give him hell.

At the house, Jewell hid in her room, most certainly traumatized by the naked man in her bed; the naked man being Sam Washington, one of Paul Washington's sons. She vaguely remembered him in school; he was two years younger. She had found her 1941 high school yearbook *The Pine Trail* and there he was. A sophomore while she was a senior. Next to his picture were two words: *Naughty Boy.* Essie would agree with that statement.

"Lester Terry, please."

Lester answered his phone with a quiet demeanor. He knew it was his niece. "Lester Terry."

Essie took a deep breath and lit right in. "Uncle Lester, that's the third time this year one of your inmates has run through here on their way to the state line. They think I'll feed them and give them water after they've sloshed through the swamp and got eat up with mosquitoes. Why, I bet Jewell's bed is full of ticks."

"Now, now, Essie." Lester soothed his niece. "Those fellas ain't in here for murder or nothing. They're just in here for drinking too much alcohol or stealing a hubcap or two. Nothing to worry about."

"Nothing to worry about?" Essie shrieked. "Poor Jewell. A naked man in her bed."

"Well, Sam Washington ain't no murderer or thief."

"Who cares? He snuck in our house and slept in Jewell's bed. What are we supposed to do? Make him a peach pie?"

"Oh, Sam's a good ole boy."

"A good old boy? What was he doing in a prison work camp if he's so good?"

"Well, you know those Washington boys. They're stubborn. Sam butted heads with Judge Earp in Madison, and the judge charged him with contempt of court. Sent him to jail for 30 days or pay a $100 fine. Well, that boy wouldn't give the county a dime of his money, so he went to jail. He had only one more day to serve, and he'd a been a free man."

"Well, now, that is stubborn. One day is all?"

"'hat's right. When I picked him up in front of your place, I blasted him up one side and down the other. I asked him why he couldn't wait just one more day. You know what he told me?"

"I can't imagine, Uncle Lester," Essie said, her words dripping with sarcasm.

"Said he was sick and tired of that hard ole mattress in his cell." Lester laughed. "Guess that's why he crawled into Jewell's soft bed."

Essie puffed out a breath. "Well, what's gonna happen now? Not that I care."

"I talked with the judge this afternoon. He slapped another $100 on the original fine and said Sam would go back to jail for another 30 days if he didn't pay."

"Does Sam know?"

"No. I can't find him. I drove him over to his daddy's this afternoon so he could get some clothes. He lives in a room over the barn at the Washington farm, so he's not far."

Essie's voice softened. "Now, Uncle Lester, I want you to listen to me carefully. If one more of your inmates comes through here, I'm just gonna blow him to Kingdom come. No questions asked. So, you put the word out. No more inmates from the prison farm are allowed on the Donnelly place. Got that?"

Lester breathed heavily into the phone. "Essie, your mama and daddy sure did raise a hard girl. Why, Jewell would make them prisoners a cake and serve it with ice cream. You know most every one of them is a Madison boy, don't you?"

"I'm not Jewell, Uncle Lester," Essie said. "So, don't you be thinking I'm gonna go easy on anybody else that comes around here. Even if they're from the gates of heaven."

Lester cleared his throat. "All right, Essie. But please don't shoot nobody. I don't believe a Donnelly has ever shot a soul."

There was quiet on both ends of the line. "I've got to go, Uncle Lester." Essie paused, a slight trickle of meanness easing up her spine. "I'm going upstairs to clean all of daddy's guns." She hung up and pulled out a kitchen drawer that held a box of cartridges.

Yes, she was a hard woman. What other kind of woman could knock a rich man off a horse without so much as a howdy-do. "I don't care if you're lost or not," she had told the stranger. "Get your horse out of my tobacco field."

"To whom do you think you are speaking, farm girl?" The stranger had looked down at her, her sweaty face, her darkened and tarred hands.

Essie had taken a step forward, a light step, the kind that gave no warning of its importance. "I'm talking to the man whose horse is trampling my tobacco." She reached out and pulled his shiny boot out of the stirrup and twisted his leg so forcefully that he flipped backward off his horse. She didn't even break a sweat.

When the man stumbled up, Essie slapped the horse's rump and watched as it galloped down the wagon lane. When she turned to the shaken man, she eyed him like she was measuring him for a coffin. Snake venom poured from her words. "You trample my tobacco plants again and I'll run you all the way to the Withlacoochee."

She was a hard woman.

CHAPTER FIVE

There were three Washington boys. Sam, in the middle, was also the most adventuresome. While he loved the fields of Madison County, he knew there was more in life. It was his opinion that life had to have balance. His balance was Florida State University in Tallahassee.

He worked tobacco all summer and went back to school in September. In the end, he was a full-fledged, bona fide attorney. This was authenticated when Judge Earp asked him to take a case in Madison County. Sam had no intention of returning to Madison County after his bar exam; he felt the big-time was New York or Atlanta. He decided to take the one case; then, after it was over, skedaddle.

That was three years ago. He had remained in Madison County, the big-time merely a figment of his imagination. He also loaded watermelons on weekends. That was called balance.

At dusk, after his lewd intrusion into the home of the Donnelly sisters and hours after he told Judge Earp he'd pay the $200 fine—anything to keep away from that cell and its hard mattress—he drove through the countryside, down the Madison/Valdosta highway, crossing the Withlacoochee to Clyattville, then back into Florida. At the Mt. Horeb church, he paused alongside the cemetery. He heard music. Somehow, it seemed angels were ushering in the softness of dusk, a distinct melodic hum that levitated above the tombstones like a fine mist.

He continued down the clay road, past Ran Terry's house and

hesitated at the Bellville road. If he turned left, he'd cross the Withlacoochee for the third time that day and again end up in Georgia. Turning left would also take him to the Donnelly farm and perhaps the yellow pillowcase on the mailbox. If he turned right, he'd pass Terryville and end up in Pinetta.

As he made his decision, he watched the sun fall behind the trees in the west, an orange glow as bright as fire. After a long moment, he pulled the steering wheel left and drove in the deep ruts of the unpaved road. He drove slowly and watched for deer. Up ahead he saw the Donnelly mailbox on his left. No yellow pillowcase. He stopped and wondered if Essie Donnelly would shoot him if he drove into her yard and stepped onto her porch. Why would she shoot him? Though he wasn't exactly a gentleman earlier that morning, he certainly could be one now. He was fully dressed— underwear, socks, slacks and a pull-over shirt. He turned into the lane and took his chances.

There were no lights in the windows except for a soft glow from an upstairs bedroom. He knew the bedroom; he had just been there. After he parked, he sat a moment and watched fireflies flit here and there, sending messages: *I'm in the mood for love.* The bright dots switched on and off all along the grass and in the lower branches of the trees. His car windows were down, and the smell of the nearby fields soothed him. He would always be a farm boy.

From the porch, he heard the creak of a swing. "That you, yellow dress?" he called. He knew it was Essie and wondered if she had cleaned her daddy's guns like she had told Lester. An hour ago, Lester had told him, 'don't go near the Donnelly place.' Yet, here he was. He was certain Essie had loaded her daddy's guns.

"Is there something inside of you that likes trouble?" she asked, her voice breathy. "I assume you've come to apologize. Jewell won't ever use that pillowcase again."

Sam opened the car door and stepped into the yard. In the faint light, his eyes found her sitting on the swing. He hoped there was no gun. "That was a sorry thing I did. And, yes, I'm here to apologize."

"I accept. Now, get the hell outta here." The swing stopped moving, and he saw her stand and walk to the porch railing.

"I'm gonna do just that." He turned and walked back to his car. He then looked back to the porch. "Hey, I want to ask you something. In the high school yearbook, by your senior picture, it says: 'Scarlett Lives.' What does that mean?"

"Scarlett O'Hara in *Gone with the Wind*."

"So?"

"So, there are Scarlett's everywhere—young women who want to run away to another place. To get off the farm. Live their life somewhere else but a small town."

"You're Madison County's Scarlett? You wanted to run away, leave Madison County?"

"No, not anymore." Her words were snippy.

"Why not?" he asked through the dark, not seeing her face.

"Jewell nearly drowned; mama died. Then daddy died. And here we are. Me and Jewell and 300 acres of farmland. Couldn't very well go to Hollywood or New York City, now could I?"

From the top of an oak tree, an owl hooted. Across the field, another one answered. To the east, a late moon crept up the sky and revealed humpbacked clouds. Sam could see Essie's silhouette leaning against the porch rail, unmoving. "I'm sorry, Essie."

"Nothing anybody could do." She did not care to slumber in times gone by. Even so, she found herself remembering the homecoming float, the yellow dress and the sweet corsage on her wrist.

Sam stepped onto the steps of the porch. "I saw in the school yearbook that your career goal was to write the sequel to *Gone with the Wind*. That true?"

He could not see her face but felt she wore an expression of sadness, perhaps some hidden reservoir of pain. He leaned on the porch rail and waited. She was a woman; he would give her time.

Essie brushed her hand across her hair, moving it back behind her ears. "My daddy told me of all vain thoughts, excuses are the vainest. I have written most of it, but…" She lifted her hands, showing the emptiness of her efforts. "But I cannot seem to…"

After a while, in the darkness, he heard the screened door open and words barely audible. "Don't ever come back here again, Sam Washington."

Essie had done more than write most of her novel. She had completed it in March, long after she began the first chapter some five years ago. And her story hadn't been the sequel to *Gone with the Wind*. She had felt she had her own story; she didn't have to write a sequel to someone else' life. Her writing was from the heart, a longing to live a life not related to fields, barns and watermelons. Though her life had been plain, ordinary days on a farm, she could write about her dreams.

She had taken a bold step and sent her manuscript to a literary agent. *Watermelon Queen of Madison County* was no longer in the bottom drawer of her dresser. Three weeks had passed since she and Jewell had traveled to a post office in Tallahassee and mailed the carefully wrapped package. After a week, she began making trips down the lane to the mailbox, hoping to receive a reply.

June 5, 1956

Mr. Thomas H. Fox
Thomas H. Fox Literary Agency
1495 Park Avenue
New York, New York

Dear Mr. Fox:

I have enclosed my manuscript *Watermelon Queen of Madison County* for your review. My novel is about a young woman who spends her youth on the family farm. In a bold move, she makes plans to leave the farm and her family to travel to New York to become a writer.

In the midst of her plans, a family tragedy prevents her from leaving her ancestral home and finding a life outside the farm. Her dreams are set aside as she cares for her ill sister after their parents' death.

Her only happiness is found in the Royal typewriter she uses to write stories that take her away to far-away places, places that do not in any way resemble a farm or fields of corn and watermelons.

It is her realization that she is destined to stay in Madison County, on the farm where she was born, that gives her courage to revitalize the family farm and make life better for her and her sister.

I look forward to the favor of your reply.

Sincerely yours,

Esther Elizabeth Donnelly
Rural Route 1
Pinetta, Florida

CHAPTER SIX

At daylight, Essie stood at the bedroom window and watched DooRay walk the lane to the road, a long cane fishing pole over his shoulder and a white goat and rooster tagging along. Again, her eyes wandered to his empty left sleeve. After a while, the absence of his arm seemed ordinary. She had watched him work in the tack room, care for Murphy and even rake around the barn. DooRay didn't need two arms; he had Jesus.

DooRay turned right at the road and was out of sight. He caught no fish the night before, but if he caught fish today, she'd fry them in a cast iron Dutch oven, along with some hushpuppies. Her daddy had engineered a small gas stove on the back porch, especially for frying. Edith Donnelly didn't like the smell of frying fish in her pristine house. And Hubert Donnelly spent his life keeping his wife happy.

Edith's hushpuppy recipe was taped to the side of the refrigerator where Essie could see it; she loved her mother's handwriting, a slightly slanted cursive to the right, with large loops in letters like A and P. The M's had long tails. It was handwriting by someone who was perhaps a bit pretentious. And that was Edith Donnelly.

Edith had kept her recipes in Hubert's many cigar boxes. Just as the fish, Hubert's cigars were not allowed in the house, the barn his hiding place for any treasures he may have. When she was a little girl, Essie collected the cigar wrappers, the cellophane printed with a picture of a horse named Alcazar. She had fervently believed if she collected one thousand wrappers, Alcazar would be her prize. So, she followed her daddy around the yard and waited for a wrapper to come flying off his cigar and into her hands.

Essie left her room and padded down to the kitchen where the coffee pot simmered on the stove. Pouring her first cup, she walked out to the porch. *Peyton Place* lay on the swing, a bookmarker poking out at page 210. She sat down and sipped her coffee.

At the opposite end of the porch, Jewell's chair sat empty. Essie's sister had sewn a cushion made from flour sack fabric her mother had saved from years past. The table next to Jewell's chair held a small tin tray advertising Pears soap. A reproduction of a painting entitled *Bubbles* by Millais was stamped on the inset of the tray. The tray held personal items: a nail file, hand cream, a small notepad and fountain pen.

A crocheted shawl draped across the back of the chair, its delicate ends touching the wood floor of the porch. Jewell had sat in the chair every day since she was twenty years old. *She was waiting for someone.*

The screened door opened and Jewell stepped out, a cup of coffee in her hand.—a porcelain cup with a saucer. It was a dainty cup, like Jewell.

"Good morning, Jewell. Sleep well?" Essie lifted her coffee mug and smiled at her sister.

Jewell nodded and settled herself in her chair. Her year in Switzerland when she was seventeen had produced a refined woman, one who sat properly, spoke properly and was fully prepared to acquire a handsome, rich husband. That was Edith Donnelly's purpose. Her beautiful daughter would marry a blueblood from Atlanta or Charleston and become a queen in a mansion on a big plantation. Edith Donnelly was a woman with a vision.

When Edith had asked Hubert for the money to send Jewell to a finishing school in Europe, Hubert's teeth sank into his cigar so fiercely that the six inches of rolled tobacco fell to his feet. His face reddened and he sputtered around in circles. "Who the hell do you think we are, Edith? Royalty? We ain't nothing but farmers. We farm tobacco, not gold."

From the porch, he stomped up the stairs to the bedroom. Edith slept on the couch. She slept there every night for a week until Hubert came down one night and whispered. "Edith, it's time you're my wife again. We'll send Jewell to finishing school."

Jewell was regal. Perhaps she had been born to rule where her Southern roots would shine. Essie studied her sister's profile. A perfect face. Lovely black hair like her daddy's. Skin as pure and creamy as fresh buttermilk.

"Our appointment with Dr. Anderson is at 3:00 today. I'll fix us a grilled cheese, and we'll leave about 1:00. That suit you?"

"That's fine," she said. "Will we have time to listen to The Gospel Hour?"

"Of course. Wouldn't want to miss what Brother Wilbur has to say today." The tinge of sarcasm was lost on Jewell, who loved her scriptures and the music that came straight from heaven.

From the lane, DooRay's high tenor reached them. *Some glad morning when this life is over, I'll fly away...* Essie looked up and smiled when she saw the string of fish slung across his arm. A can was tied to his belt loop. Worms, she supposed.

"Oh, Miss Essie," he hollered when he saw her. "Them fish done wore out my hook this mornin'. Look here at these bream. Big fat ones." He grinned wide, his teeth arctic white against the tar black skin.

"Oh, my, DooRay. I can taste them now."

"That's right, Miss Essie. You get that grease hot and we'll have a fine, fine feast."

"Sounds good, DooRay. You clean them up good and I'll do the rest." She stood and walked down the steps into the yard. "My goodness. Those are the fattest bream I've ever seen. I bet they're at least half a pound each."

"Good eatin' size, I'd say, Miss Essie."

She counted them. "Twenty-three fish. What a grand string, DooRay." She noticed the arrangement of DooRay's cane pole across his shoulder. The string of fish weighed heavy from the crook of his arm; the can of worms affixed to his belt loop. Fishhooks stuck out from the black man's shirt pocket along with the tip of a small knife. She found herself tearing up. What more could a body want: fresh fish, a warm bed, a goat and a killer rooster.

"Tell you what, DooRay. Jewell and I must drive over to Tallahassee. We'll be back around 5:30 or 6:00 o'clock. You be okay? By the way, I put some of daddy's clothes out in the tack room for you."

"Yes, mam. You don't worry about ole DooRay." He left the yard humming, and then the chorus of *I'll Fly Away* burst forth like July 4th fireworks. *I'll fly away, fly away, oh Glory, I'll fly away. When I die, Hallelujah, by and by, I'll fly away.*

At 1:00 o'clock Essie and Jewell drove to Pinetta and turned left on 145 toward Madison, where they would pick up U. S. 90 to Tallahassee. Madison County straddled the Florida-Georgia border where only nine miles north, northeast of the Town of Madison, an abundance of pine trees not only brought in the woodcutters but also gave the name to an area that became a small cocoon for families whose origins were mostly Irish, Scots and English.

Well over a hundred years ago, in Pinetta, Florida, a settlement evolved that begat families named Allen, Bass, Buchanan, Cash, Coody, Crafton, Crews, Gaston, Gibson, Herring, Hollingsworth, Keeling, Leslie, Sapp, Terry, Townsend, Washington, Wiglesworth, and Woodward—their pioneering spirit the foundation of a community filled with beautiful farmlands that rivaled the old South's plantations.

Essie sighed as she drove slowly down 145; her life was between the meandering dirt roads and the miles of cornrows, slipping away into a gray dullness interrupted only by the care of Jewell.

In Madison, they drove south on Duval Street, then right on Base Street, where the Madison County Courthouse with its neo-classical architecture stood bright in the early afternoon sun.

Essie's eyes caught sight of a tall man jauntily walking down the sidewalk, the briefcase in his hand swinging as he walked. It was Sam Washington. He wore a dark suit, the white cuffs of his shirt stark against the long-sleeved jacket. He looked as good in a suit as he did naked. She hoped Jewell would not recognize him as they slid by in her daddy's 1948 Buick Century Riviera.

Essie turned her head slightly to the right. It was Sam all right. She'd recognize a Washington boy anywhere. Handsome, almost pompous, Sam looked her way, and she saw the hesitation in his step and then the smile and the wave. She pressed her foot on the accelerator and stared straight ahead.

Almost to Greenville, they passed the Hixtown Swamp on the left.

29

It was nothing but a cypress swamp full of alligators and rattlesnakes.

"Have we been here before, Essie?" Jewell's voice sounded anxious as she peered out the window.

"Sure have. We've made many trips to Tallahassee. We'll be there in another hour or so."

"Why are we going to Tallahassee? I want to go home."

Essie reached over and patted Jewell's arm. "We are, sister. But, first, we've got to see Dr. Anderson. Then, let's go get some ice cream."

Outside Monticello, off to their right, they passed Lake Miccosukee where their daddy had duck hunted all his life. He had come home with a dozen or so on a cold December afternoon and wanted Edith to cook them, call in the neighbors and feast on roasted duck. She scrunched up her face and went upstairs. Hubert cleaned the ducks and drove his truck over to Negro Town along the Withlacoochee. "This here is some of the finest eatin' in the world. Get a fire going and we'll roast these things."

Hubert stayed all night, drank their whiskey and slept until noon in a ramshackle lean-to next to the river. A hairy dog named Ebenezer had kept him warm while he listened to the sounds of the Withlacoochee roll along and thanked God for His glorious bounty. When he arrived home, he went directly to the barn and lit one of his cigars. He knew Edith would not let him in the house.

The skyline of Tallahassee loomed ahead, and Essie eased the Buick over one last hill and drove to Dr. Anderson's office. Jewell had dozed the last thirty miles and woke when Essie turned off the car's motor. "We're here, Jewell."

The sisters saw Dr. Anderson together. Essie answered most questions while the doctor looked into Jewell's eyes and ears, listened to her heart, took her pulse.

"You feeling good, Jewell?" He smiled as he looked at her hands and tapped a rubber hammer at her knee.

Jewell glanced at Essie, then back to Dr. Anderson. "Very well, thank you." She folded her hands neatly in her lap. She was a lady even if she was undressed and in a medical gown.

"Ah, that's good." Dr. Anderson picked up Jewell's chart. "Your weight is down about ten pounds, Jewell. Why's that?" He studied Jewell's face.

"I'm not as hungry as I used to be, I guess."

"You eat breakfast?"

"Every morning."

"How about lunch and dinner?"

"Always." Jewell's eyes flitted around the room.

Dr. Anderson made a few notes on Jewell's chart. "Tell you what, I'm going to have Alice take some blood. That okay?"

"Do you have to?"

"Yes. We haven't drawn your blood for about six months. Let's see how you're doing."

Dr. Anderson called in his nurse, took Essie by the elbow, and they left the room. "And how are you, Essie?" he asked as he settled at his desk and pointed to a chair for Essie.

"Same as always. Nothing new."

Dr. Anderson was silent for a moment, never taking his eyes from Essie. "You getting out? Doing things?"

"Not really. Jewell is full-time care."

"She'll never be better than she is right now, Essie."

"I know that." Essie seemed irritated.

"What I'm saying is that you can never expect anything to change. It will always be this way. So, I'd like to suggest you think about a place for Jewell to go, to be cared for so you can have a life. You're a young woman."

Essie sucked in a quick breath. "Jewell in a home of some kind? How could I? She's my sister. Mama and daddy left her in my care."

"I know. But I'm thinking Jewell would be happy anywhere she might be."

"That's not true," Essie shot out. "The farm's her home. I'm her sister. No place could be better." A flush crept up her neck, her cheeks hot.

Dr. Anderson swiveled his chair to a bookcase and pulled out a book. "Ever read *The Social Animal*?"

"No. What is it?"

"It's about the mind. Jewell's mind is in a certain place and it will never go backward or forward." He paused. "Does she ever mention Jimmy?"

Jewell turned away. *Jimmy? Did Jewell ever mention Jimmy? Of course, she did. She thought he was still alive.* "Jimmy? Yes. Most every day."

"What do you say to her?"

Essie looked at her hands. Her fingers were not slim and graceful like Jewell's. When she looked up, Dr. Anderson had leaned back and folded his arms across his chest, waiting.

"I don't say anything. I just... just let her believe." Her words caught, and she returned Dr. Anderson's stare. "What could I say?"

The doctor shook his head. "Who knows? You're probably doing the right thing by just listening. How many years has it been?"

"Fifteen. Fifteen years of waiting." Essie's throat tightened. Not only had Jewell waited, but Essie had also waited. "I think about it a lot. If only they hadn't gone swimming that day. Nobody knew Jimmy had seizures. Nobody. Not even Jewell."

"She tried to save him?" Dr. Anderson's voice was just a whisper.

"Yes. She tried to save him." A tear rolled down Essie's cheek. "She watches the field across the road all day. Looks over there thinking any minute he'll be coming over the hill to see her."

"And when he doesn't?" Dr. Anderson handed Essie a tissue.

Essie lifted her hands. "Nothing."

A soft knock on the door. "Yes," called Dr. Anderson.

Alice poked her head inside. "All through and Jewell is dressed."

The doctor stood. "Okay, Essie. I'll get back with you on the blood work and, if necessary, I'll have Jewell come back in. She's too thin. Make sure she's eating enough."

Essie nodded. "Thank you, Dr. Anderson."

The sisters went for ice cream like Essie had promised and picked up U. S. 90 east toward Madison, skirting the same little towns they had passed earlier. The clouds in the west had darkened and followed them, a late afternoon shower heading their way.

They passed through Madison and Essie scanned the lawn of the courthouse. The crepe myrtles were in bloom: watermelon red, lilac and a lollipop pink. Confederate jasmine twirled around the bottom of the flagpole, reaching for the sky. There was no sign of Sam Washington.

CHAPTER SEVEN

The Buick turned north on Highway 145, through Hanson, then slowed at the Bellville road and found Pinetta settling down for a quiet evening. The train depot was dark, but a few people lingered around J. T. Woodward's store. Behind his store, down the lane, Essie could see lights in the windows of their white house, where J. T.'s wife, Miss Abby, and their daughters Carolyn and Abigail lived.

For a moment, Essie considered stopping at the post office and getting a Coca Cola for Jewell. She smiled at the thought of Maude White and Mrs. Gussie fussing over the ice cream box full of Dixie Doodle ice cream and the nickel bags of plain potato chips hanging on clips on the counter.

And there was Jeanette Coody. Essie tooted the horn and waved at one of Pinetta's most beloved citizens, a philanthropic woman who delighted in turning little country girls into fabulous beauties at proms and weddings. She introduced the young girls in Pinetta to the joys of taffeta and lace, despite their hard work in the tobacco fields of Madison County.

The car's tires found the soft dirt of the country road and traveled smoothly, a bump or two here or there. They passed Lon Terry's general store, a sign above the store proclaiming it *Terryville*. Across the road from the store, a small gristmill lay shaded from the evening sun, its boards gray and worn, a Coca Cola sign tacked to the side.

Hog wire stretched around the mill, where hogs lay in the mud, a faucet dripping over the fence. Mr. Terry was proud of his Tamworth hogs; not a summer day passed that he didn't heave a few watermelons over the fence into their pen.

They passed Ran Terry's road on the left where cypress knees poked up through the swampy water of his pond, promising big bass at the first light of day. DooRay's worms caught the slyest of bass, the fattest of catfish.

Around the next curve, Essie slowed and turned left onto the lane leading to the grand Donnelly house, a house built by the Hughes side of the family, her mother's father—a man they called Purvis.

The sight of the house caused a soft squeezing in her chest. Fifteen years ago, she had almost left it all, sat on the Greyhound bus waiting for it to pull out of the bus station, wanting to see the last of Madison County and feel the last of field-hand sweat. She wondered if she had left, would she have ever returned. What if she had been like Scarlett, met a man like Rhett Butler and lived a whirlwind life in Atlanta.

If truth be told, she had met a man like Rhett Butler. She had loved him passionately, not a honky-tonk love. A tall farm boy, born and raised in Madison County. Then, like a puff of smoke, he was gone. He had promised her many things—would give her the moon. *Had he really loved her?* He had told her many times that he did. Told her she was the sun, the moon and the stars. And she believed him. Believed him until he left town on her 18th birthday.

Autrey Browning had not returned to Madison County, had not picked the daisies along the Bellville road and brought them to her. Had not danced with her under the moonlight at Cherry Lake. Fifteen years had passed without a word.

She mourned him for a year, watched the road from her upstairs bedroom window, looking for him until her eyes spilled over with tears. Sometimes she imagined him drowned in Grassy Pond—that he would never have left her intentionally. But, he did. Months later someone had told her they saw him in Tallahassee, another woman holding his hand. Her mourning turned to hate.

She drove slowly down the lane, acorns popping under the tires. The house seemed almost majestic, a cupola at the high pitch of the roof where at least a half dozen old bird nests filled the inside. The copper top was dull with age, a green patina here and there. The slate gray shingles ran neatly along the roof, shaded from the sun most all day except for early morning. Long, leaded windows along the front allowed the rising sun to sweep in and, for just a few moments, illuminate Edith Donnelly's prized Dresden lace figurines a cousin had sent from Germany.

The porch was a house in itself. One could live there, feel the rain spatter on their face when the wind blew, sleep in the swing made of cypress and dream of distant places. The paddle fans kept the lazy days cool and the bugs away at night. And, best of all, in the midst of the wooden planks and the rockers and swings, people laughed and loved.

It wasn't the same porch as it was years ago, the ghosts of another time lingering high in the porch rafters. A sadness crept over Essie and covered her as the car came to a stop. If she squinted real hard, maybe she could see smoke coming from the smokehouse, horses grazing in the south pasture and smell cane syrup boiling in the big kettles. After her mama and daddy died, the farm grew everything but happiness.

Dr. Anderson had said Jewell's mind would never move backwards or forwards. *Well, neither will mine. I'm here, right where I was born. Here to stay.*

Essie parked alongside the house and looked for DooRay. "You go on in, Jewell. I'll be there in a minute."

Essie stepped out of the car and walked to the barn, idleness in her steps. She hesitated, a feeling of something being out of sorts. A smell. A few steps and she stopped. The oak tree to her right, at eye level, had something nailed to it. She studied it for a long moment in the waning light before she realized it was an ear from an animal. A goat's ear dripping blood. *Murphy's ear.*

Around her feet she saw feathers. Long tail feathers. *Killer's feathers.* From the barn, she heard a moan. *DooRay.*

A shrill scream. Essie pivoted toward the house. Another scream. In seconds, she was at the back porch picking up an ax that leaned against the steps and rushing through the back screened door into the kitchen. Leaning against the far kitchen wall, Jewell clutched her chest, her face white, her body stiff.

"Well, well, little lady. 'bout time somebody came home."

Prisoner #458 stood in the kitchen, a butcher knife in one hand, a jar of peanut butter in the other.

"Get out of this house," Essie snarled. She held the ax in the air in front of her. Both hands wrapped the handle, ready to swing.

"Now, now. I just need me somethin' to eat and I'll be on my way." The man was small and scrawny, his prison garb wet to the waist after sludging through the swamp from the prison farm. Mud smeared his face and arms. The odor of sweat filled the kitchen.

Essie circled him, her chest heaving. "What'd you do to DooRay?"

"DooRay? Oh, that's that nigger you got out there in the barn. Don't you know better than to have a nigger on your place? I had to teach him a thing or two when I got here. He told me to leave." Prisoner #458 laughed, a mouth full of crooked, brown teeth snapping the air. "Now, I ask you, what can a one-armed, black son-of-a-bitch do to make me leave?" He threw the jar of peanut butter against the wall, shattering the glass. "Nothin'. Absolutely nothin'."

Essie glanced at Jewell, whose body pressed against the wall behind the prisoner. She shifted her eyes to the stairs. *Go upstairs, Jewell.* "You bastard. This ax is gonna split your head wide open if you don't leave this very minute."

"Leave? Now, I'm wondering where I'm gonna sleep. Not in the barn with that nigger, for sure. Certainly not with that one-eared goat." He chuckled. "I figured if the nigger had only one arm that his goat should have only one ear. Don't you think that's reasonable?"

"No way you're staying here. Just get going or I'll call the sheriff."

The man's face darkened. "The sheriff? They's no way I'm gonna let you call the sheriff." He thrashed the butcher knife in the air toward Essie.

Essie squeezed the ax handle harder, sweat forming on her brow, her heart beating as though she had just run a mile. "I'm ready for you, mister. You just come on. I just sharpened this ax this mornin'." She began waving it back and forth like a flag, ready to push the blade into the sweaty head of the swamp rat. The man grinned as he lunged toward her.

The gunshot was so loud Essie became disoriented, her ears full of cotton. She blinked, stunned. Her eyes blurred, and she thought she was going to faint.

The prisoner grabbed the side of his face and whipped around. "My ear. You done shot off my ear." Blood ran through his fingers, his eyes searching the floor for his ear. "Where's my ear?"

His mouth open in shock, he stared at Jewell and the pistol in her hand. "You bitch, you. You done shot off my ear." He lifted the knife. "I'm gonna slit your throat for sure." He took a step toward Jewell and the gun exploded again, knocking the man to the floor, the butcher knife falling from his fist and sliding across the floor.

"Jewell! Give me that pistol." Essie jumped across the kitchen, across the man who lay quiet and unmoving. "Oh, dear Lord." She lifted the pistol and kept it aimed straight at the man's head.

"The phone. We've got to call the sheriff, Jewell." With trembling hands, Essie picked up the phone and rang the operator.

"Hello," she barked into the phone. "This is an emergency. I need the sheriff and an ambulance out here." She paused and listened. "Yes, mam. An emergency. Pinetta. The Bellville road. The Donnelly place."

When Essie hung up, she opened her arms toward Jewell. "Come here, Jewell. It's gonna be all right." The sisters held each other, and Essie felt Jewell slump into her arms. "It's okay. It's okay." She gently pushed Jewell away and looked into the large green eyes. "Jewell, where in the hell did you learn to shoot daddy's pistol?"

Out in the yard and waiting for the sheriff, Essie sat Jewell down in a lawn chair. "Sit here, Jewell, and watch for the sheriff. I've got to go find DooRay."

She half-walked, half-ran to the barn. She saw no signs of Murphy or Killer. When she spotted a trail of blood leading into the cornfield, her body trembled. Easing up to the tack room door, she whispered. "DooRay." She poked her head inside. "DooRay," she called louder. Her eyes adjusted to the dim light and she stepped inside.

At first, she thought it was a pile of rags and debris. She took a step farther and leaned over the pile. It was DooRay. He lay in a fetal position, his head covered with his one hand. She sunk to her knees. "Oh, DooRay." She pulled at his shoulder. "It's me. Essie."

Her eyes fell to his bloodied head. Gently, she turned his face toward her. "DooRay, can you hear me?" His eyes were shut;

abrasions covered his face. He was unrecognizable. Were it not for his missing arm, she would never have known it was DooRay. "You get up from here, DooRay." Her voice was harsh. "Nobody's gonna hurt you anymore, you hear?"

She saw one eyelid flutter. "Hey," she said softly. "We've gotta fry those fish." She smiled and smoothed his head, blood staining her fingers.

His voice came in a hoarse whisper. "Miss Essie, I told him to leave."

"I know. I know, DooRay."

"He jus' laugh at me and started swinging a two by four at me." DooRay closed his eyes. "He had a butcher knife, too. He saw Murphy tied up to the tree and done cut off his ear." Tears rolled from his eyes.

"Shhhhh. Don't talk, DooRay. The ambulance is on the way. We'll get you fixed up good as new."

"Killer. Killer attacked that feller. Spurred him real good in the leg. That butcher knife sliced through the air and got all Killer's tail feathers." DooRay coughed and blood ran from his mouth.

The faint sound of a siren filled the air. Mournful and sad, the wail became louder. Two cars pulled into the yard and parked between the house and the barn. Behind them, an ambulance, its red lights twirling, jerked to a stop and left its motor running. *Valdosta, Georgia* was written alongside *Ambulance,* and two men jumped out.

"Out here," yelled Essie. She waved her arms and felt her knees weaken. Her throat closed and she gasped for more air. "Hurry. It's DooRay Aikens. He's hurt real bad."

Essie stepped aside and watched as two men carrying medical bags slipped quickly into the tack room. She heard one say: "Didn't know we'd be workin' on a nigger, did you?"

Essie grabbed a nearby hoe and lunged into the tack room. "So help me, you better treat him like he was gold. You hear me?" Essie raised the hoe and glared at the two men. She knew them both—went to high school with them. Both the men shrunk back and nodded. "Yes, mam." Essie backed up into the yard.

"What's going on, Essie?" Sheriff Simmie Moore hurried across the yard. His deputy, Son Stokely, all three-hundred and sixty pounds of him, followed close behind.

"Oh, hell, Simmie. One of them damn inmates over at the inmate work camp came through the swamp on his way to Georgia. He stopped off here while Jewell and I were in Tallahassee." She caught her breath. "I told Uncle Lester I'd shoot the next inmate that showed up here."

"That right?" Sheriff Moore looked around. "Where is he now?"

Essie shrugged. "In the house on the kitchen floor. Two bullets in him."

Sheriff Moore jerked back. "Two bullets? He dead?"

"I certainly hope so. He was about to slice me and Jewell with a butcher knife."

The sheriff turned and nodded at his deputy. "Go in and see if he's still alive. Don't touch anything."

"Where's the gun?" Simmie studied Essie, then turned and looked at Jewell sitting near the picnic table.

"Right here." Essie pulled up her shirt and pulled out a .38 pistol and handed it to the sheriff.

Simmie Moore glanced at the gun. He knew it well. It was Hubert Donnelly's. A Beaumont-Adams .38 revolver made in the United Kingdom. Hubert's brother had brought it back from World War I. The proud farmer had shown it to anyone who visited the Donnelly farm.

Simmie sniffed the barrel and smelled fresh cordite. He turned when he heard the back screened door slam. Son Stokely looked his way and nodded. The man was dead.

"Essie, you and Jewell want to come sit on the front porch and tell me what happened?"

"Be glad to, Simmie." She hesitated. "Mind if I check on DooRay?"

"DooRay?" Simmie glanced at the barn.

"DooRay Aikens. He's living in my barn. That man beat DooRay something fierce."

"Let's take a look." The big man left the back yard and followed Essie to the barn. Jewell remained in the lawn chair under an oak tree, staring out at the cornfield.

In the tack room Essie leaned over the back of Malcolm, a Madison boy, and watched as he tended DooRay's wounds. "How's he doing?"

"We've got most of the bleeding stopped. He needs a few stitches, but other than that he looks okay. He's badly bruised, but I don't think anything is broken. He's one tough nig—one tough fellow."

"Don't you think he needs to go to the hospital?" She reached out and touched the top of DooRay's head.

"Naw, don't think so. You can take him to see Dr. Bush and he'll stitch him up if he needs to."

"What about pain. You got anything for pain?"

"Can't give him anything. I imagine the doc will take care of that."

DooRay moaned. Both eyes were swollen shut; his cheeks raw with blood oozing from them. His lips were cut open in three places. He pulled his tongue over the cuts. "Miss Essie, can you find Murphy and Killer for me?"

"Sure, DooRay. I'll do that and then we'll run over to Dr. Bush for some stitches and pain medication."

DooRay half smiled and nodded. "Thank you, Miss Essie."

The big sheriff knelt beside DooRay. "Hey, DooRay," he said gently. "Just rest for now. We'll get Dr. Bush over here in a minute and take a look at you." The sheriff patted the black man's shoulder.

Essie left the tack room and looked for the trail of blood she'd seen earlier. When she found it, she followed it into the cornfield, where corn five feet high grew in long rows almost to the river. She'd only gone about a hundred and fifty feet when she saw Murphy curled beneath the corn stalks. He bleated softly. The side of his head where his ear had been was matted with blood. On Murphy's rump, a tail-less Killer set watching Essie. Killer's eyes blinked rapidly; his beak lay open, and she could see the end of his arrow-shaped tongue.

She eased up to them and crouched down. "Want to go home now?" she said softly. Murphy bleated again. A low caw came from Killer. "Come on. Follow me." Murphy understood. He stood up and dutifully followed Essie; Killer not far behind.

When they got to the tack room, the goat and the rooster went inside, and Murphy's bleating became louder. She heard DooRay talking to them. "Gone be fine. Gone be fine."

40

CHAPTER EIGHT

On the Donnelly front porch, Simmie Moore and Son Stokely had settled into some chairs. Simmie Moore was an affable man, wore no badge, no uniform, just plain country clothes, but he did carry a pistol in the right front pocket of his pants. His county car was plain, with no markings—a '56 Ford that was almost as fast as the moonshiners. Essie walked up the steps and wearily sat down in the swing. If she pushed it slowly, perhaps the rhythm would calm her beating heart.

"Where's Jewell?" The sheriff asked.

"Let's not bother Jewell with this, Simmie. She's been traumatized enough, don't you think?" Essie held his steady eyes with hers. An awkward silence followed, and she touched her foot to the porch floor and began a slow swing.

Simmie reached up and scratched his head. He appeared casual, but Essie knew it was just his way of putting her at ease. "Who shot the inmate?"

"Jewell," she said, her words barely audible. "Jewell saved my life. Had she not pulled that trigger, we'd both be dead." Essie stared off into the distance for a long minute and then came back to the fixed eyes of the sheriff. "It was that simple."

Simmie cleared his throat and glanced at Son, then back to Essie. "Well, Essie, I wish it was that simple. But, there has to be an inquest and Jewell and you will be subpoenaed and appear before a judge. There's a dead man and that's not simple. We'll have to follow the law." His words were gentle.

Essie nodded and kept swinging. "Will Jewell have to go into Madison—to the courthouse?"

"I'm thinking so. It's a formal inquest in front of the judge. This is a death regardless of the mitigating circumstances."

"Jewell's so frail, Simmie. I don't want to put her through this."

Simmie nodded his understanding. "I'll talk to Judge Earp. Dr. Bush is on his way out here now, so we'll try to get things wrapped up quickly." His big chest heaved. "Any place you can go for a few hours?"

The swing stopped. "No. No place to go. We'll just go out to the barn. Look after DooRay. I'll ask Dr. Bush to take a look at DooRay and maybe give him some pain medication. Doc might think he'll need to x-ray him."

Simmie Moore stood and patted Essie on the shoulder. "Everything will be alright, Essie." His deputy walked down the brick steps in front of him. "We'll take a few pictures and wait for the doc. I'll keep your daddy's pistol for a while, if you don't mind."

Essie followed the men down the steps and into the yard. "Go ahead and keep it. He's got a half dozen more upstairs."

Headlights shone from the road as a black sedan moved slowly down the lane. "There's Dr. Bush. He'll make a few preliminary statements and release the body to be driven to the morgue. It's his call about an autopsy, but I think two bullets will be enough proof of cause of death."

Essie nodded and watched Dr. Bush get out of his car. He was a meticulous man; there would be no mistakes on his part. A bullet hole was a bullet hole.

"Dr. Bush," she called. "After you finish your examination of that dead man, can you come look at DooRay? He's in the tack room all beat up."

"I sure will, Essie." Following the sheriff, Dr. Bush climbed the front steps and went into the house.

Essie found Jewell asleep in the lawn chair, her face peaceful. She gently smoothed her silky hair. She was the beautiful sister.

She met the ambulance attendants as they loaded up their bags and prepared to leave. "Thank you so much," she said. "Is there anything I should do?"

"No, Essie. We're thinking he'll be fine. A few days recuperating, but after that he'll feel much better."

"What about the cuts that need stitches?"

"We bandaged them tightly. If he'll leave the bandages alone, I think he'll heal okay. Don't let him get the areas wet. I left some alcohol and gauze for cleaning the area. Do you think you can do that okay?"

Essie pushed a lock of hair behind her ear. "I'm sure I can. Dr. Bush is here and he's going to take a look at him."

The men nodded and loaded up. The red flashing lights of the ambulance became still. Just as they began to turn around in the yard, Sheriff Moore waved them down. "Hold on, fellas. I think Dr. Bush wants you to take the body to the morgue. Give me a minute."

The men looked at each other and shrugged. "I didn't know there was a body. Did you?"

"First I heard of it." The men glanced at Essie. "You know anything about a body, Essie?"

"Oh, some fella escaped from the inmate work camp and met up with two women who shot him full of holes. That's all I know." She turned away, and a vision of a butcher knife swept through her head.

In a half hour, Dr. Bush left the kitchen and walked to the barn. "What have we got here, Essie?" He knelt next to DooRay. "Oh, my. Looks like DooRay's been beat up pretty bad."

Dr. Bush examined DooRay's head and face, checked his chest. "I know he's hurting, Essie, but there are no major, life-threatening injuries. The ambulance boys cleaned him up just right. I'll give him an injection of pain medication and he'll feel better. Also sleep some."

"Thank you, Dr. Bush." Essie knelt and smoothed a blanket over DooRay.

"Don't worry, Essie, he'll be fine. Call me at the office if you see that he worsens. Just let him rest. Give him lots of water, too."

"Yes, sir. I'll do just that."

Essie stood on the porch until the yard was empty of cars. From the back yard, she heard Jewell call her. "I'm coming, Jewell."

The two sisters climbed the stairs together, Jewell somber and wanting sleep. Essie pulled back the bed covers and fluffed the pillow. "You okay, Jewell?"

"I'm just fine, Essie." She seemed puzzled. "I wonder where that ear went?" She snuggled into her pillow, a half smile on her face and was asleep in seconds.

Wearily, Essie walked down the dark hall to her mother and father's bedroom where her father's gun case rested against the far wall, the same wall that held Edith Donnelly's gold-leafed French provincial mirror. She opened the case and pulled another one of her daddy's pistols from the glass case. She'd be darned if she'd get caught without a pistol should another of her Uncle Lester's prisoners escape and decide to stop at the Donnelly farm.

It was a Colt M1917, a service revolver from World War I, its swing out cylinder easy to load. Her daddy had shown her every detail of the gun. Essie lifted it and aimed it across the room—she knew she could load and shoot it without missing a beat. Indeed, she was a hard woman.

At the bottom of the gun case, a drawer held a myriad of cartridges, at least two boxes for every gun Hubert owned.

She rummaged through the boxes looking for a box of .45 cartridges. Just as she picked up a box of .45 ACP's, she saw a folded piece of paper, yellowed, a little ragged along the edges, tucked in the back of the drawer. Even before she unfolded the fragile paper, she knew it was hidden for a reason, that its contents were secret. She hesitated and almost pushed it back into the dark corner of the drawer. She let her fingers rest on the thin paper for a moment, then slid it forward where her eyes could see it.

Slowly, she unfolded it and saw neat, feminine handwriting, beautiful cursive letters that spoke of... of love. *Dear Hubert, please forgive me. I know my love for you is wrong, but I can't help loving you. L.*

CHAPTER NINE

The sun had set across Grassy Pond hours ago, leaving the fields awash with moonlight from a three-quarter moon. Essie smoothed salve on Murphy's ear and smiled when the goat stuck out its tongue and spoke a goat language. Essie knew the goat was thanking her. "You're going to be fine, Murphy. It's Killer we've got to worry about. Don't you think he looks depressed? I think he realizes he doesn't look like a yard rooster anymore. The absence of those brilliant tail feathers has hurt his ego."

She left Murphy and moved over to DooRay. Earlier she had placed a bale of hay in the tack room and spread it out into a bed, not only for DooRay but also for Murphy and Killer. She had made chicken broth and spooned it gently into DooRay's mouth, past his swollen lips. He never opened his eyes; he couldn't.

He slept peacefully, especially after Dr. Bush' injection. She listened to him breathe and watched as his body twitched now and then. He was in a deep sleep; a healing sleep.

"I'll check on you first thing in the morning, DooRay," she whispered. She patted him gently on the shoulder and left a quart jar of water on a brick by his bed of hay. She scratched Murphy on the head. "Sleep tight, you pretty goat." Killer's head was tucked under his wing. He wasn't so pretty, so she said nothing to him.

Simmie Moore and his deputy had cleaned the kitchen floor and removed all traces of inmate #458. The butcher knife was taken as evidence, along with her daddy's .38 pistol. She wondered if her daddy's prized gun had ever killed a man before.

Her walk back to the house was slow; her thoughts many. Oddly, she wondered if the sheriff and his deputies had found inmate #458's ear. An ear for an ear. How ironic. Maybe that was karma. She'd have to tell Murphy about the inmate's ear flying across the kitchen. She became angry; by God, she'd nail the inmate's ear to a tree if she found it.

She turned the corner of the house and smelled smoke. Cigar smoke. She stilled when she heard the squeak of the chain on the porch swing. She stood on tiptoe and looked over the top of her mother's azaleas but saw nothing. The faint notes of a melody drifted into the night air; a song she recognized. *Beautiful, beautiful brown eyes.* The voice was lovely, a Burl Ives raspyness that lured one into wanting to sing along. In her head, she followed the notes and for a moment felt the softness of her heart. *There is softness*, she told herself. Uncle Lester told her she was a hard woman, but she knew underneath that hardness, a tender spot waited to be discovered.

"I reckon I could go in the house and get one of daddy's guns, or you could just leave." She leaned against the oak tree at the end of the house.

"Don't do that," Sam Washington replied.

"Didn't I tell you not to come back here again?" she said matter-of-factly, no real animosity evident in her words.

"That you did. But I'm not known for doing anything just because somebody told me to do it."

"The way I see it, that will get you into a lot of trouble." She knew he was smiling.

"Well, come on up to the porch and let's discuss it."

She left the oak tree and climbed the brick steps to the porch. Sam was stretched out in the swing, a cigar clutched in his teeth. The moonlight revealed he had thought it best to wear clothes.

"Are you always so audacious?" she asked.

A chuckle. "Always. Have to be. I'm an obnoxious attorney, you know."

Essie sighed and sat in a nearby rocker. "Why are you here?"

"Easy," he said, puffing on his cigar. "Word got around you had some trouble here earlier this evening. I thought I might be able to assist in some way."

"Assist?" Essie shook her head. "There's nothing you can do for me that I can't do for myself."

"Ah, not true, Essie Donnelly." He sat up from the swing and tapped the ashes of his cigar over the porch railing. "I'm thinking you just might need my... my expertise."

"Expertise? How so?" Essie heard the irritation in her words. She closed her eyes and thought about reaching over and slapping the cigar out of his hand. His arrogance needed tempering, and she was very capable of doing just that.

"The deposition. The inquest."

"And?"

"I'll talk to the judge. With his approval, the state attorney will take Jewell's deposition out here at the farm. Hopefully, Jewell won't have to appear in court."

"How'd you figure that out?"

"Eight years of college. Bar exam. Brilliant attorney."

Essie rocked a few minutes, her gaze finding the moonlight on the field across the road. From the oaks, an owl called before she saw it dip to the ground and swoop up something in its beak.

"What is your fee, may I ask?" Essie pulled a clasp from her shirt pocket, lifted her long hair and clasped it on top of her head.

"No fee," he said, relighting his cigar. The glow of the match lit Sam's face. When she saw his twinkling eyes, she thought of the yellow pillowcase and her sexual being. She glanced around for the copy of *Peyton Place*.

"No fee because of your abundant generosity?" Again, blatant sarcasm puffed her words.

"Not at all. I'd like a date with you." He blew cigar smoke into the night air and leaned forward, elbows on his knees. He was only a few feet away, the cigar resting between his thumb and forefinger. "That fair?"

Essie felt her heart tremble. A date. A date with Sam Washington. She was thirty-three years old, well past the dating age from her point of view.

"That's a high price for me to pay," she said, unsmiling.

"It's worth it." He grinned.

A few moments of silence. Essie cleared her throat. "What if I sold these 300 acres, the house, the barn, daddy's guns, all the tractors and equipment and mama's jewelry? Would you take that instead of a date with me?" There was not one shred of humor in her voice.

Sam leaned back into the swing and placed the cigar back into his mouth. He lifted his chin in thought, ran a hand over the top of his head and pushed the swing back and forth. Minutes passed while he deliberated his response. Essie rocked and waited.

"No. No, I wouldn't. A date with you is much more valuable than 300 hundred acres of prime farmland right in the middle of Madison County. Your mother's jewelry—a mere pittance compared to spending a few hours with you. The house? Couldn't even be a down payment. Your daddy's guns? Not a chance in hell those guns could hold a candle to you."

In the distance, heat lightening traveled across the sky. From the field to the west, a calf bawled, and its cry made Essie stand up and walk to the end of the porch and peer out into the night. "What kind of date?" she asked, not turning around, her back unyielding.

She heard him taking fast puffs on his cigar. "I come to your house in a car to pick you up. You dress up in a pretty dress. I hold open the car door for you. You slide in and we play music on the radio while we drive to Tallahassee to a nice restaurant. You tell me how nice my after-shave smells. I tell you I like your perfume. You tell me you like my tie. I tell you I like your shoes.

"When *Allegheny Moon* comes on the radio, we sing along with Patti Page. When we get to the restaurant, I park and open the car door for you, reach out and take your hand and we walk into the restaurant where the maître de asks if we have reservations. I tell him yes and he shows us to our table. And, we eat a delicious meal and talk about our lives."

The quiet lasted four or five minutes. Sam said, "Hello?"

"I'm here," said Essie. "We talking four or five hours altogether?"

"I'm thinking so."

"So, the state attorney will take Jewell's statement and you'll represent Jewell at the inquest?"

"That's right."

"Five hours. No more," Essie said, with quiet finality.

The swing stilled, and she heard him relight his cigar. "Well, now. I think we're making progress."

She turned from the porch railing. "Mr. Washington," she said

48

through the dark, "this will be my first and only date with you. Understood?"

"Yes, mam."

Long after midnight, long after Sam had driven his 1952 Pontiac down the lane and onto the Bellville road, Essie walked back to the barn and stood at the tack room door. Murphy lifted his head when he heard Essie; Killer remained still, his head under his wing. Essie listened for DooRay's breathing and heard him whimper softly.

"I'm here, DooRay," she whispered. She left the barn and walked along the path to the well and lifted the arm of the hand pump. She primed the pump and cool water spilled out into a pint Mason jar. She sipped the water and looked out over the cornfield. The moonlight was so bright she could clearly see the tin roofs of the tobacco barns a quarter of a mile away.

Walking back down the path to the house, her only thought was how to break the date with Sam Washington.

CHAPTER TEN

E arly the next morning, Lester Terry banged on the back screen of the Donnelly house. "Essie! Essie, you up?" He pulled open the door and hurried into the kitchen. He smelled coffee and looked around for a cup. "Essie, come down here right this minute."

Lester heard his niece coming down the stairs. "Hurry up," he said, sipping his coffee. He picked up an old biscuit and opened a jar of fig preserves.

"Uncle Lester, does Aunt Shelly know you're eating sugar?"

"No, and don't you tell her."

"Yes, I am. Dr. Bush told you to lose weight and to watch your sugar."

"Now, Essie. Neither Dr. Bush nor Shelly need to know what I eat."

Essie stared her uncle down. "Come on out to the porch. I haven't had my coffee." Essie poured a cup and meandered to the porch, with Lester right behind her, licking fig preserves from his fingers.

She sat on the swing; Lester sat in the rocker. "Why are you over here so early?" She looked over at the county car and knew it was business.

"Well, Simmie Moore paid me a visit before daylight with all kinds of information. That dead man is at the morgue and his next of kin has been notified. That's why I'm here."

"Who's the dead man?"

"George Barnwell is his name—a fella who's been in Madison

County about a year. He got off a Greyhound to buy some whiskey and never left. I know he didn't get any whiskey in Madison unless it was moonshine. That's why he was at the work camp—public drunkenness."

"Where was he from?" Essie furrowed her brow. "And he was no harmless drunk, either."

"That's what I'm here to tell you. That fella was from New York City, and his brother is his next of kin." Lester licked his lips, leaned toward Essie and dropped his voice to a low, nervous pitch. "Now, listen to this. His brother is a big-time New York City lawyer, and he's coming down to 'straighten things out.' And, those are his exact words. He wasn't very nice on the telephone to Simmie Moore, and I figure he's comin' to stir up trouble.

"He said something about a wrongful death, whatever that means." Lester slurped his coffee and shook his head. "Looks to me like he's coming for nothin'. His brother threatened you and Jewell with a big butcher knife, and I'd say that was worthy of a pistol whippin', wouldn't you?"

"Well, he sure got more than a pistol whipping, didn't he?" Essie shuddered. She saw the man lifting the large knife and waving it in the air.

"Anyway, I'm here to let you know about that lawyer fella. Done told Sam about it, too. By the way, how do you think Jewell is doing?"

"I checked on her several times during the night. She slept well, especially after taking some medication. When she gets up, I'll talk with her about her statement. Amazingly, she seems unscathed by what happened."

"That's a relief. What about DooRay?" Lester drained his coffee cup and wiped his mouth with the back of his hand. Essie saw fig preserves on his cheek.

"He seemed alright when I checked on him late last night. I'll check on him in a few minutes."

"Whatever you do, don't let the poor fella die. It wouldn't be the same without DooRay." Lester stood and walked down the porch steps and into the yard. "Look, Essie. Please be nice to Sam. He's a good boy, and he don't mean no harm to anybody."

Essie nodded and smiled at Lester. "Uncle Lester, when have I ever not been nice to someone?"

Lester waved his hand in the air, a perplexed expression forming on the chubby face. "Oh, I ain't got time to tell you all the times I've seen you slingin' buckets of corn cobs at folks who don't behave themselves. Got to go. See you."

Essie walked out into the yard and watched her uncle head toward the Bellville road. *So, the big-time New York lawyer was coming to Madison County. His baby brother was shot by a fragile, sweet Southern belle, and he's going to set things straight. Well, come on down, Mr. Big City Lawyer. You've never met the Donnelly sisters, so I'd be careful if I were you.*

CHAPTER ELEVEN

Essie picked up *Peyton Place* and turned to the first page of Chapter 23; she desperately wanted to learn more about her *sexual being*. But, first she wanted to check on DooRay, Murphy and Killer.

At the barn, DooRay sat on an overturned bucket, the jar of water in his hand. He smiled a crooked smile, and she saw a front tooth was missing. "Oh, DooRay. You poor thing." She pulled up another bucket and sat beside him and looked at his swollen face. "How much do you hurt, DooRay?"

His fat lips cracked open, one eye peering at her, the other one tightly shut, blood dried along the lid. "Miss Essie, that was a mean man, wasn't he?" He pointed over to Murphy. "Look at my beautiful Murphy. His ear done gone."

"I know. I know, DooRay. I'm so sorry. And, look at poor Killer. He looks so sad."

"Yes, 'em. I don't believe he even crowed this mornin'."

Essie reached out and touched DooRay's cheek. "DooRay, tell me. Does it hurt real bad?"

DooRay winced when she touched his cheek. Dried blood covered his face and head. The lobe on his right ear was cut and covered in dried blood. "I's kinda sore all over. But, I'm not paining too much."

"I'll take you to Dr. Bush, DooRay. Let's get some stitches in that ear."

"Oh, no, Miss Essie. My ear is jus' fine." He looked over at Murphy. "It's Murphy I'm worried about. His ear done gone."

Murphy bleated and walked over to DooRay.

"DooRay, you know that man who beat you? Well, he's dead."

DooRay jerked back. "Dead? What happened, Miss Essie."

"Well, when Jewell and I got back from Tallahassee, he was in the kitchen and had one a mama's big butcher knives and threatened Jewell and me."

"Oh, my. I'm so sorry, Miss Essie."

"No need to be sorry, DooRay. He was meaner than a snake. Jewell got daddy's pistol and shot him right through the heart." Essie paused. "If it hadn't been for Jewell, I don't know what that man would've done. Probably killed us."

Murphy bleated loudly and kicked up his heels, perhaps rejoicing the death of the man who cut off his ear.

"I'll bring you something to eat, DooRay. Maybe some warm chicken soup would be best."

Essie walked back to the house just as a car pulled up in the yard. Sunlight glinted off the chrome grill. It was an unfamiliar car, and the man who opened the door and stood in the yard was unknown to her.

He was tall and thin, his large nose the most prominent feature on his face. He wore a dark suit and tie. His hat was brown, a felt fedora with a center crown crease and narrow brim. The brim turned down in the front with a slight tilt forward, giving Essie the feeling that everything about him was mysterious. Like he was hiding something. The brim of his hat cast a shadow on the top half of his face, like a veil covering his eyes.

She watched him as he studied the house and the yard. "You there," she called. "Can I help you?"

He didn't smile and stood a moment looking her way, waiting for her to approach him. He never removed his hand from the top of the car door, as if he wanted to make a quick get-away.

Essie walked slowly past the house and under a big oak. "You lost?"

"No, not lost."

"Don't believe I know you." Essie looked him over for the second time.

"No, mam. I'm looking for someone—a man named DooRay Aikens."

54

"DooRay Aikens?" Hesitating only a fraction of a second, Essie shook her head. "Don't believe I know a DooRay Aikens."

"Someone in Pinetta told me he lived out this way." The man's eyes scoured the yard while his head slowly swiveled to his right and then left."

"Not here on this farm. Maybe down the road. What do you need him for?"

The man reached into the inside pocket of his suit and pulled out a card. He walked a few steps toward Essie and held it out for her. "Here. If you see Mr. Aikens, give him this card. I'd like to speak with him."

Essie looked at the card. *Earle Knight Washington, D. C. Telephone 55572.* She felt the hairs prick on the back of her neck, an anxiousness flushing her skin. When she looked up, the man was getting into his car. She heard the motor start and watched as he rounded the circular drive and drove the lane to the Bellville road. He turned right and headed to Pinetta.

Her hand shook as she reread the card. *Washington, D. C.*

She turned and ran to the barn. "DooRay! DooRay!" She turned the corner and stopped at the tack room door. "DooRay, there's a man lookin' for you. He's from Washington, D. C. What have you done? Are you making moonshine, DooRay?"

DooRay squinted up at Essie. "Washington D. C. A government man?"

"Yes! You're right! He looked just like a government man."

"I surely don't know, Miss Essie. I surely don't."

"DooRay, you know it's illegal to make moonshine, don't you? You get caught doing that and you're going to jail, for sure. You know ole Lewis Hill drives his mule to Madison and sells moonshine out behind a store, in an empty lot. You know that, don't you, DooRay."

"Yes, mam. I knowed some peoples who do it, but not DooRay."

"I told that government man I didn't know you. Who sent him over here lookin' for you? Oh, DooRay. How could a one-armed man make moonshine anyway?"

DooRay laughed. "'member I tole you DooRay can do most anythin', Miss Essie, even if I's only got one arm."

Essie rushed to the house and called Lester. 'Uncle Lester, there's a government man lookin' for DooRay. You know anything about it?

"A government man? How do you know it's a government man?"

"His business card says so. Washington, D. C."

"Hmmmm. No, don't know a thing. Is DooRay in some kinda trouble? Making moonshine or somethin'?"

"He said not."

"I remember a few years back he kinda disappeared for a while. Came back with his arm gone. Never did know what happened or where he went."

Essie took a deep breath. "Nobody knew where he went. Not even his mama."

"Well, I'll let you know if I hear anything about a government man snooping around."

"Okay, Uncle Lester. I'll talk to you later."

Behind her, Jewell stepped into the kitchen. "Good morning, sister."

"Good morning, Jewell. Sleep well?" Essie studied her sister and looked for signs of distress. She saw none. Her green eyes were clear and focused. She wondered if Jewell remembered shooting George Barnwell. Remembered the blood? The knife?

Dr. Anderson said Jewell went neither backward nor forward. Essie felt Jewell would not dwell on the shooting of George Barnwell. She would listen to The Gospel Hour and look for Jimmy at the top of the hill. She would laugh as the sunlight caught Jimmy's blond hair, and he'd lift his arm and wave and begin to run across the field.

"My goodness!" Jewell looked at the kitchen clock. "It's time for The Gospel Hour."

On the front porch, The Gospel Hour had begun, and the voice of Brother Wilbur boomed through the speaker. The gospel coursed through the radio as if it were on fire, leaving trails of smoke and sparking and snapping like cracklings in a hot oven. "And thou shalt not kill…"

CHAPTER TWELVE

The motor on the mail car was loud, a clunk-clunk as it pulled up to the Donnelly mailbox. Waldo Kinsey, a mail carrier for thirty years, sat a moment and stuffed mail into the box, then pulled out toward the Withlachoochee, where he'd turn around and continue his route on the south side of the Bellville road.

Essie set aside her book and hurried down the lane. It had been weeks since she submitted her manuscript to the literary agent in New York City. Anxiously, she opened the mailbox and found a Sears catalog, an electric bill and a letter from a cousin in Tallahassee. Nothing from Mr. Thomas H. Fox, supposedly a renowned literary agent known for his discovery of new writers. Essie let out a breath; there was no acceptance letter for her manuscript.

She slowly walked the lane home, the sun warm on her back. Though disappointed, she could not regret her hours at her typewriter. She wouldn't trade her Royal for a solid gold pitchfork. Her life had shifted and tumbled off balance, but her fingers still found the cool keys of the typewriter and felt the life force of her dreams and imagination through the words she wrote.

A pot of chicken soup simmered on the stove. It was Edith Donnelly's recipe. Thick and creamy with lots of carrots and celery and hunks of tender chicken, Essie ladled it into a bowl and took it out to the barn. DooRay was fast asleep, Murphy right beside him. Killer sat cleaning his feathers on top of Murphy's back. She left the soup nearby, refilled his water jar from the well and walked back to the house.

Essie eased into the swing, opened *Peyton Place* and began reading, gently pushing the swing with her foot. Like Constance in the novel, she wondered if she, too, had been forced to come to terms with her identity, both as a woman and a sexual being. The three women in the story carried scandalous secrets, were lonely and repressed. Essie carried no scandalous secrets, nor did she feel repressed. She couldn't even determine if she had any forbidden thoughts, which the novel's characters certainly had.

Just who was Essie Donnelly? She turned the page and there were those words again: *sexual being*. Coming to terms with her identity did not seem to be foremost on her mind. She had wanted to leave the farm. Leave Madison County. She was Scarlett in *Gone With The Wind* and searched for... for a place—a place where she would be more than who she was in Pinetta, Florida.

Her eyes left the pages of the book and drifted across the field south of the house. She felt an ache in her throat. From the moment she got off the Greyhound in Madison and went to the funeral home to see her mother, she knew she would spend the remainder of her life on the farm, day-to-day existence that entailed caring for Jewell and her daddy.

Hubert Donnelly had died only seven years after Edith and left his daughters with a large farm, cows, hogs, chickens and three employees who managed the daily operations. A field of corn there, a field of watermelons there, tobacco barns full of drying tobacco and plenty of money in the bank.

Suddenly, Essie had the urge to see the Greyhound bus ticket she had bought so long ago, to hold it in her hands. A bus ticket to Atlanta. From there, she didn't know. Where would she have gone? Anywhere would do—anywhere away from Madison County.

She was nothing but a farmer's daughter. Now, the farmer's daughter owned the farm. Within three months after her daddy's death, she leased the entire 300 acres out to Emmett Gaston. She sold the cows and hogs at the Madison stockyards and kept only a few chickens. She would never load another watermelon.

At the other end of the porch, the gospel hour over, Jewell closed her bible. Her eyes swept the south field for the millionth time. She raised up in her chair, her chin tilted upward. Always searching.

"Jewell, Sam Washington is coming here later this afternoon to talk to you. Do you remember Sam Washington?"

"I am certain I do, Essie." She closed her eyes and when she opened them, she turned to Essie. "Sam Washington. A handsome man if I recollect correctly," she said, a primness in her voice. Poised, her back erect, she straightened her skirt and swept her hand across her hair.

"That's right. The Washington's farm's over on the Madison highway, around the Washington loop."

Jewell said nothing, her fingers twirling the red silk bookmarker in her bible, her eyes gazing south, south to the field and the crest of the hill.

"Sam's a lawyer. He needs to talk to you about some things. Do you remember shooting daddy's pistol?"

Jewell narrowed her eyes and nodded. "Oh, yes, I do, Essie. That man in our kitchen. The one with mama's butcher knife." A scowl on her face, Jewell blurted to Essie. "You know that was mama's favorite butcher knife, don't you?"

Essie nodded. "Well, Sam needs to talk to you about the man from the prison farm. Do you think you can remember everything that happened?"

Jewell watched a redbird peck the ground around the bottom of an oak tree and slowly nodded. "I remember." She turned to Essie and smiled. "Essie, let's go to Lon Terry's store and get some candy today."

"We can do that, but let's wait until after Mr. Washington pays us a visit."

Jewell smiled and opened her bible. "You know, Essie, I think we should invite Jimmy over for dinner tonight. Fry some chicken. I could make mama's buttered rum pound cake. Then, maybe we can ride out to Cherry Lake."

"Cherry Lake?" Essie closed her book. Jewell hadn't mentioned Cherry Lake in years. They had found Jimmy's body in eight feet of water five hours after Jewell was dragged to shore. She was revived, but things were never the same. Jewell's memory was forever tainted, never realizing Jimmy was gone.

Jewell's face was beaming. "We could have mashed potatoes, you know how Jimmy likes mashed potatoes."

Essie smiled. "Yes, mashed potatoes. I could make some biscuits, too."

Jewell clapped her hands and jumped from her chair. "I'll start that pound cake. Do you think we have enough eggs?"

"I'm sure we do."

Jewell opened the screened door and turned back around to Essie. "I'll set the table in mama's good china."

"Yes, mama's favorite china."

The screened door slammed shut and Essie heard the rattle of cake pans in her mama's kitchen. Jewell talked to herself, but Essie couldn't hear what she was saying.

Essie leaned back in the swing and tucked her legs beneath her and opened *Peyton Place*. So, Constance went to New York and fell in love with a rich married man named Allison MacKenzie. She became pregnant with his baby and Allison died shortly after the baby was born. Constance went back to Peyton Place as a widow with a child. The scandalous secrets were beginning to pile up in that small town. One after the other, they tormented the women who all along had had forbidden thoughts.

Essie closed the book when she heard a car slow and turn down the lane. Sam Washington. She'd tell him the date was off after he talked with Jewell. She watched him park in the shade under an oak tree and step into the yard, a smile on his face. Yes, he was handsome. No doubt about it. But handsome was nothing compared to intelligence. So far, in Essie's opinion, Sam had not displayed an abundance of intelligence by escaping the prison work camp and sleeping naked in Jewell's bed.

"Miss Essie," he called. "You're lookin' mighty fine today."

Mighty fine? She wore her daddy's overalls and a work shirt. Her hair was pinned up off her neck, not even brushed. She gave him a concierge smile when he stepped onto the porch.

He sat next to the swing and leaned back into the big rocker. "How's Jewell? And DooRay? Lester said that fella beat DooRay with a two by four."

"Jewell's fine. She's inside baking a cake. DooRay's sleeping." Essie found herself looking at Sam's eyelashes, his nose, his mouth and the brown hair combed neatly to the side, a neat part. His skin was dark, tanned she supposed from working on the road crew. A cigar poked out of his shirt pocket. Could she really spend five hours with him?

Essie felt a moment of malicious glee. "Lester says that dead fella's brother is a lawyer from New York City, and he's on his way to Madison. He's gonna whip you up one side and down the other when he gets here," said Essie, the corners of her mouth promising a smile.

Sam laughed and slapped his knee. "Oh, that'll be the day. He's never tangled with a Madison County lawyer before."

Essie noticed Sam's fingers were long, his hands strong. She wondered what work he did while he was on the prison road crew. "Why do you think he's coming down here?"

"Oh, I suspect he's looking for some answers. Wants to make sure he has the facts. He told Simmie Moore he was filing a wrongful death suit. From what Simmie told me, Jewell didn't commit any wrongful conduct. It's a clear case of self-defense from what I gather." He paused and pulled the cigar from his pocket. "You were there and saw everything. Your statement will be just as important as Jewell's."

"Has a date been set for the inquest?"

"Monday, July 23. 10:00 a.m. Judge Curtis Earp residing. Judge Earp is a good man; he'll handle things well. In his court, that New York lawyer won't get away with anything."

Sam unwrapped his cigar and moistened the end in his mouth. "So, I'm thinking Saturday night would be a good time for you and me to go to Tallahassee. Have a fine dinner." He was so casual his words did not register with Essie for a few seconds.

"Saturday night?"

He looked at her and smiled. "Saturday night." She held his eyes and saw glitters of humor in them, a laughter that waited on the fringes.

"I'm not sure I can leave Jewell alone." She fiddled with the straps of her overalls.

"Already talked with your Uncle Lester and Aunt Shelly. They're going to come over and sit with her for a few hours while we're over in Tallahassee."

"Well, how convenient. You take care of everything, don't you?" They were not kind words. She turned away and felt anger heating up.

Sam pulled a stool to the front of his rocker and propped up his feet. He clipped off the end of his cigar and lit it, puffing hard until he saw the embers glow bright. "I've been thinking. Let's don't call this a date. A date might be too complex. Let's just say I'm very attracted to you and want to get to know you better. We'll spend some time together at dinner and, at the end of dinner, we'll see where we stand."

Essie cocked her head at Sam. "I do believe I stated my preferences the other night. I already *know* where we stand. You're my sister's lawyer. That's all. There's no need to prolong the agony I feel by getting in a car with you and driving to a restaurant in Tallahassee." *Damn, she was a hard woman.*

Essie jumped from the swing. "I'll get Jewell for you."

She half-stomped to the screened door and yelled for Jewell. "Jewell, Sam Washington is here."

"I'm sorry, Essie." Jewell called. "I've got to watch this cake. It's about ready to come out of the oven."

Behind her, Essie heard Sam chuckle. "Agony? It would be agony for you to get in the car with me and drive to Tallahassee?"

He stood and walked the length of the porch and looked out over the yard. His chin lifted as he watched a buzzard circle the east pasture. He turned and grinned. '*Contact with a high-minded woman is good for the life of any man.*' Henry Vincent.'" He bounded down the steps. "Think I'll walk out and talk to DooRay." He left the porch and headed toward the barn, cigar smoke following him.

Essie watched his long legs cover the distance. He was a Washington, all right. All those boys had long legs. They were stubborn, too. Wild and crazy in their teens, if there was trouble in Pinetta, it was usually one of the Washington boys, either Paul's sons or Tillman's sons, Joe and John. They hung out around the train depot at night or the Pinetta Garage and smoked and, for sure, had some of Lewis Hill's shine.

Lewis was Madison County's most prolific shiner, his still hidden in dark bends of the Withlacoochee, where fat water moccasins kept watch on the old man. His shine, pale gold and as safe as buttermilk, would not affect a man's private parts, break him out in warts or cause him to run naked through the cornfields under a full moon. But Lewis' shine would smother a man's brain like soft vanilla custard and make him think he was the smartest man on earth.

The stills were never hidden well enough to fool the Washington boys, as every Saturday night they were hootin' and hollerin' clear across The Prairie. One night they made so much noise that Lum Townsend raised his shotgun into the air with a promise to use it on their behinds if they didn't go home.

She stood watching Sam until he was out of sight, admitting her anger was no less than a hurtling freight train whose brakes had failed. Somehow, she must refuse to spend one more moment with that cocky man.

Essie went inside the house, the fragrance of pound cake heavy in the air. *I never considered myself to be a high-minded woman.*

"Jewell, I'll take care of the cake. You go on out on the porch and talk with Mr. Washington."

Jewell wiped her hands on a dishtowel and took off her apron. "Oh, my, Essie. What was it you said I'd have to say? Something about daddy's pistol?"

Essie stared at her sister. "Remember yesterday, Jewell? The man with mama's butcher knife?"

Jewell pursed her lips and frowned. "I'm not sure I put vanilla in that cake."

CHAPTER THIRTEEN

Sam meandered from the barn and pulled a briefcase out of his car. On the porch, he waited for Jewell while he finished smoking his cigar. In the west, black clouds billowed on the horizon and moved slowly toward Madison County. He watched the tops of the pine trees sway as the wind picked up and blew pine needles across the yard. He felt the temperature drop and knew rain was on the way.

His love for Madison County was heartfelt. He knew Atlanta or New York would have been a short-lived adventure after his bar exam. In the beginning, his quest to go out into the world with his newfound knowledge had not included Madison County.

He'd had restless dreams where he had walked alone in large cities with narrow streets; cold cities where thousands of people walked without speaking or looking at one another. His homesickness would have atrophied his mind and debilitated his body. He tilted his head onto the back of the rocker, closed his eyes and felt a surge of joy. He was in the right place.

Jewell left the kitchen and stepped onto the porch where Sam held a notebook and pen. "Jewell," he began, "the state attorney will be visiting you next week along with a court recorder. Do you understand what he'll be asking you?" He sat across from her and saw what an amazingly beautiful woman she was.

"I'm so happy to help," she said, her voice a soft whisper. Her green eyes were wide and eager.

"Just tell him the truth. Always the truth. If you can't remember something, tell him you can't remember."

Jewell nodded and took a deep breath. There was a slight fragrance of vanilla in the air, perhaps the remnants of her pound cake.

Her skin was as pale as moonlight, her facial bones prominent, revealing a delicate, oval face. Her hands rested in her lap, pressed together as if in prayer. Her thinness troubled him as though she were the fragile wing of a hummingbird. He found himself wanting to shelter her from whatever it was that might harm her.

"Do you have questions for me, Jewell?"

Sam waited for Jewell to continue. A splatter of raindrops fell on the brick steps. Jewell suddenly left her chair and stood at the porch railing. "Oh, my. Jimmy will get drenched."

"Jimmy?"

"Jimmy—my fiancé. He's coming for dinner." She pointed to the far hill. "He'll be coming over that hill any minute." She turned and smiled. "I'd like you to meet him, Mr. Washington."

Sam moved to Jewell's side. Wind blew soft mist onto their faces. "Jewell." He knew the interview was over. Jewell had gone to another place; he could see it in her eyes.

A low echoing of thunder rolled across the hill like a slow-moving freight train. For a moment, everything seemed to still, even the wind. Then, a streak of hot silver split the sky. Thunder boomed like artillery, and sheets of warm rain raced across the road toward them. "Let's go inside, Jewell."

Inside, the Donnelly kitchen smelled of cake and frying chicken. Essie stood at the stove and stirred a pot of potatoes. She looked up when she heard Sam and Jewell. "Finished?" she asked, returning to the frying chicken.

Sam wiped the rain from his face with his hand. "Yes, we're finished except for a few details. The state attorney will visit next Thursday and take Jewell's deposition." He noticed Essie was barefooted.

Jewell placed china plates on the table over a white cotton tablecloth. "Essie, Mr. Washington is going to stay for dinner. The weather is so horrible I don't believe Jimmy will be able to join us." She fretted over the placement of cloth napkins, then glanced at Sam. "Mr. Washington, I think I'll place you at the head of the table. Is that acceptable to you?"

Sam nodded. "Of course." His eyes cut over to Essie who placed a platter on the counter and began arranging the chicken. He saw a pan of biscuits on the stove, butter melting on their tops. Steam rose from a bowl of mashed potatoes and he hoped there was chicken gravy.

When they sat down for dinner, Essie passed the platter of chicken to Sam. "Mr. Washington, don't you think this marvelous dinner will suffice as payment for your legal services."

Sam took the platter and placed a large drumstick on his plate. He couldn't help but smile, his eyes locking onto Essie's. "I will have to refrain from answering that question until I have finished my meal. After all, you may not have salted the chicken enough. Also, I like a lot of pepper on my chicken." He raised his eyebrows in question, mischief in his eyes. "You did pepper the chicken, didn't you?"

Chapter Fourteen

The autopsy report on George Barnwell did, indeed, show a bullet wound right through the heart. It also showed a large laceration on the side of his head where his ear used to be. A notation on the report mentioned the ear was not available for analysis. A curious wound on the calf of his right leg was noted as *perhaps a gouge by the spur of a rooster.*

At the request of Sheriff Simmie Moore, a copy of the autopsy report was sent to Stanley Barnwell, Attorney, Barnwell, Smith and Wolfson law firm in New York City. In response, Barnwell had notified Sheriff Moore that he would arrive prior to the inquest scheduled for Monday, July 23.

Stanley Barnwell also notified Judge Curtis Earp of the Third Judicial Circuit Court of Florida that he would be attending the inquest. After the inquest, Mr. Barnwell stated he would have his brother's body shipped back to New York.

Sam wondered about DooRay Aikens. An escaped inmate of the Madison County Correctional Institution had beaten DooRay, almost killed him. Somehow DooRay needed restitution. The correctional institution was most likely entitled to immunity under the state tort claims act.

Sam thought of laws grinding the poor and rich men ruling the law. He became melancholy. He felt universal and absolute law was a natural justice, a justice that could not be written down but would appeal to the hearts of all.

In law school, his professor talked of unalterable law—those words convinced Sam the man was an unalterable fool. He decided he would research the law library and, hopefully, provide justice for DooRay through the courts.

On Friday morning, Sam decided to drive out to the Donnelly farm. There were questions to be asked.

In Pinetta, he stopped in J. T. Woodward's store and found Fred Huggins behind the counter. "Mr. Fred, it's good to see you."

"Hello, Sam. Heard you were working for Judge Earp."

"Well, let's just say I'm at the courthouse quite often." Sam smiled at the soft-spoken man who seemed to always be wearing a Cardigan sweater, whether it was ninety-five degrees or freezing.

Fred nodded. "Got you a big murder case working? That prisoner from the road gang?"

"Well, it's not exactly what I'd call a murder. Guess the inquest will decide based on the circumstances."

"I see." Fred smoothed his hair. "What are you looking for today, Sam."

"I need something for my mama. Let me look in that glass case over there." Sam walked up front and found the long glass case that had all kinds of knick-knacks that his mama might like. He pointed to the silver pin in the corner. "How 'bout that butterfly pin."

Fred slid the back of the case open and reached inside. "Yep. This is nice. Just right for your beautiful mama."

Sam grinned. "I'll take it."

Fred placed the pin in a small box and wrapped it in brown paper and tied it with a string, just like it was a pork chop or a steak. Sam smiled to himself. His mama would like it no matter what it was wrapped in.

"Where's J. T. today?"

"Oh, he's out back. Got a load of fertilizer in and he might be unloading it. Or could be he went home to eat lunch. Miss Abby's not feeling too good so maybe he's checking on her."

"While you're working on that, I'll run down to the telephone."

Sam walked over to the little wood house that served as a telephone booth by J. T. Woodward's store. He sat on the small wooden seat and cranked the telephone and waited for the operator. "Operator."

"Hey, Doris. Can you try Judge Earp for me?"

"His number 4321?"

"That's right."

Sam heard it ring a few times. Doris came in on the line. "Nobody there, Sam."

"No problem. I'll try again later."

A farm truck pulled next to the post office. Tillman Washington jumped out. "Hey, Sam. Good morning to you."

"Hey, Tillman. Where you going with all those younguns? Hey, Mary Nell! Hey, Abigail!"

"Oh, we're headed to the movies in Madison. New Lone Ranger show today."

"Where's Inez?"

"Oh, she's getting ready for a church meeting at Mr. Horeb."

"Tell her I said hello. Your mom doing all right?"

"Sure is, Sam."

Back in the store, Fred handed Sam the wrapped package. "That'll be $4.00, Sam."

Sam pulled out a $5 bill and handed it to Fred. "Thank you so much, Fred."

"My pleasure."

Sam glanced at the white house where J. T. lived and thought about stopping in. He changed his mind when he bumped into Dr. Bush coming out of his office. "Dr. Bush." He said, reaching out his hand.

"Hey, Sam. Guess I'll see you in court on the 23rd. I'll be testifying on the cause of death on that Barnwell fellow."

"That's right, Dr. Bush. I'll see you then."

Sam crossed the railroad tracks and passed V. S. Smith's store and over 145 to the Bellville road. In Terryville he pulled into Lon Terry's general store for an ice-cold Nehi orange soda. Mr. Terry was behind the counter smoking a Chesterfield. His gruff voice bellowed across the small store. "Here comes one a them Washington boys. How are you, Sam?"

"Doin' fine, Mr. Terry. How about you?"

"I'm kinda tired. Me and Rana had to cut out some hogs early this morning. Get them ready for the stockyard.

"Your Tamworth hogs are worth a mint."

"Yeah. Big fat fellers all right."

Sam pulled a Nehi out of the cooler, sat on a stool and looked around the store. "You've got everything in here, Mr. Terry. I see blue jeans, shoes, sacks of flour." Sam pointed past Lon. "And you've got that lean-to next door loaded with televisions and freezers."

"Well, it's a general store, Sam. Got everything but whiskey." Lon Terry leaned across the counter. "Say, speakin' of whiskey, a feller came in yesterday asking about DooRay Aikens. He wasn't from around here. Looked like one of them Yankees to me. In a suit, hat. Serious looking man. Reckon he's one of those revenuers?"

"A government man? Did he give you his name?"

"Nope. I told him I never heard of DooRay Aikens. Don't think he believed me, though. You reckon DooRay's in some kind a trouble?"

Sam shook his head. "I have no idea, Mr. Terry."

The back-screen door of the store opened and Lon's wife, Rana, came in. "Oh, Miss Rana. I would kill for some of your macaroni and cheese."

Rana laughed. "You been eatin' my macaroni and cheese since you was a little boy, Sam. I'd think you'd get tired of it."

"Oh, no, Miss Rana. Never." Sipping his soda, Sam put a dime on the counter. "Those are some mighty good-lookin' hogs you got over there."

Rana nodded. "Yep. They're headed to the stockyard.

"That's what Lon said. I'd like to go with you, Lon. Help out."

"Be here early and we'll ride together."

Sam wandered around the store and ended up at the front door. "Guess I'll be getting' on down the road. Good to see you nice folks."

"Take a watermelon with you, Sam. If you don't, I'll just throw it to the hogs."

"Believe I will. Appreciate it." Sam picked up a small watermelon and started for the door.

"Oh, hold on a minute, Sam." Lon Terry came from around the counter. He was a tall man, Irish through and through. Red hair turned almost white, thick and curled, freckled skin. "I got somethin' to tell you." He paused and looked over his shoulder at Rana, then back to Sam. "If you see DooRay, tell him he can hide up here at the grist mill if he needs to."

"I'll do that, Mr. Terry." Sam left, the watermelon on his shoulder, and headed for the Donnelly place.

When he braked for the turn onto the Donnelly lane, Sam heard the watermelon roll around in the back of his car. He'd take it out to the barn and split it. While there, he'd talk with DooRay and see if he knew anything about the man who was looking for him.

Sam parked under the spreading limbs of a great oak tree. Both Essie and Jewell sat on the porch. Jewell waved; Essie did not. "Be back in a minute," he called. "Going to the barn to see DooRay." He pulled out the watermelon and hoisted it to his shoulder.

DooRay sat on a bucket outside the tack room, Murphy and Killer nearby. "DooRay! How's it going?" Sam winced when he looked at the black man. His face was swollen and bruised. Scabs had begun to form on his lips where they had been split. He still had gauze around his head wounds.

"Mr. Sam, that looks like a mighty good watermelon."

"It's for you, DooRay. I'll have to get a knife, so we can cut it. Be right back."

Sam walked from the barn to the front of the house and onto the brick steps. "You ladies mind if I borrow a knife? Mr. Terry gave me a watermelon—I'd be willing to share it."

Jewell smiled and stood from her chair. "Hello, Mr. Washington. We'd be glad to lend you a knife. I'll be right back."

There was no response from Essie, who sat in the swing reading her book. She turned a page, her foot slowly pushing the swing. Sam saw the words *Peyton Place* on the book's cover. "Miss Essie, I'm quite certain that book's been banned in Madison County."

Essie looked up, unsmiling. "You're thinking of *Lady Chatterley's Lover.*"

Sam continued up the steps and leaned against the railing. In an almost whisper, he spoke as though he were alone in the middle of a Madison County cornfield. *"Indian summer is like a woman. Ripe, hotly passionate, but fickle, she comes and goes as she pleases so that one is never sure whether she will come out at all, nor for how long she will stay."*

Essie closed the book, never taking her eyes off Sam. "That's the first paragraph in the first chapter of *Peyton Place.*"

"Indeed, it is. A passage that is not as torrid as most in the book."

Essie's eyes narrowed. "You read the book." It wasn't a question but rather a statement. She stared at the small-town farm boy who went off to college and returned to an isolated town whose cupboards surely held skeletons much like those in the fictitious town of Peyton Place.

Sam nodded. "*Peyton Place* is a small-town peep show."

Essie left the swing and took a few steps toward Sam, the book in her hands. "I feel it is a work of absorbing interest and of considerable literary value."

"Have you learned anything from the book?" Sam countered, a slight smile hovering on his lips.

Essie lifted her chin, her back stiffened. "I'm learning it's okay to be a sexual being and to have the aspirations men have."

Sam took a slow step toward her. He was so close he could smell the fragrance of soap; he noticed the pinkness of her cheeks and the way her eyebrows curved slightly. There was a small dark mole near her lips. His words came soft, as tender as a Brahms lullaby. "Why, Essie Donnelly, I would have thought you learned that a very long time ago."

The screen door opened, and Jewell stepped onto the porch. "I positively could not find mama's big butcher knife to cut that watermelon. But I've got a knife, some plates, forks, a lovely tablecloth and four of mama's white linen table napkins. Let's have a picnic out under the oak tree near the barn."

Sam reached out and took the knife and plates. "Miss Jewell, you are the best hostess in Madison County. May I accompany you to the picnic table?"

She took his arm. "By all means, kind sir."

They stepped from the porch and walked across the lawn. "Come on, Essie," chirped Jewell. "We're going on a picnic."

Sam glanced over his shoulder and saw Essie watching him. Her expression was quizzical, as if he were a mystery man and she wondered who he was. He held her eyes for a moment until Jewell pulled on his arm. "Hurry up, Sam! I'm dying for a slice of that watermelon."

Sam helped Jewell spread the tablecloth and listened to her chatter away. "Wouldn't it be lovely if Jimmy were here. But, he's probably helping his daddy with tobacco."

"I'm sure Jimmy would like to be here." Sam called over to

DooRay. "DooRay, would you bring that watermelon over here? It looks like we're having a picnic."

DooRay obliged and carried the watermelon with his one arm to the table. He hung his head. "I can jus' eat watermelon in the barn."

Jewell stilled. "In the barn? Now why would you do that, DooRay?" She pointed to the bench. "You sit there. Sam, you sit there." She turned and looked toward the house. "Essie!"

Essie opened the screen door at the back porch and stepped into the yard. She had brushed her hair and twirled it up on top of her head. A hint of pink lipstick swept across her lips. She came slowly as if in thought. She felt each step was just a little gleam of time between two eternities; no second chance.

She wondered if God had let her fall in just the niche she was ordained to fill. A little work, a little sleep, a little love and life was over. *Where is the love*, she thought? Maybe her soul had its own ears to hear the things her heart was too fragile to hear.

She sat at the picnic table, next to Sam. She couldn't help herself. "Do I need to get pepper for the watermelon, Mr. Washington?"

After their picnic, Sam meandered to the barn and found DooRay pumping water from the well. "Mr. Sam, would you like some cool water?"

"That sounds good, DooRay."

The two men sat outside the barn while Murphy grazed slowly toward the tobacco barns. Killer rode along on the goat's back.

"DooRay, I stopped by Mr. Terry's store on my way out here. He tells me a fella is going around town asking about you."

DooRay, through his bruised and swollen lips, smiled. The eye with the laceration above it drooped considerably. "I done heard about that from Miss Essie. He was here lookin' for me. Said she thought he was a government man since his card said Washington, D. C."

"Have any idea why he's looking for you?"

"I has no idea, Mr. Sam. I ain't makin' no moonshine or nothin'."

Sam nodded. "Well, I better get on my way. Got to go back to the courthouse." He hesitated. "DooRay, you're going to receive a subpoena to appear as a witness at the inquest."

DooRay looked surprised. "Me? DooRay?"

"I think you'll make an excellent witness. And, besides that, you are a victim. That fella beat you real bad."

"That he did. Tried to kill me." DooRay closed his eyes as if remembering.

"You'll be hearing from the state attorney's office."

"Yes, suh, Mr. Sam."

"By the way, Mr. Terry said if you need to lay low for a while, you can come up to the grist mill. He said it was dry and there was a stack of hay in there. Said he'd feed you, too."

"Uh, huh. Mr. Terry. I knowed him since I was born."

"I'll see you later, DooRay."

Sam passed the front porch and called to Essie. "See you tomorrow night, Essie."

She gave him a reticent nod. He could almost see anger washing over her; she was a thunderclap in a summer storm.

CHAPTER FIFTEEN

Sam had provided information to the state attorney's office to subpoena DooRay as a witness at the inquest. Late into the night, he studied at the law library at the courthouse. DooRay Aiken needed a voice and Sam was determined to be that voice. He was considering a personal injury lawsuit against the estate of George Barnwell.

It was near midnight when he left downtown Madison and drove to his father's barn where he had a small cozy room in the corner in the rafters. His brothers had helped him frame in the space; the room even had two windows as well as a ladder to climb to his lair.

He walked a path to the rambling house to use the bathroom on the lower floor, as well as the kitchen, over which his mother so diligently presided. He was thirty-three years old and found himself quite content to remain on the big farm. Balance—that's what it was all about.

The next morning, Sam helped his father load hay, feed cows and gather in dozens of eggs from the hen house. His mother would use a few dozen of the eggs to make cakes for the members of her Sunday school class at church; she was a saint. Afterwards, she fixed a breakfast of grits, eggs and ham from one of their homegrown hogs. Life on the farm, though hard, was idyllic.

Around three o'clock, he showered and shaved. He whistled a tune from Tennessee Ernie Ford's new album: *Sixteen Tons*. He then found himself thinking about Essie Donnelly. He felt she was like an invented persona, worn like a cloak and then changed on a whim. He knew not to make the blunder of underestimating her, yet he decided beneath the harshness of his conversations with her that she held within her a softness. It was as if she walked a tightrope that stretched from hot to cold, from hard to soft.

Was he being romantic? One is said to be romantic if one admires finer things. He felt Essie Donnelly was definitely a finer thing.

He dressed in navy slacks, a white oxford shirt and a red and blue striped tie. He carried a jacket, though one was not required at The Embers restaurant in Tallahassee. Oddly, he felt nervous. Yes, he would not underestimate the younger Donnelly sister.

Sam passed through Pinetta on the Belleville road, the clay road riddled with ruts at least six inches deep. An earlier rain had made the mixture of clay and sand thick enough to work a potter's mold. When he passed by Lon Terry's store, several of Mr. Terry's hogs had escaped their pen and lay rooted in the cool mud of the road. He eased by them; they hardly blinked an eye. It was their mud.

At the Donnelly drive, he turned slowly into the lane and saw Lester Terry's truck. Lester was Lon Terry's brother. Spastic and energetic, Lester kept the Pinetta community within his grasp with his rowdy guitar playing and his love of boiled peanuts.

There was no one in the county who didn't like him, except maybe the prisoners at the county prison farm. The ten hours he worked each day at the prison farm turned Lester into a pump-action shotgun. He took no nonsense from any of them—unless, of course, they happened to be Sam Washington, a Pinetta boy made good.

The cool of a late June evening spread along the Donnelly front porch, the ceiling fans twirling slowly, and where Lester and Shelly sat arguing about whether barbecue should be chopped or pulled.

Lester puffed loudly. "Why, my daddy would roast a pig on a spit over a fire made with fine oak wood and, my darling wife, he would let it cool ever so slightly and begin to pull the strips of delicious meat from the bones as if it were pure gold."

Shelly was not to be outdone. "Well, my daddy had an open pit on which he roasted big cuts of pork and when it was perfectly tender, he would get his sharpest knife and chop it into the most delicate pieces—just right for my tiny mouth."

She took a deep breath and leaned over toward Jewell. Then, a hoarse whisper to ensure Lester heard. "And my mama made barbecue sauce with a secret ingredient." She looked over her shoulder at Lester. "She put pureed oranges and tangerines in her sauce." She leaned back in her chair, a look of pride on her face. "Best barbecue sauce in the county."

Sam parked his car along the lane next to the house. "Evenin', everybody," he called. He had flowers for Essie but left them in the car. He had told her not to call their outing a date, but rather a casual get-together. Perhaps the flowers were not a good idea.

Lester stood from his chair and leaned out over the porch rail. "Well, I thought I heard a Washington out there in the yard. How are you, boy?"

Laughing, Sam bounded up the steps. "Yep, it's a Washington all right."

"My goodness, Sam. You are quite handsome tonight," said Shelly, her rounded, squat body ambling toward Sam. She reached up and hugged him.

"Good to see you, Shelly. And you, too, Jewell." He found Jewell in her chair and picked up her hand. "You're quite lovely on this Saturday evening."

"Thank you. We're so glad to see you." Jewell's eyes lingered as if she wasn't quite sure who he was. Then, Sam saw the light of recognition. "Oh, yes," she said sweetly, "one of the Washington boys."

Sam sat in the swing at the west end of the porch where the tops of azalea bushes lined the edge. "Thank you, Lester and Shelly, for allowing Essie to have a little bit of leisure time."

"Oh, it's our pleasure, Sam," said Shelly. "We enjoy Jewell's company so much. She is such a lovely girl."

Sam found himself watching Jewell. She sat slightly forward in her chair, her eyes far away on the fields across the road. There was a smile on her lips.

From the upstairs window, the one above the porch, they heard 'shit' and then 'damn' and then a crash of glass. No one spoke; only the rocking chairs moved. Shelly fiddled with her wedding rings. Lester's fingers twiddled along the edge of his chair arm. Sam found himself with a sly smile on his lips—was he truly about to woo this woman?

The front screened door opened wide and like a mirage on a desert, Essie appeared. Her hair, the color of a burnished tobacco leaf in full sun, was swept up into a French twist and held by a jeweled comb that had belonged to her mother. She took a step forward and dipped her chin toward Sam. A belligerent smile followed. "Ready?"

Her dress was like a peach soufflé, perhaps borrowed from her mother's closet and most likely seldom worn. Soft and flowing, it wrapped around her in gentle folds, cinched at the waist and falling just below her knees. A single strand of pearls hung around her slim neck.

Sam jumped from the swing and moved toward her, his eyes steady, but unbelieving. He held out his hand. Essie ignored it.

"How lovely you are, Essie," he said in his most gentlemanly voice.

"Let's go." Essie turned toward Lester and Shelly. "We'll be back by 10:00 o'clock." Then, she turned to Jewell. "Good night, Jewell. Don't worry—I'll be back soon. Do what Uncle Lester and Aunt Shelly tell you. Okay?"

Jewell beamed at her sister. "I will, Essie."

CHAPTER SIXTEEN

They rode to Madison in silence before picking up U. S. 90 toward Greenville and Monticello. When they passed the courthouse, Sam turned on the radio to WMAF, Madison's country music station. He hummed along to Elvis' new hit *I Want You, I Need You, I Love You.*

They traveled west into the setting sun, passing fields laden with planted corn and tobacco. The hills rolled by gently, the crops standing in almost perfect lines as far as the eye could see. Cattle roamed some fields, cattle egrets following them for a last chance to dine on insects the cows' hooves stirred up.

Lake Miccosukee reflected the setting sun with blazing orange clouds, perhaps painted by Van Gogh. In his mind, Sam titled the painting *Sunset on Lake Miccosukee.* He was a tender man, a man who loved his family and his life in Madison County.

He took a deep breath. "I like your shoes."

"I like your tie."

"You smell good."

"So do you."

He would give her quiet attention, not so pointed as to alarm her, but not so vague as to be misunderstood. "I've been thinking about your writing, your sequel to *Gone With The Wind.*" There was no response from Essie. He continued, "I'm wondering what Scarlett is going to do since ole Rhett left her in the end. I feel like he'd had enough of her high-mindedness."

Essie turned and looked at him for a long moment. Then, stared at the asphalt highway. "Scarlett is an independent woman who loves her individuality—she will get along just fine without Rhett." Sam had no idea her manuscript had been sent to New York, its content far from the fields of Tara and the illusive Scarlett O'Hara.

Sam pondered her words. "If I were Rhett, I would appreciate her strength."

Essie didn't hesitate. "You have to realize the era in which they lived. Women were to be genteel and helpless." She smoothed her dress and wished the night were over.

Sam glanced at her profile. Even if he were going to woo this woman, there was absolutely no chance he could win her. She was the Scarlett of Madison County, and there was nothing helpless about her. "Write the book your way; make Scarlett the woman you want her to be."

"Perhaps. My responsibilities in other areas are many."

"Jewell?"

"Yes, Jewell." Her chin lifted, her words containing a knife's edge of resentment. Surprisingly, she continued. "Her doctor suggested I send Jewell to a home somewhere to be cared for. Can you envision her somewhere but the farm? Away from her imagined Jimmy? I could not tolerate her unhappiness."

Sam nodded. "You feel it is your duty as her sister to care for her?"

"Yes," Essie said, emphatically.

"I understand. I am certain, in her own way, she is aware of your care of her."

Essie made no comment as they edged closer to the lighted skyline of Tallahassee. Her hands lay in her lap, her breathing quiet. She was with a man—a man she knew who empirically found her attractive. What did she care—she was who she was: the high-minded Scarlett. What need did she have of him?

Approaching Tallahassee, Sam turned left off U.S. 90 onto Capitol Circle, then left again to the edge of Upper Lake Lafayette where the Embers Restaurant set on a pier-like structure over the water.

After he parked, he leaned toward Essie. A smile played across his lips. "Please allow me to open your car door."

Essie raised her eyebrows. "But, of course." He noticed she had darkened the small mole on her chin by her mouth. Faint soft green eyeshadow glistened on her eyelids. If he kissed her, would she somehow brandish the ax she was so adept at using?

Sam opened her door and extended his hand. Essie quickly took it, but released it immediately upon stepping out of the car. Sam chuckled softly. Her eyes, glinting with a trace of treachery, crossed his face for a split second. Again, he caught a whiff of her soft perfume. At the moment, there was nothing hard about this woman.

The maître de met them at the front of the restaurant. His attire was formal, a bowtie and dark suit. "Reservations?"

"Washington," said Sam.

The thin man with an angular face found Sam's name. "Ah, would you like to sit on the deck above the lake?"

Sam turned to Essie. "I'd like to. Would you?"

"Only if there are no gnats." Sam shrugged, and they followed the black suited man to their table. Sam pulled out Essie's chair and she sat primly at the table.

"Wine for you and the lady?"

Sam glanced at Essie. "May I order wine for you?"

Essie nodded again as she looked around the deck. Candles glittered on the tables, which were set with crisp white tablecloths. Essie's mother would be delighted at the crystal and silver that filled the tables.

"I ordered a white wine. A Riesling. I think you'll like it."

"Thank you. I'm sure I will." Her eyes lingered a moment before she took her napkin and placed it in her lap. "This is lovely. I've never been here before."

"Their food is excellent. I believe their chef is from Austria of all places."

"Austria? I believe Jewell visited Austria while she was in Europe."

"When was that?"

"1938. She spent a year in Switzerland at Alpin Videmanette. Mama wanted Jewell to have an irreproachable foundation in all aspects of social etiquette." Essie half smiled. "You know, more marriageable."

"A charm school?"

"Somewhat—though it's not all about balancing a book on your head or how to hold a teacup. The exposure of Europe had an affect

81

on Jewell."

"How so?"

Essie gave him a full smile. "She got out of Madison County for an entire year. An extraordinary thing, wouldn't you say?"

Sam leaned back while the waiter placed their wine on the table. He picked up his glass and held it toward Essie. "Salute," he said in a voice that held a peculiar softness. He found himself enchanted by the younger Donnelly sister. He didn't quite know why, but it was certainly there.

Essie gently touched his glass with hers. "Salute."

A soft breeze skimmed across the waters of the lake and found the handsome man and his lovely woman at ease with one another. Sam sipped his wine. "So why didn't you go to Europe?"

Sam saw Essie's jaw line harden, her eyes darkening as they swept across his face. "Mama had only one daughter and that was Jewell. Jewell was the princess in the family and mama had big plans for her. Marriage to a blue blood of some kind. Maybe in Charleston or Atlanta. But, that all changed."

Essie ran her finger around the top of her wine glass. "It changed on a hot summer day in August fifteen years ago when Jimmy drowned. Mama never really recovered. She died in 1941, the year I turned eighteen, almost a year after Jewell's near drowning."

"That must have been very hard for you."

"It was. I had my dreams like any young girl. Leave Madison County on that Greyhound bus—just like in the country songs." She sent him a warm smile. She knew he was watching her with the intensity of a portrait artist studying his subject.

Essie continued with soft words, not really wanting to speak of the past and its incongruities. Even so, she talked of the summer she turned seventeen. In meticulous detail, she described her manuscript, her Royal typewriter and the reams of paper her daddy had to buy for her. She was a writer through and through, she told him, resting her chin on top of her folded hands.

From across the table, Sam began to see the slow fading of the harshness around Essie's mouth, the relaxing of her jaw; the liquid shine in her eyes became more vibrant. She was the smiling girl in the yellow dress on the homecoming float. He had never forgotten her.

On the ride home, he wanted to hold her hand. It was only a few inches away, resting in her lap. If he reached out and placed his hand of top of hers, would she pull away?

Sam drove slowly; it was that slow drive taking a girl home after a date, a slowness that said he didn't want the evening to end. He turned down the radio. "I brought you flowers."

She turned and looked at him, the light from the dashboard lighting his face. "Where are they?"

"In the backseat."

"Why didn't you give them to me?"

"I was afraid to—thought you might think this was a date if I gave you flowers."

She looked over her shoulder into the back seat. "They're lovely. Yellow mums."

At that moment Sam placed his hand over hers. He waited for rejection, but there was none. He settled back into the car seat and felt the wooing of Essie Donnelly wash over him like a gentle rain. He was glad she had never left Madison County.

CHAPTER SEVENTEEN

S am spent a few days researching the possibility of DooRay filing a personal injury lawsuit against the estate of George Barnwell. George Barnwell was a degenerate; how could a degenerate have an estate? Especially a dead degenerate.

DooRay, as the plaintiff, would have to comply with statutory procedural requirements. The first order of business for Sam was to determine if George Barnwell's estate existed and if he had collectible assets.

He called Sidney Davis, his college roommate and now an attorney in New York City. "Sid, buddy! How are you?"

"Is that you, Sam?"

"It's me all right. Still in Madison County. Didn't get too far away from Florida State University, did I? What's going on with you?"

"Still with the same firm. A junior partner. You gotta come up to New York—it's on fire, Sam."

"Oh, no, Sid. This is my home. I don't see myself in New York." He paused. "Sid, I need you to do some snooping for me."

"Snooping? Tell me more."

"I'm working on a case down here in Madison. A prisoner on a road gang here in the county was shot and killed by a local family after he threatened them. Before he was killed, he beat up a black man and near about killed him. The black man is a caretaker on the farm where the man was killed. I'd like to know if the deceased has an estate that might have some collectible assets. I'm thinking about a personal injury lawsuit against the estate."

"Why don't you do the snooping?"

"Because the man was from New York City. And guess what else?"

"What?"

"The deceased is George Barnwell. His brother is Stanley Barnwell of Barnwell, Smith and Wolfson."

A dead quiet from the other end of the phone. "Sid? You there?"

"Yes, yes, I'm here. Sam, I wouldn't go near Stan Barnwell. I hear he's tight with Johnny Dioguardi."

"You'll have to explain that, Sid. I know nothing about a Johnny Dioguardi."

"Let me refresh your memory. He's the guy who committed the acid-blinding of a journalist by the name of Victor Riesel, because Victor was getting too close to finding out some things that would send Dioguardi to prison for life. Would you believe they couldn't make the charges against Dioguardi stick?

"Listen, Sam. The Kefauver Committee is working hard against organized crime along with the FBI, but these guys are not to be messed with. We're the little people. You, more than I."

Sam listened intently. "Look, Sid. Just find out what you can about the Barnwell family and their assets and let me know. Can you do that? George Barnwell may have been a reprobate, but he could still have an estate, especially if his family has money."

A deep sigh from Sid. "Yeah. I'll do it, Sammie. Be back with you in a few days."

CHAPTER EIGHTEEN

The Donnelly farm eased into the summer, the crops planted by Emmett Gaston flourishing after generous rains moved across the panhandle and into Madison County. Early one morning, Dr. Anderson called Essie. "Essie, I've looked over the report on Jewell's blood work and there's not a thing wrong with that gal."

Essie became thoughtful. "Well, she's still losing weight, Dr. Anderson. She doesn't eat very much and she sleeps quite a bit."

"Hmmm. You know what I think, Essie? I think Jewell is depressed."

"Depressed?"

"That's right. Keep an eye on her. If she's depressed, she'll wither away. Come back in around the middle of the month if she doesn't get better, and let's take another look."

Essie meandered to the front porch and found Jewell sitting in her chair, a slight whiffle coming from her lips. She was asleep. She touched her shoulder. "Jewell, would you like some iced tea?"

"Oh, hello, Essie." She shifted in her chair and smoothed her skirt. "No, thank you. I had a glass of water earlier," she said sleepily.

Essie went to the other end of the porch and sat in the swing. She picked up *Peyton Place,* all the while watching Jewell. "Jewell, how are you feeling today?"

"A little tired. I was thinking about mama?"

"About mama?"

"Yes," Jewell said in a whisper. "Remember when mama made a buttered rum pound cake just about every day and folks would be stopping by all the time?" She closed her eyes, then looked down the porch at Essie, her fragile face recalling the neighbors who filled the porch chairs and swings. Her smile was full of memories. "I remember mama was making those cakes, pouring iced tea and shooing the chickens off the porch." She turned away and her eyes traveled down the empty lane to the road. "No one comes to visit anymore."

Essie's thoughts became measured, a putting together of her sister's life in tiny increments. *Lonely.* Jewell was lonely. Her heart ached for love, the human touch. Perhaps she wanted to dance on the edge of time, to feel it all again. She knew it had to be there somewhere, laughter once again on the long, shaded porch in the middle of three-hundred acres of farmland.

Jewell's malady had not taken away her desire for happiness nor the need for laughter in a life that was somewhat remote and hidden among the acres in which they lived.

Jewell leaned back in her chair and closed her eyes. "It's time for The Gospel Hour, Essie."

Essie reached over and turned on the radio. The soft strains of *The Old Rugged Cross* floated high into the oak limbs hanging over the porch. Essie felt her throat tighten and her eyes mist over. *Jewell was lonely.*

"You listen to your program, Jewell. I've got a few chores."

Essie eased out the back door, across the yard and into the cavernous barn where years of farm life lay stored in the rafters, hung on the walls and crammed the corners and stalls of the fifty-year old structure. She had probably been in and out of the barn thousands of times over the years. The hay, the grain for the cows and horses. Chicken feed in large burlap bags. The earthy smell was glorious, a smell like no other.

She stood in the middle of the huge barn and felt so small. Her earliest memory seemed only yesterday; the discovery of a saddle for her fifth birthday, her daddy swinging her up on Princess, a small quarter horse about fourteen and a half hands high, who did exactly what Essie wanted her to do, go where she wanted her to go.

So long ago. Her eyes scanned the massive space and fell on a darkened corner at the south end of the barn, a place stuffed with a plethora of farm items. An old one-bottom plow, a tractor tire, shovels, hay rakes, all rusted and worn from years of use, yet vibrant with memories.

Essie pulled a few two by fours from the barn wall. Covered with spider webs, dust and debris from the passage of time, she moved them aside. Next, she shifted an iron gate to another wall. And smiled. There it was. The detour sign—a reminder of the '48 flood.

The sign had saved lives—anyone who lived in Pinetta during the flood depended on the sign as their escape route, an escape from the rising waters that would ravage the entire area. As the waters rose, the county placed the sign on the Bellville road at the Donnelly farm lane and directed people across the Donnelly farm to the Madison highway and safety.

Panting, Essie dragged the heavy two-sided sign to the barn door and stood back, staring at it. Essie may not have known it, but the sign was about to alter the course of the sisters' lives, unleash a sweet havoc on anyone who may stumble upon its magic.

Essie heard Jewell call. "Essie, there's a car coming this way."

Essie stepped outside the barn and watched as a familiar car eased down the lane. She knew the car; it was the government man.

She waited while he parked and opened the car door. He wore the same dark suit and tilted felt fedora hat with a narrow brim, a brim that cast a shadow over the top half of his face that once again caused a slight shiver across Essie's neck.

"You lost again?" she called, irritation in her voice.

"No, mam." He stepped a few paces toward the porch and stopped. His eyes scanned the yard, the house and finally the barn. "You'll recall I'm looking for DooRay Aikens. Can't seem to locate him. I've been told he's somewhere in these parts, but no one knows exactly where."

"That right?" Essie walked on the porch and lifted herself to the rail of the porch and sat without speaking. She swung her legs in obvious boredom.

"Yes, mam. Funny thing, though. I keep thinking he's here on this farm." He removed his hat and fanned himself. A slight baldness spread across the top of his head, his hair damp with sweat. Essie could see the indention the hat rim had made on his forehead.

"My advice is for you to go back to Washington, D. C. You're wasting your time. Looks like DooRay Aikens has disappeared."

A slight smile formed on the man's lips. "You sure 'bout that?"

"Yes, sir, I am." Essie held her eyes level and dared him to question her again.

"Do you still have my card?" he asked, placing his hat back on his head.

"I do, Mr. Knight." Essie recalled the name on the card: *Earle Knight, Washington, D. C.*

The government man looked around the yard once more before he walked back to his car. He placed his hand on the door handle and pulled open the car door. Before he slid onto the seat, he looked up once more at Essie. "I'll be back."

Essie's eyes held the car until it turned onto the Bellville road. From her right, she saw DooRay ease around the corner of the house. "That the government man again, Miss Essie?" The one-armed black man cowered in the azaleas, his eyes wide.

"That's him, DooRay."

CHAPTER NINETEEN

L ike clockwork, clouds in the west darkened. They rolled and
rumbled and readied for their afternoon encore. Emmett
Gaston and Jim Al Townsend would be happy to see their
fields showered with warm June rains. The Withlacoochee was
rising but had a long way to go before it reached flood stage.

In the hen house, Essie gathered the eggs and added them to the
ones in the kitchen: twenty-four altogether. Enough for six buttered
rum pound cakes. She checked the flour bin, the sugar bin, the
butter, the vanilla and rum extract. Of course, her daddy's bottled
rum was only a few feet away in the end of the buffet. Visions of her
mother getting ready for the county fair flashed across the kitchen.

"Jewell," Essie called. "Please help me crack these eggs." She
turned the radio to WMAF and Johnny Cash's *I Walked The Line*
rocked the Donnelly kitchen. She measured out flour, sugar, butter,
and eggs. And, of course, three cups of Hubert Donnelly's dark rum.
In minutes, Edith Donnelly's kitchen exploded into the makings of
six buttered rum pound cakes.

Jewell eased into the kitchen, hesitant. She wrung her hands, all
the while watching Essie. "Crack eggs?" she finally asked.

"Yes! Over there!" Essie pointed to the breakfast table where a
mountain of eggs filled a large ceramic bowl. "Four eggs to a bowl,
Jewell. Don't let any shells get into the bowls. Then, we need to
think about that glaze. You'll find more butter in the refrigerator."
Essie counted on her fingers. "That's plenty of eggs! Now, get busy,
sister."

Jewell nodded slowly, all the while staring at the bowl of eggs. "We're making mama's buttered rum pound cake?"

"Yes. Four of them." Essie measured out the flour.

"Who's coming?"

"I don't know."

Jewell lingered around the table and considered the bowl of eggs again. Her expression was one of confusion. "Are we baking these cakes for anyone in particular?" Her hands flitted over the table, not sure what to do.

"Don't know." Essie threw a dishtowel at Jewell. "Get busy."

Johnny Cash thumped along—*Because you're mine, I walk the line.* Essie cranked the handle on the eggbeater at a furious pace and creamed the butter and sugar for the first cake. The music changed to Marty Robbin's *Singing The Blues.*

At the small breakfast table, Jewell meticulously cracked eggs into a small bowl, four at a time. Her slim fingers searched for any eggshells but found none. Color came to her cheeks, her eyes glistened and slowly, ever so slowly, her hips began to wiggle to Arthur Smith and His Cracker-Jacks' *Guitar Boogie.*

Near midnight, six buttered rum pound cakes lined the buffet in the dining room. They were perfection; their tops sprinkled with pecans and puffs of powdered sugar. Essie was sure her mother would have approved.

Jewell hummed as she went up the stairs and collapsed into bed. She told Essie she didn't need her sedative; she would sleep just fine.

After midnight, in the light of the full moon, Essie walked to the barn and pulled the detour sign into the yard. Essie lugged the sign down the lane a few inches at a time. Behind her, she heard DooRay mumbling something about nobody being able to sleep around the farm. "What you doin', Miss Essie?" He grabbed one end of the sign and together they inched it down the lane and to the middle of the Bellville road.

"Okay, DooRay. You're a dear. Now, go back to bed."

Confused, DooRay shuffled to the barn, once in a while looking over his shoulder at Essie.

Essie stood back and studied the sign. Coming from the east, the arrow pointed right; coming from the west, the arrow pointed left. Either way, anyone traveling the Bellville road would turn down the

Donnelly drive and take the farm lane two miles to the Madison/Valdosta highway to continue their journey.

But, first, they would stop for a slice of Edith Donnelly's prized buttered rum pound cake and a glass of sweet iced tea.

CHAPTER TWENTY

At 1:00 a.m., though exhausted, Essie stretched out on the swing and listened to music from a Tallahassee station. Soothing music about love. Her date that wasn't a date with Sam Washington had been more pleasant than she had expected. She rather enjoyed his company or perhaps it was the fine dinner over Upper Lake Lafayette.

From the end of the drive, headlights swept the lane and eased toward the house. Essie sat up in the swing and watched the car park under the oak. Sam Washington, of course.

"Lost?" she called. Essie heard him chuckle and move up the steps.

"No. Just curious."

"About what?"

"The detour sign." Sam sat in a chair near the swing. "River gonna flood?"

"No. The river's fine."

"Then, why the detour?" He pulled a cigar from his pocket and lit it, leaning back in the chair and crossing his legs.

Essie pulled a light blanket across her lap. From the pasture north of the house, one of Emmet's cows gave a long, mournful bawl. Essie closed her eyes.

From a far-away memory, she saw a place of happiness. It was the porch; always the porch. "Why the detour?" Essie tried to find Sam's eyes in the dark. "I remember in '48 when the Withlacoochee flooded this area and the road department detoured everyone across our farm over to the Madison/Valdosta highway. We fed everyone who came through. We wouldn't let them pass without at least a glass of iced tea."

Sam became thoughtful, puffing his cigar gently. "So, you're needing some company? That why you're detouring folks this way?"

"No, but Jewell's needing company. Dr. Anderson thinks she's depressed. I think so, too. More than that, she's lonely." Essie sat up quickly, as if remembering something. "What are you doing out at this time of night?"

Sam laughed. "Detour sign pointed me in this direction."

She asked again. "What were you doing on the Bellville road at 1:00 a.m.?"

Sam blew cigar smoke into the night air, then tapped the ashes into a nearby flowerpot. "Just ridin' around. Couldn't sleep."

They sat in silence; Essie pushed the swing slowly. Sam leaned his head on the back of his chair. The chain on the swing creaked softly, almost in tune with a nearby tree frog.

"I wouldn't mind sitting in that swing with you," he said, a hint of tenderness in his words.

Essie opened her eyes and watched the soft embers at the end of Sam's cigar. "Why would you want to do that?"

"Because I like you."

Essie didn't consent, but neither did she deny. Sam slowly left his chair and tucked himself into the swing. He pulled her to him. "Come here. I want to hold you."

Essie leaned into the warmth of Sam Washington and, for only an instant, wondered if this was why she had never left Madison County.

Chapter Twenty-One

At daylight, a truck horn blared across the yard in front of the Donnelly house. Dr. James Aubrey Davis, Madison County's veterinarian, stomped onto the porch just as Essie ploughed through the screen door, her robe barely buttoned.

"What's going on, Essie? The river's as low as it can get. What's that detour sign doing out there?"

"Oh, goodness, Dr. Davis. There's a big ole tree down across the road but you can go through the field to the Madison/Valdosta highway. It's just a two-mile detour." *A tree down? She didn't know she could lie so easily.*

Dr. Davis, flustered, plopped himself into a rocking chair. "It's been a terrible morning. Just terrible."

"Let me get you some coffee, Dr. Davis." Essie ran into the kitchen and heard the doctor yell: "Black will do." She poured his coffee and heard Jewell coming down the stairs.

"Who's that on the porch?" she asked, her words full of sleep.

"Dr. Davis. Slice him a piece of cake, would you?"

Essie hurried to the front porch and placed the doctor's coffee on a nearby tray. "Where're you headed, Dr. Davis?"

"Over to the Gibson farm. Dale Gibson bought himself a two-thousand-dollar bull and that bull's done worn out."

Jewell arrived with a slice of pound cake. "Good morning, Dr. Davis," she said sweetly. "Here's a slice of the best buttered rum pound cake you've ever eaten." Jewell's cheeks flushed pink, she had quickly pulled her hair into a ponytail, her smile warm and welcoming.

Dr. Davis's face softened. "Oh, my, Jewell. You're just too kind." He picked up his fork and raked a big bite into his mouth. He followed it with a slurp of coffee. "I adore you Donnelly girls," he smiled. "I guess you're waitin' on me to marry the both of you."

The country vet shook his head. "Yes, sir. That bull has been so busy with those heifers he's done... he's done..." The doctor looked at Essie and Jewell, who both listened attentively. "Well, I don't really know how to say this... with ladies present and all. It's rather... delicate."

"Go on," urged Jewell, her eyes wide in question.

"Well, he's done broke his pecker. That's all I can say. Broke it and can't use it anymore and Dale Gibson's wasted two thousand smackeroos."

"Oh, my," said Jewell, her hands clasped together.

Dr. Davis jumped up. "Got to go. Hoot's waitin' on me. Dang if I know what I can do about a broken pecker." He bounded down the steps and into the yard. "Thank you, ladies. That was a wonderful surprise—I may be back later!" He got into his truck laughing, his dog beside him sitting upright and looking out the window, his tongue lolling around. He looked like he was laughing, too.

Essie watched Dr. Davis' truck roar down the farm lane toward the Valdosta highway, dust billowing up into the air. At the edge of the barn, she caught sight of DooRay. "DooRay, come get a slice of pound cake and a cup of coffee."

DooRay waved, then placed a fishing pole across his shoulder. Essie assumed the can tied to his belt loop held big fat worms. He was barefooted and behind him trailed Murphy and Killer.

"Thank you, Miss Essie. I sure do like pound cake."

"Well, come on up on the porch. Jewell will slice you a big piece."

DooRay lumbered up the steps. He pointed to his goat. "Stay down in the yard, Murphy. You, too, Killer. This cake ain't for you."

Jewell dutifully sliced the cake and placed it on one of her mother's china cake plates—the one with tiny roses twirling around the edge. DooRay's big black hand reached out and took the dainty plate. "Mighty nice, Miss Jewell. Mighty nice."

"Here's some coffee, DooRay. A little cream and sugar in it."

"Well, Miss Essie, I'll have to catch a lot of fish today to repay you for this good coffee and cake."

Essie poured herself some coffee. "You catch the fish, DooRay, and we'll fry them."

"I surely will, Miss Essie." The black man, with his one arm, balanced the cake plate on his knees and held the fork in his long fingers while he cut into his cake. The left sleeve on his shirt hung loosely by his side, empty.

"You be careful walking down to Grassy Pond, DooRay. That government man said he'd be back."

"Yes, mam. DooRay will be careful. He surely will." DooRay lifted the dainty teacup by its rim, making no noise as he tipped the cup and sipped the hot coffee. Nearby, Murphy bleated. He was ready to go fishing.

Around 2:00, a shiny black Mercedes sat at the end of the lane. Its chrome glistened like diamonds in the bright sunlight of July. As if in doubt, the car lurched forward, then backward, then forward again and settled a few moments before it gradually moved down the lane.

Essie tried to recall who owned a Mercedes in the tiny community of Pinetta or in Madison. Probably no one. Perhaps whoever was driving was just passing through on their way to Tallahassee or Jacksonville or Atlanta. Why they were on the Bellville road, she didn't know.

The windows of the car were mysteriously dark as if its occupant did not want to be seen. When the car parked under the oak tree near the house, Essie saw a flash of bright pink through the windshield. The car door flew open and out stepped the one and only Alice June Wiglesworth. Of course, it was Alice June who drove the black Mercedes. She had wanted one since elementary school.

She squealed and ran to the porch. "Oh, is that you, Essie? Is it really yooooooou?" In a cloud of perfume, she gathered Essie in her arms and squeezed—squealed and squeezed so long that Essie pushed the skinny girl away.

"Yes. It's me, Alice June." Essie tried to remember the last time she'd seen her high school classmate. Not since graduation. Fifteen years ago.

"Oh, I can't believe it's you! Where's Jewell?"

"Jewell's napping for a while." Essie led Alice June to a rocker while she sat in the nearby swing. She then prepared herself for the onslaught simply known as Alice June.

In high school, Alice June had strutted through the halls with her bleached hair and hot pink lipstick like she owned the world. She'd talked big: "Well, you can stay in this little ole town, but I'm going to New York City."

And she did. Essie had, indeed, seen Alice June since high school—on the cover of numerous fashion magazines. She wasn't hard to recognize even though her hair went from blond, to red, to black and back to blond. She was little ole Pinetta's rising star.

"What are you doing here, Alice June?"

"Oh, I came to see mama. She's not doing too well. Her heart." Alice June frowned. "You know daddy died last year."

She nodded. "I'm sorry to hear that. How long will you stay?"

"Oh, I've got to go to Paris in a few days. Their runways are so busy this time of year." She ran her hand along her slim leg and Essie saw three or four diamond rings on her hand.

"Say, why's there a detour sign out on the road? I thought I was lost."

"Oh, there's a big tree across the Bellville road. You can go on through to the Valdosta highway—just follow the farm lane along the fence. It's just two miles."

Alice June became thoughtful and when she spoke, her words were soft, inquiring. Her luminous skin, her lips full and moist, a photographer's perfect model. She leaned toward Essie and spoke in a conspiratorial whisper. "Essie, what happened to you? I thought you were going to write a book, go to New York."

Essie watched a mockingbird light on the porch rail, its tail going up and down like a seesaw. It flitted along the rail, then flew up into an oak tree. She turned back to Alice June. Her words came slowly, like molasses pouring from a pitcher. Once again, her eyes found the mockingbird on the oak limb. Perhaps Alice June would not see the mist in her eyes. "Sometimes life just gets in the way, Alice June."

Moments went by and left the two women to their own thoughts. Suddenly, Alice June clapped her hands. "Essie! Come to New York with me. I've got a huge apartment we can share. Of course, I'll be traveling a lot, but that doesn't matter." She jumped from her rocker and laughed like a school girl. "Oh, Essie. This is a grand idea. Let me help you pack."

Alice June's long, pink nails swept the air as if she were leading a band. Her flimsy pink skirt bounced as she walked the length of the porch and almost pirouetted back to Essie.

"Oh, Essie. You belong in New York. I can just see—"

Essie left the swing and leaned against the porch rail. "Alice June. Don't. I can't leave Jewell."

Alice June's pink lips parted. Her vibrant blue eyes opened wide, her long dark lashes almost touching her brows. She waved her hand through the air. "Oh, Essie. Put Jewell in a home and come with me. This is your ch—"

Essie's words shot out of her mouth like hot bullets. "Get off my porch, Alice June, before I beat the shit out of you."

Alice June shrieked as she backed away and ran off the porch. "You maniac you. You've always been crazy, Essie." The pink skirt Alice June wore twirled into the Mercedes, the skinny blond squealing in short bursts. "Maniac!" The Mercedes whipped around the yard and flew out of sight down the farm lane.

By late afternoon, all of Edith Donnelly's cake plates had been used—all twelve of them. A pound cake and two pitchers of tea remained on a small table on the porch. While Jewell washed plates, iced tea glasses and silverware, Essie snuck down to the end of the lane and moved the detour sign behind a maple tree. She also checked the mailbox. No letter from the literary agency.

From the lane, Essie took a moment to savor the magnificent house, the lovely pitch of its roof, the cupola, and the old brick chimney. What a grand house it was. She felt the sprawling porch had been built as an invitation, an invitation written in big gold letters and painted across the porch front: *Welcome. come sit with us and have a slice of cake.* The memories were all there, every last one of them. All she had to do was sit in her swing and wait for them.

When she stepped onto the porch, she heard Jewell. She was singing like an angel. *I'll fly away, fly away, oh glory, I'll fly away.* She couldn't remember the last time she'd heard Jewell sing.

Chapter Twenty-Two

In a few days Sam Washington received a call from his college roommate, Sidney Davis, an attorney in New York City. "Hey, Sam. It's me, Sidney."

Sam grabbed his note pad. "Go, Sidney. What did you find?"

"Well, you were right. The deceased, one George W. Barnwell, does indeed have an estate. A fairly large one, at that. Seems his wealthy parents gave both their boys a significant amount of money upon their twenty-first birthday.

"From what I've determined, the younger son, George W. Barnwell, also known as the deceased, became a rebellious jackass. Left New York, his family and, of course, his money."

Sam released a long breath. "Well, it looks like there are some collectible assets. I'll get this thing rolling, Sidney. I'll file the personal injury claim in a week or so."

"Looks like you have a good case, Sam." He hesitated. "Just fly low, buddy. George's brother is not exactly Mr. Congeniality.

Sam scoffed. "Sidney, Barnwell will have no power here. Madison County is a long way from New York City."

Sam decided he would file the personal injury claim for the plaintiff, DooRay Aikens, in the Third Judicial Circuit Court of Florida. Stan Barnwell couldn't do a darn thing about it.

In the case of Jewell Donnelly, the state attorney's office had issued a subpoena for DooRay Aikens to appear as a witness at the inquest. Essie Donnelly had also been served.

Sam left the courthouse whistling a happy tune. Hopefully, DooRay

Aikens would receive restitution for the injuries caused by George W. Barnwell.

CHAPTER TWENTY-THREE

L ate in the day, like a returning boomerang, the government man came back like he said he would. He did not say, however, that he'd bring someone with him. There were now two government men, each wearing a dark suit, fedoras and no smiles. Essie watched them from the upstairs window as they stepped into the yard.

"Hey, down there. Reckon you're lost again." Essie hollered in her hog-calling voice. Stern and slightly mean. Maybe Uncle Lester was right: she was a hard woman.

Mr. Knight looked up to the upper floor windows and searched for Essie. The other man moved beside him, his eyes squinting along the rooftop. "Not lost," said Mr. Knight. His hand moved to the inside of his coat jacket and rested there.

Essie left the bedroom, stomped down the hall, flew down the stairs and slammed open the front screened door. "It seems to me that you are wearing out your welcome, Mr. Knight."

For the first time, Mr. Knight smiled. "I apologize." He gestured to the man beside him. "This is Mr. Whittington, my superior. I felt perhaps you would tell *him* how to find DooRay Aikens."

Essie gave the men a blank stare. "I'm confused, Mr. Knight. I didn't know where DooRay Aikens was yesterday morning, and I sure don't know where he is this afternoon."

The men moved closer to the porch. In unison, they removed their hats. "That pound cake up there on the porch? On that table?" asked Mr. Whittington, with a hint of a smile.

Essie slumped. "Yes, that's pound cake." She ran an exasperated hand across her face.

At that moment, Jewell walked outside, removing her apron. When she looked up and saw the two men, she yelped. "Oh, my. More guests. Come." She motioned them onto the porch and ran back into the kitchen to get two plates and two glasses. A wave of frustration washed over Essie before the telltale prickling feeling ran across the back of her neck. *Who were these men and what did they want with DooRay?*

Mr. Knight and Mr. Whittington climbed up the porch steps and sat in rockers, placing their hats on their knees. "This is a lovely porch," said Mr. Whittington. He admired the climbing jasmine, the English ivy, the clematis, all clinging to the white pillars surrounding the porch. His eyes then fell on *Peyton Place*. He quickly looked away.

Essie sat in the swing and stared at the two men while Jewell served them cake. "So, where are you from, Mr. Whittington? Washington, D. C.?"

"Yes. I flew into Tallahassee around noon. Mr. Knight picked me up at the airport."

Essie nodded. "So, it takes two of you government men to go on a rabbit chase."

"Excuse me," asked Mr. Knight, leaning forward.

"Like I told you numerous times, DooRay Aikens is nowhere on this farm." Essie folded her arms across her chest and gave the two men her best glare.

From the lane, the baritone voice of DooRay Aikens lifted to the skies. *Do Lord, Oh, do Lord, oh, do remember me...* He ambled along, a string of fish hanging from the bend of his elbow, and the cane pole balancing across his shoulder. A few feet behind him, a white goat followed him, a tailless rooster on its back

DooRay's bare feet shuffled him along; his face turned upward, his eyes closed, as he sang the praises of his Lord and Savior. *Oh, do remember me...* All the while, the string of fish swinging to high heaven.

The glaring eyes of Essie Donnelly watched the one-armed skinny black man with quiet disdain. Not only did DooRay live on her farm, she also fed and clothed him. He was a fugitive and she had given him aid. She was going to jail.

"Well, now," said Mr. Knight, rising from his rocker, "I do believe that is DooRay Aikens."

CHAPTER TWENTY-FOUR

Murphy, the most beautiful, one-eared white goat in Madison County, stopped dead still in the farm lane leading to the Donnelly house. He lifted his head and bleated one long mournful bleat. Killer, the snake-killing rooster who rode the goat's back, squawked as though its neck was being wrung.

DooRay spun around mid-chorus in *I'll Fly Away* and hollered at Murphy and Killer. "What in the world are you two belly-aching about?" Murphy and Killer stood like statues. Murphy closed his eyes and Killer pushed himself farther into Murphy's hide.

As if the heavens had warned him—*run, DooRay, run*—DooRay slowly turned around, a shudder riding up his back, and saw the two government men run down the steps of the porch, both hollering: "Mr. Aikens! Mr. Aikens." They galloped across the yard like Shetland ponies, their arms waving as furious as a flag in a hurricane. Panting hard, they stumbled to a stop a few feet from DooRay. "Mr. Aikens," Mr. Knight said, trying to catch his breath, "we'd like a moment of your time."

DooRay stood before the two men, a string of fish hanging on the crook of his arm, the cane pole across his shoulders and a can of worms hooked to his belt loop. His feet were covered in dried mud, his one hand smeared with the remains of big fat red earthworms. "Me? You want a moment of DooRay's time?"

"Yes, sir. We'd like to talk to you privately, if we may."

"Privately?" DooRay saw Essie standing on the porch, her face in quiet torment. "Cain't we jus' sit on the porch?"

"The porch?" Mr. Whittington turned to cast a glance at the rambling porch behind him. "Well, certainly. We can do that."

"What about these fish?" DooRay lifted his arm and the stringer of fish swayed out into the air toward Mr. Knight, who yelped and jumped back, stumbling to the ground.

Mr. Whittington reached out and took the cane pole off DooRay's shoulder. "Let's find a bucket and fill it with water—"

"Yeah!" said Mr. Knight, regaining his composure. "Let's put them in a bucket of water until we can clean them."

Wide-eyed, DooRay licked his wide lips. "We can do that, all right."

In one swipe, Mr. Knight pulled the string of fish off DooRay's arm. "You just show us where the bucket is."

DooRay gave the men a stoic nod and ambled toward the barn, Murphy and Killer behind him. Without turning around, he called over his shoulder. "Don't mess with my goat and my rooster," he said.

"No, no. We won't," said the men in unison.

DooRay found a large farm bucket and filled it with well water and eased the heavy string of fish into the water. At the well, he washed his hands. He told Murphy and Killer to go into the barn. They obeyed, but not without a soft bleat of foreboding and a low throaty rumble of rooster malice.

The two government men waited silently by the barn door, watching DooRay's every move.

DooRay pulled the worm can off his belt loop and placed it on the ground and steadied a brick over the top. "Well, I reckon we best go on up to the porch and talk this thing out. Clean these fish later."

The men nodded and followed DooRay down the path to the house. They walked past Edith Donnelly's azaleas and up the old brick steps. Essie sat frozen in the swing. Pale and wordless, she watched the government men sit down, then remove their hats. *I should have shot those men and buried their bodies in the Hixtown swamp.*

"DooRay, I'm gonna sit right here and make sure these government men don't hurt you. Okay?" Her voice quavered, and her hands shook as she watched Pinetta's beloved DooRay Aikens. His eyes downcast, the one arm limp by his side, and standing in resolute quiet, DooRay seemed to have shriveled into nothingness.

Hardly breathing, DooRay's long face, sweaty from walking the two miles from Grassy Pond, nodded. "Thank you, Miss Essie. I reckon everything's gonna be all right." The black man sat down in a nearby rocker and leaned back.

From the barn, they heard Murphy bleat loudly. DooRay forced a smiled. "I think that goat's in love with me."

The government men laughed. Essie didn't; her mind was in utter chaos.

"Mr. Aikens," Mr. Whittington began, nervous to the point of stuttering, "we apologize if we have caused you any anxiety this past week. You see, we have been working on your case for quite a long time and—"

"My case?" DooRay scratched his head. He winced when he touched a bruise that had not healed. His wide eyes seemed childlike— he had committed no sins, his conscious was clear.

"Yes. We've been searching for you for quite some time. The Department of Defense, namely the army, wants to award you a Silver Star as well as the Purple Heart for your service during the war."

"The war?"

"Yes. For your actions at Lucca, Italy, on September 7, 1944; Massa, Italty, in November 1944 and Coburg, Germany, on April 25, 1945. Although it's been eleven years, your heroism has been authenticated by the 92nd Division's commander and by your company commander, as well as your captain and sergeant. After the war ended, all of these men made recommendations for a commendation." Mr. Whittington paused. "That's why we're here, Mr. Aikens."

DooRay Aikens closed his eyes. A solitary tear ran down his smooth black cheek and hung on the bottom of his chin. His chest shuddered, a sob hovering there and fighting with the memories of war. His lips trembled. "Yes, sir," he said in just a whisper of words, "that was a mighty terrible war."

The government men, silent and still, merely waited until the soldier opened his eyes. Mr. Whittington, his voice soft, leaned over toward DooRay. "It's our privilege to give you these awards, Mr. Aikens." His eyes fell to DooRay's empty sleeve.

Essie, evermore the hog calling, watermelon queen of Madison County, broke the spell.

"Wait a minute. You're just gonna give DooRay the Silver Star and the Purple Heart in an old ugly brown envelope? She rolled her eyes. "Without some kind of awards ceremony or dinner? A trip to Washington to meet the President?"

She stood from the swing and towered over the two sitting men, hands on her hips, a spark or two in her brown eyes. She was an ominous presence. There was just something about the girl who loaded watermelons and plucked chickens that nobody wanted to mess with.

The men, still reeling from Essie's earlier verbal snarls, looked at one another. Their lips moved, but they could not find the words. At last, Mr. Whittington stuttered. "Well... well, we..."

Essie raised her arm and pointed to the barn. "Get out there and get those fish cleaned. We're gonna have a fish fry, and" shaking her finger at each of the men, "you're going to do this right."

She swiveled to DooRay. "DooRay, you get cleaned up. Tonight's your night!"

All three men said, "Yes, mam" and left the porch, their feet moving as if ants were biting them. Halfway to the barn, DooRay's voice lifted high into the oak trees. *Mine eyes have seen the glory of the coming of the Lord...* She wasn't sure, but she thought she heard the hesitant voices of the two men from Washington singing along.

CHAPTER TWENTY-FIVE

"Jewell," Essie hollered as she entered the house from the back porch. She stood at the bottom of the stairs. "Get up from your nap. We've got company coming."

The Donnelly kitchen buzzed as if Edith Donnelly was still alive. "Jewell, make mama's buttered rum pound cake right away. The dining room table will have to be set for eighteen people, so we'll have to get out the extra leaf."

Jewell stood in the middle of the kitchen, sleepy-eyed, confused, her cheeks flushed from sleep. "Eighteen people?" She looked around. "Where are they?"

"They're coming. I'm leaving right now to drive over to Ran and Inez', then to Lon and Rana's. Got to let everybody know. I'll be back in thirty minutes or so. Get busy."

Essie flew down the back-porch steps, fired up her daddy's '48 Buick and tore down the Bellville road. She swerved right and drove up the hill to Ran and Inez Terry's house. She honked the horn, and Inez' head popped out the side door. "Hey, Essie."

"Inez, you and Ran are invited to a fish fry at 5:30. Can you bring a pie or something?"

"I sure can, Essie. I'll get a peach pie in the oven right away. How 'bout a pan of corn pudding, too?"

"Yum! How about Mavis and Bob? Have them come with you."

"They'd love that."

"See you at 5:30."

The Buick backed out of the yard, almost running over two of

Inez's ducks. She drove down to the Mr. Horeb cemetery and turned left to Tom and Barnie Mae Keeling's. She whipped by their pond and saw Barnie Mae working in her garden. "Barnie Mae, you and Tom come over for a fish fry around 5:30."

Barnie Mae wiped her hands on her dress. "Why we'd love that, Essie. We haven't had any good fish in a month of Sundays. This pond here's got 'em but don't have no time to fish for 'em."

"Can you bring something good to eat with you? Enough for a crowd?"

Barnie Mae wiped her forehead, pushing her damp hair off her face. Her blue eyes danced. "Seems like I got a half bushel of green beans ready to snap. How about a pot with some ham in it?"

"That'll go wonderful with fish. See you at 5:30."

Essie flew back down the road by Ran and Inez's house and skidded right onto the Bellville road to Lon Terry's store. She parked under the big oak tree behind the store where Mr. Lon sat in an old wooden chair smoking a Chesterfield and talking with Paul Ellington.

"Hey, Mr. Lon. You, too, Paul. I guess Rana's in the store doing all the work?"

Lon Terry's big chest shook with laughter. "That is some woman. That Rana. She and I chased coons until 5:00 this morning. Those dogs led us everywhere and ended up near Grassy Pond."

"Mr. Lon, you ought to be ashamed of yourself. Miss Rana is the hardest working woman I know, and now she's huntin' coons with you."

"That's true, Essie." Lon puffed on his cigarette, his Irish eyes laughing.

"Mr. Lon, I'm here to invite you and Paul to a fish fry at 5:30. We've got the fattest bream you ever saw. DooRay's cooking them for us."

"I'll go anywhere for some fresh fried bream. We'll be there." Lon lit another cigarette. "Go in and let Rana know."

"I will. Paul, you think Wilma can make a big bowl of potato salad? Maybe some deviled eggs, too?"

Paul Ellington nodded, his dark eyes serious. "Wilma loves to cook, you know that, Essie. She'll bring whatever you need, and we'll be there at 5:30."

"Thanks, Paul. See you at 5:30."

Essie slipped inside the store and became dead still. She found Rana sharing a Coca Cola with Sam Washington. She glanced at him, hesitant, almost shy. His eyes held hers for only a moment until she looked away.

Rana Terry, a short, round woman with lovely brown eyes, smiled and in a weathered voice said, "Well, there's one a them Donnelly sisters. How are you, Essie?"

Essie walked to the drink box and pulled out a Nehi orange soda, its bottle so cold it hurt her fingers. "Doing just fine, Miss Rana." She turned away from the drink box and found Sam watching her. She sent him a half smile. "Miss Rana, I want you and Mr. Lon to come have some fried fish with us. About 5:30. Can you bring some of your macaroni and cheese?"

"Fried fish? Oh, my. Lon will love that. Of course, we'll be there and so will that macaroni and cheese."

Essie glanced at Sam who had folded his arms and leaned against the doorframe, a puzzling smile on his face. She stuttered. "How... how about you, Sam? Would you like to come over for a fish fry?"

"A fish fry at the Donnelly's. I can't think of anything I'd like more." His eyes filled with mischief. "How about I bring an iced cold watermelon?"

Essie nodded. "Watermelon is good." She turned to leave when Sam called out.

"Essie, after the fish fry, why don't we settle on the front porch? Talk about... watermelons?" Such a casual invitation, stated with such innocence. A roguish smile lingered in the handsome face. He was courting her—just as sure as eggs is eggs, Sam Washington had his eye on Essie Donnelly. It was true—he had thought about her since that homecoming night, the yellow dress, her shining face, the smile that went from Canada to Key West.

Essie glanced at Rana who arranged apples in a box on the counter and hummed to herself. Then, back at Sam. "Maybe. See you later."

CHAPTER TWENTY-SIX

Almost home, Essie stopped at Deedie Gregol's house. Deedie was at her mailbox and looked up when she heard Essie's car. "Deedie, how are you?"

Deedie, a pretty woman whose cherry round face smiled all the time, closed the mailbox with a snap. "We're doing just fine, Essie. Thank you for asking."

"Deedee, why don't you and Dom come on up to the house about 5:30 and eat some fried fish with us. Maybe you can bring something good to eat. How about sliced tomatoes and cucumbers?"

"A fish fry. Dom's gonna love that. We'll be there with some sweet, fresh tomatoes."

"Wonderful." The Buick pulled down the clay road for a short way and turned into the Buchanan drive and tooted the horn. Their truck was nowhere to be seen so she scribbled a note and stuck it in their door: *Fish Fry 5:30 Donnelly's.*

Essie zipped around in the Buchanan's drive and scooted back down the Donnelly lane. She saw DooRay and the government men at the picnic table. DooRay was evidently showing them how to clean fish. The men from Washington D. C. had their jackets off and their shirtsleeves rolled up, but she did not see a knife in their hands.

Inside the house, Jewell flitted around the kitchen, her apron on, and Edith Donnelly's china plates stacked on the counter. "I wish you'd please tell me who is coming to have fried fish with us. Eighteen people! Oh, Essie. What have you done?"

"It's for DooRay, Jewell. And everybody will be here at 5:30.

We've got exactly two hours to get the table set." Essie threw teabags in a big tin pot and filled it with water. "Thank goodness, Mama loved her china. We'll have a full table setting for everyone."

"Mama's Moss Rose? Or the other set—Glenlea?" Jewell held one salad plate out toward Essie. "This is the Moss Rose."

Essie flipped open the oven door and lit the gas stove. "My favorite is Glenlea."

"Oh, my, Essie. Eighteen people. Do we have enough napkins?"

Essie pulled six eggs out of the refrigerator. "Jewell, run out and get some more eggs from the hen house. And watch out for that big rat snake. He's been making the hen house his home for a couple of weeks now. I'm surprised Killer hasn't found him. And, yes, we have plenty of the white linen napkins. They're bleached and ironed."

"A party," Jewell said, her eyes shining like holiday sparklers. "What about flowers? I think I'll cut some of mama's roses; the pink ones. Maybe a few sprigs of ivy."

"Lovely. Just lovely. Now, get those eggs."

Essie wished Dr. Anderson could see Jewell now. There was no sign of depression, and she certainly couldn't be lonely. The house had been Grand Central Station for a week.

The dining room table, with its extra leaf, took up most of the space in the dining room. Twelve places had been set with meticulous attention to the placement of silverware, crystal and china. Essie had the government men pull in the small breakfast room table to the edge of the living room where six table settings had been arranged, only a few feet from the main dining room.

Jewell, humming *In the Garden* from page 210 in the church hymnal, fussed over every detail. Her cake sat proudly on the buffet, powdered sugar strewn across the top, a sprig of mint in the center.

Essie and DooRay readied the big black kettle Hubert Donnelly had set up to keep Edith happy all those years. At ten minutes to five, she ran upstairs and got one of her daddy's Sunday shirts out of his closet. A starched light blue shirt with a stiff collar. Her father had died years ago yet the contents of his closet remained the same. She cornered DooRay on the back porch.

"DooRay, come over here a minute." She removed the shirt from the hanger. "Let's get you dressed up for your special night."

DooRay shied away. He moved down the back steps, his head

hung low to his chest.

"DooRay. What's wrong?" Essie patted his arm. "Tell me, DooRay."

DooRay lowered his eyes. "Miss Essie, I don't want you to see my... my hole."

"Your hole?"

"Yes, mam. Where my arm used to be."

Essie stared unblinking, then reached up and gently touched the black man's cheek. "Oh, DooRay. It's all right." She handed DooRay her daddy's shirt. "I'll go inside while you change your shirt."

"Yes, mam."

At 5:00 o'clock, the grease hot, DooRay and the government men dropped the first fat bream into the hot grease. The fish sizzled, its coating of corn meal turning as golden as the first leaves of autumn. A whiff of frying fish drifted into the early evening air. Its aroma had a taste to it—it tasted of friendship and laughter. That's what fish fries did to neighbors; they made them touch each other with the memories of where they came from and the joys of the present.

By 5:30 the Donnelly front porch overflowed with Pinetta folk who found themselves in a place they had been before. The only ones missing were Hubert and Edith Donnelly. Perhaps if one squinted hard and looked at the railing on the west end of the porch, they would see Hubert with a cigar, its wrapper with a picture of the horse Alcazar emblazoned in full color. They would also see Edith Donnelly flitting around ensuring everyone's glass was full of fresh tea.

Laughter bellowed from the end of the porch where Ran Terry entertained a half dozen people with his latest, outrageous story. "Well, after those ducks landed, I eased into the water, plunked down my head and breathed through a reed I had cut from Inez's stand of bamboo. I moved along slowly and felt each of the ducks, and when I found a fat one, I pulled it into my croaker sack."

Whoops and hollers filled the porch. "Ran, wasn't that the same pond where you sneezed, and your teeth flew out into the water?

Ran furrowed his brow. "Yep. And it was in the dead of winter, too. I was in shallow water and could see those teeth down there, but my dip net couldn't reach them. Finally, I eased into the water and got my teeth. I wasn't about to leave 'em down there—they cost me $75.00."

The ladies listened in awe as Rana Terry told about her and Lon's run through the woods after a raccoon. Their hunting dogs bayed long and hard and finally ended up at Grassy Pond. "I was still in my nightgown," she said. "And there was Lon, gun in one hand and Chesterfield in the other. That man."

By 5:45 the fried fish piled high on platters and bowls of food sat on the long mahogany buffet that took up an entire wall in the dining room. There were no place cards on the table settings, but Jewell directed everyone to their assigned seats.

DooRay was pushed into the chair at the head of the table, a chair from which Hubert Donnelly had ruled until his death. Hubert's dress shirt was too big for DooRay and hung loosely across his chest. Essie had folded the left sleeve and pinned it at the last fold.

Jewell sat queen-like by Sam, smiling and her hands demurely folded in her lap.

Essie, leaving her hog-calling voice for another time, addressed the Terry's, the Ellington's, the Smith's, the Keeling's, the Gregol's, the two government men, Sam Washington and, of course, DooRay Aikens.

"I want to thank everyone for coming over on such short notice. I guess the words 'fish fry' created quite a stir throughout Pinetta. All of you good cooks brought some delicious food, and I know we'll enjoy every bite."

Essie paused and pointed at the two government men. "We have two guests here today that I don't think you know. I must apologize to these gentlemen—they've been searching for DooRay for quite some time, and most of Pinetta has not been particularly helpful in helping them locate him." Essie glanced around the table at the faces watching the government men and saw sheepish expressions. Each of them knew they had been a part of the great deception.

"Mr. Knight and Mr. Whittington are from the Department of Defense—the army to be more specific—out of Washington, D. C. We welcome you to our small town. Usually, we're quite friendly." She motioned to Ran Terry. "Especially that man over there. He'll keep you laughing from here to sunset."

Essie walked around to where DooRay sat. She placed a hand on his shoulder. "The folks here in Pinetta don't know this, but DooRay, when he was nineteen years old, decided to join the army. He didn't tell his mama; he just went to Madison and joined up."

DooRay sat silent at the end of the long dining room table, his eyes downcast. In the army, as a black man, he had suffered the prejudices that accompanied every man of color, no matter who he was. But that didn't stop DooRay from excelling on the rifle range or enduring the dreadfulness of boot camp. He had become a soldier and he would bleed like any white man.

In the army, he had been taught obedience and discipline. Had they asked him, he would have told them his mama had taught him all of that. For DooRay, bravery on the battlefront had become a habit. Though an uneducated man, he felt the army was a good book in which to study human life. He observed that the delicate and rich who fought alongside him were forced to see hardship and live with it—something he had learned since birth.

DooRay had also understood and maintained a sound understanding, a tender conscious, and a gracious spirit throughout the darkest trenches in the middle of the war. And, he had kept his candle lighted throughout.

Essie, her words softer, flowing slow like a gentle stream, squeezed DooRay's shoulder. "DooRay came back to Pinetta at the end of 1945." She looked at the empty sleeve. "He never told us how he lost his arm; where he had been for four years. When his mama asked him where he'd been, he'd simply say. "Just amblin', mama. Just amblin'.

"We know now that he had been fighting the war in Europe." Essie walked around the table. "Like many returning soldiers, DooRay never discussed the war. It was too difficult for him.

"You folks here tonight have been invited to see our friend DooRay Aikens receive the Purple Heart as well as the Silver Star." She nodded to Mr. Whittington. "Mr. Whittington, would you like to take over?"

Richard Whittington left his seat and walked to the end of the table where a somber DooRay sat, his lips still swollen and bruised from his encounter with prisoner #458. "Thank you, Miss Donnelly, for your gracious hospitality and for providing a venue in which to present these awards to Mr. Aikens."

The box was small, but its content was priceless, a remembrance that paid tribute to a man who had probably never been out of Madison County until World War II. "Mr. Aikens, I'd like you to stand." Mr. Whittington turned to the remainder of the room, "Would everyone please stand?"

The government man gently placed the Purple Heart on DooRay Aikens, pinned on Hubert Donnelly's starched blue shirt. "By order of the President of the United States, Dwight D. Eisenhower, I present you the Purple Heart for wounds received in November 1944 in the Battle of Massa, Italy, while serving in the United States Army, 92nd Division."

DooRay lifted his chin, back erect and smartly saluted the room. His lips quivered as he stepped back and eased into parade rest. The room was silent, its inhabitants mesmerized by the sight of their very own DooRay Aikens receiving the Purple Heart.

Mr. Whittington continued. "As a member of a Negro combat patrol, DooRay Aikens advanced three miles north of Lucca, Italy, to engage the enemy in an attack on September 7, 1944. For conspicuous gallantry, bravery and overt battle cunning, you are hereby awarded the Silver Star." The Silver Star was pinned next to the Purple Heart and Mr. Whittington stepped back.

Again, DooRay stiffened and released a sharp salute. His eyes traveled the room, to the people who sat in awe at the black man's history of heroism.

Sam Washington began the applause, his hands swinging together loudly. The rest of the room joined in; whoops and hollers followed.

DooRay smiled as best he could through his injured lips. His eyes misted over as he shook hands and said, 'thank you' over and over again. The two government men stood nearby and watched their gallant soldier—he had just been decorated for valor in combat, and his friends honored him just as fervently as Dwight D. Eisenhower would have had he been there.

Essie and Jewell poured iced tea and directed the hungry crowd to the buffet table. "Rana brought a tray of sliced ham from one of Lon's hogs. You eat up now."

Jewell leaned over and whispered to Sam. "I do wish Jimmy could have come."

Sam found her large green eyes wide and full of hope. "Me, too, Jewell. Me, too."

CHAPTER TWENTY-SEVEN

E ssie and Jewell had waved their good-byes from the porch as their neighbors called goodnight, some of them hopping on their tractors and riding through the fields to their homes.

DooRay Aikens had floated on air as he drifted out to the barn, full of Inez Terry's peach pie and Jewell's pound cake. He offered to return the crisp blue shirt that had belonged to her father, but Essie told him it looked very smart on him and to keep it, maybe to wear to Sunday school.

Mary Lou and Belton Buchanan popped in at the last minute and brought a pot of chicken and dumplings. They had been in Valdosta picking up chicken feed. Essie sent them home with cake and pie.

The two government men fit right in with the Pinetta folk, even though they were from Washington, D. C. and didn't know a hen from a rooster. They smoked on the porch with the neighboring farmers and marveled at the stories about Lon Terry's hogs. Lon's hog 'Pony,' a Tamworth, weighed almost nine hundred pounds. Lon moved Pony from one field to the other, crossing the Bellville road, using only his walking stick and hollering, 'Pig! Git pig!', in his gruff voice.

Mr. Knight and Mr. Whittington left the Donnelly farm in high spirits. They had fulfilled their duties: they had followed President Dwight D. Eisenhower's orders and presented the Purple Heart and the Silver Star to one of America's brave soldiers.

Sam helped Jewell wash the few remaining dishes while Essie

dried. Jewell chattered about their mama's china and the lack of place cards at the place settings. "Why, Essie. We can't be having any more dinners without a proper setting."

"Everyone knew where to sit, Jewell. The table was perfect."

"I'm glad you chose the Glenlea pattern, Essie. Mama would have been so pleased."

Jewell climbed the stairs to her bed while Essie turned out the lights in the kitchen and dining room. "Well, Mr. Washington, thank you for all your dish-washing skills," she said, opening the door to the porch and finding the swing, while Sam pulled a rocker nearby.

The sun had set long ago on the Donnelly farm, shrouding the porch in a quiet darkness, the paddle fan slowly pushing air across the painted boards, the creak of the swing's chains moving in a song-like rhythm that matched the chirps of nearby crickets.

"I loved tonight," said Sam, a hint of longing in his voice. "You know, the people. DooRay. The medals." His voice caught. "I'm glad I decided to come back to Madison County. I don't think you'd find tonight in New York City, do you?"

"Not at all. Some of us want to stay and some of us want to go and all because of our hearts."

"Is that in your book?" Sam pulled a cigar from his pocket and unwrapped it.

"Hmmmm. My book is a heart book—you know, the kind of story that compels you to go through life with love the primary focus."

"Really? Like your love for Jewell? Staying here and caring for her?

"Yes. Exactly."

Sam lit his cigar and puffed loudly. He threw the spent match over the porch rail into the yard. "What about man/woman love?"

The cadence of the swing did not change. Essie watched the glow at the end of Sam's cigar. "What about it?"

"Is that not important to you?"

"Of course, it is. But you must understand—I'm here in this small place with a huge responsibility. Meaning Jewell. My opportunities for a relationship are few. My focus is on Jewell, not a knight in shining armor on a white horse."

"What about that fellow?"

"What fellow?"

"That knight on a horse when you were a senior in high school. Autrey Browning."

The swing stopped. "That was long ago."

"Did you love him?"

The swing began again. "Very much. But that was in another time." A small sliver of time. Essie felt the pain as if it were new—heart pain that never healed. She still remembered him as though he was on this very same porch, holding her hand.

Essie pushed the swing. Sam smoked his cigar. They both breathed the night air and watched fireflies flit unhurriedly in the dark.

"This is the kind of night I'd strum a guitar and sing to you—if I had a guitar... if I could sing."

Although Sam couldn't see it, Essie smiled. "What would you sing?"

Sam took in a breath and let it out slowly. "I think I'd make up a song of my own."

Essie half-giggled. "A song of your own? About what?"

"About a hound dog that howls to the moon 'cause he's in love."

Laughter came from the swing. "That would be a #1 hit, I'm sure."

"Oh, I'm positive it would be, too. I think I should have become a song writer, not a lawyer."

"Why is that?"

"Because I could write songs better than I could lawyer."

"Okay, sing me one of your songs and I'll decide."

Sam lifted himself out of the rocker and gently pulled Essie from the swing and began to slow dance. He hummed softly. "This is a song I wrote," he said as he began to sing. *"Got me a little farm girl who loaded watermelons all summer long. Uh, huh. Uh, huh. She arm wrestled me cause lifting watermelons made her strong. Uh, huh. Uh, huh."*

"That's it? That's the song?"

"Yep. That's it. What do you think?"

Essie felt Sam's arms pull her in closer. She smelled his aftershave and hair cream. She leaned her head on his chest. "I think I would stick to lawyering," she whispered.

"I do, too." Sam lifted Essie's chin with his finger and kissed her. Such beautiful lips. The kiss, like lightening, went tingling to his panting heart and when their lips parted, the sense of it stayed, the sweetness of it clinging to his lips like drops of honey. He could not have known until he fell—he was in love.

She didn't kiss him back, but she didn't draw away. His lips moved to her cheek, her brow, her ears. "You were the most beautiful girl in the homecoming parade, Essie Donnelly," he whispered, smoothing her hair back from her face and again kissing her soft lips.

CHAPTER TWENTY-EIGHT

Only moments after sunrise, Essie made coffee in her mama's tall peculator with its curving spout, given to her by her mama's mama, Grandma Hughes. She filled two cups and walked down the back steps to the barn. DooRay, Murphy and Killer were stirring. Despite his lack of tail feathers, Killer had flapped to the top of the well house and released a magnificent crow that surely woke the folks in the Mt. Horeb cemetery. The rooster sputtered and cawed and then arched his great neck and crowed a second time, followed by a long melodious bleat from nearby Murphy, Madison County's most beautiful goat.

"I cain't ever sleep in," said DooRay, his face groggy. "Those two start their duet 'bout the same time ever' mornin'."

Essie handed DooRay his coffee, full of cream and sugar, and sat down on a nearby bucket. "There's just something about hearing a rooster crow. Kinda calming. You know you've awakened to a new day." She'd rather hear a rooster crow than a dog bark or a cat meow.

"It's a new day, all right, Miss Essie." DooRay sipped his coffee. "Yes, sir. I sure do like my medals. Mighty fine."

The black man smiled through his full lips. "Them government mens sure had a good time last night, didn't they?"

"That they did, DooRay. Everybody did. You need to catch more fish, so we can do that again."

"I can do that for sure, Miss Essie. Gots to find me some more worms first."

The rays of the rising sun found them, and Essie moved her bucket into the shade. She studied the black man and decided he looked a lot like his mama, a woman the color of light rum, who picked cotton as efficiently as a surgeon removed an appendix. "DooRay, you understand about the subpoena you received, don't you?"

"Oh, for sure, I do. Mr. Sam told me all about it. All I has to do is tell the truth, and I can sure do that."

Essie nodded. "That's what we have to do. Tell the truth." She stood. "I'll fry up some eggs for us after a while, DooRay. Maybe some grits, too."

"Mighty fine, Miss Essie." DooRay emptied his cup and handed it back to Essie. "Guess I'll go find some worms."

Essie walked the worn path to the back porch. In the kitchen, she poured another cup of coffee and found the porch swing, her evening with Sam still on her mind. They had talked long into the night—him about his college days—her about farm life.

They had eased into a comfortable camaraderie, neither of them feeling the stress of courtship. She was thirty-three; he was thirty-one—they were certainly not teenagers.

Finishing her coffee, Essie left the front porch and walked the lane to the Bellville road. She pulled the detour sign to the middle of the road and readied herself for the onslaught of visitors. She felt the Bellville road was a lonely road, its travelers always searching, going from one place to the other, never really arriving. Just searching.

In the kitchen, Jewell stirred her coffee, as always in a delicate china cup and saucer. "Good morning, Jewell. I'm thinking maybe we'd better make a few more cakes today," said Essie as she lit the gas stove.

"Oh, yes. No telling who's coming to see us today," Jewell said, giving Essie a smile over the rim of her coffee cup. "I'll put new cushions in the rockers on the front porch and maybe some ferns along the porch."

Essie smiled. Dr. Anderson would not believe the change in Jewell. If only she did not have to lug the detour sign out into the road and then back again in late afternoon.

"When you finish your coffee, why don't you run out and get all the eggs out of the nests, and I'll start measuring out flour. I see we have a half a cake on the buffet so that'll do in case someone comes before these cakes are ready. I'm thinking three cakes—hope there are enough eggs."

"Oh, Essie," Jewell said in her sweet voice, "I just know mama has another cake recipe we could make. Remember the orange upside down cake."

Essie nodded, while starting a pot of grits. "That was one of my favorites. Easy to make." She pulled out the iron skillet and threw in a few slices of bacon. "We don't have any oranges though."

Jewell took the egg basket from the cabinet. "Be right back."

The skillet heated up and soon the sound of sizzling bacon filled the kitchen. Essie cracked four eggs in a bowl, beating with a fork and adding salt and pepper.

The sound of a scream pierced the air. Shrill and long, it kept coming as Essie flew out the kitchen and ran into the yard. Jewell, her face pale, stood on top of the picnic table, little yelps came and went as she jumped up and down.

On the ground, a mass of flailing snake and one tailless rooster battled, rolling together over and over. Killer on top and then the bottom. The snake, long and flailing and then coiled, wrapped around Killer. Killer broke free and jumped onto the back of the snake, his feet holding him down while his long, pointed beak punctured the snake's head.

DooRay came running from the barn. "Oh, Miss Jewell! Miss Essie."

Killer jumped off the snake and ruffled his feathers and strutted around the yard. The snake lay unmoving. Feathers floated in the air, wisps of orange and black raining down in the back yard.

DooRay arrived panting, his eyes wide. "Oh, Lord Jesus! That's the biggest moccasin I ever seen."

"Moccasin? I thought that was a rat snake," said Essie, her voice trembling. She peered at the snake and shuddered.

"Oh, no, mam. That there is a moccasin."

"Killer killed a moccasin?"

"Yes, em. Him's the best snake rooster I ever did see."

Jewell, standing on the picnic table, said weakly. "Can I come down now?"

DooRay waved at her. "Yes, mam. You come on down. This snake is dead as can be."

Essie picked up the egg basket and handed it to DooRay. "DooRay, please empty those nests for me. Then bury that damn snake."

"Yes, 'em. I surely will." DooRay took the basket and headed for the chicken house, Killer close behind. Killer pranced in circles as if singing *I killed a snake I killed a snake*. From the field, Murphy came running, bleating every step of the way.

"Come on, Jewell. Let's get those cakes in the oven."

Jewell climbed down from the picnic table and walked to the house, giving the dead snake a wide berth. "Oh, Essie. That snake coiled and was going to bite me and then here comes Killer flying through the air and lands right on top of him."

"I'm so sorry, Jewell. I saw that snake several times and thought it was a rat snake. I bet he's been getting eggs out of the nests."

"I'm okay, Essie." She took a deep breath. "I'll grease the cake pans and cream the butter and eggs."

Inside the kitchen, Essie rushed to the stove. The bacon was just right. She stirred the grits, removed the pot from the burner and dropped in a pat of butter. She scrambled the eggs and put bread into the toaster. "Jewell, would you get some peach preserves from the pantry?"

Essie took a plate out to the barn for DooRay. The sisters ate and then began work on their cakes, humming as they worked. They finished just in time for Jewell to hear her gospel radio program and for Essie to continue *Peyton Place*.

The porch was cool, shaded by the limbs of the oak trees in the front yard, trees that had outlived generations of Donnelly's. A soft breeze blew from the west, running down the porch and lifting Jewell's hair and the hem of her dress. Essie turned on the radio and the sound of Brother Wilbur and Sister Gladys Gospel Hour filled the air. Jewell opened her bible and leaned back in her chair.

Essie opened *Peyton Place* to page 273 and began a paragraph about Constance's daughter. The women in the novel were tormented, lost and unaware of their potential in a world, where opportunities abounded. Leave, thought Essie, leave and go somewhere else—get away from all that hate and sorrow. Don't waste your life struggling.

A horn tooted along the drive as a truck pulled up alongside the porch. It looked like Rob Crafton's truck. Essie could hardly see anyone behind the wheel when out jumped his seventeen-year-old daughter. She seemed troubled, a frown on her face, her hair in tumbles around her shoulders. "Hey, Miss Essie. How come there's a detour out there on the road?"

"I'm not sure, but you can take the farm lane over to the Valdosta highway. It's about two miles. Where're you going? Aren't you supposed to be in school?"

Essie moved closer and could see evidence of tears, a splotched face, trembling lips. "Come on up on the porch, honey."

"No. I got to go." The girl, very thin, moved to get back into the truck.

"Wait," called Essie. "Let's talk awhile. Have you eaten? We've got a wonderful cake. Let me fix you some iced tea." She wasn't sure which Crafton daughter hovered on the brick steps, obviously in distress.

The girl hesitated. "Maybe. For a few minutes." She squinted up at Essie. "Could I use your bathroom?"

"Why, sure you can. Go on through the kitchen. It's down the hall, past the living room."

At the buffet, Jewell uncovered the buttered rum pound cake and sliced several pieces. Essie poured iced tea. It was only noon; their day had begun with a rabid rooster and a fat poisonous snake in a fight to the death. Now, it seemed a young girl was in some kind of trouble. The detour sign was beginning to bring a multitude of troubled lives onto the Donnelly's front porch.

The girl returned, her face had been washed, her hair smoothed back. "Come sit on the swing with me for a while." Essie patted the swing and handed her a cake plate. She placed the tea on a small nearby table.

"Please forgive me, but I'm not quite sure which Crafton you are."

With timid fingers, the girl picked up a piece of cake. "Patty."

Essie gave the swing a little push with her foot and the two sat a moment, swinging and listening to the music from Jewell's gospel program. "I'm wondering where you were headed, Patty."

Patty looked away, her eyes watching Killer scratching in the yard, a mockingbird giving him a warning sweep.

"I wasn't going anywhere really. Just… going."

"School's about out, isn't it? Another week?"

"School's out." Her mind was somewhere else. The cake plate

rested in her hand, the cake half eaten.

"School's a good thing," said Essie, casually. "Just one more year and you'll be ready for college."

The girl's head whipped around. "College. How can I go to college? I'll have to work the farm for sure."

"That right?"

"Uh, huh. Hate that farm. All I do is work." Her shoulders slumped. Essie saw her lips tremble.

"Oh, my. I know about that. I was your age and loading watermelons day after day. I bet I loaded over a thousand watermelons in one day." She leaned over conspiratorially, her voice lowering. "But you know what? I noticed my bra size went from A cup to a C cup before the summer was over. So, I didn't mind so much after all."

The girl smiled. "I never thought about that." She looked down at her almost flat chest."

Essie let the girl nibble at her cake. "You were taking your daddy's truck?"

"That's the only way I could get away. I couldn't stand it any longer."

"Stand what?"

"The work. I'm so tired of the farm. I want to go to Valdosta or even Atlanta."

"Well, you can certainly do that." Essie let a few minutes go by. "But, first things first. Finish school, then you can go anywhere. Tell you what—you finish school and come back here, and I'll give you the money to travel to Atlanta or even New York, if that's what you want. But the deal is you finish school."

"You'd do that? Why?"

"Why? Because I was seventeen once and wanted to leave the farm."

There was quiet deliberation. Patty's eyes were wide when she turned and studied Essie. "But you're still here."

Essie glanced down the porch to Jewell who held her bible and followed along with scriptures from her gospel program. "Sometimes we don't get to do what we want. You know, Patty, maturity is doing what we should do, not what we want to do. Do you understand that?"

The young girl was quiet for a few moments. "Are you saying I need to go back to the farm? To school?"

"See that truck out there?" Essie pointed to the old blue pickup. She knew it had carried watermelons, hogs and anything else the Crafton farm needed. "Your daddy needs that truck more than you do right now. And I'm not telling you to do anything—that's up to you."

Patty picked up her tea and sipped it, thinking. A tear rolled down her cheek and dropped on her blouse. "I know mama and daddy need me."

"Yes, they do. But there will come a time, and very soon, that you'll leave the farm and have a life of your own. But right now, you're part of a family—an important part."

The girl sniffed and wiped her nose with her hand. Seventeen but still a child. Essie patted her arm. "You know what I think? I think anytime you need some company, Jewell and I will be here. We can churn some peach ice cream, put a saddle on Murphy and ride him around."

"Who's Murphy?"

"Murphy's DooRay's goat."

"DooRay Aikens? One-armed DooRay?"

"The one and only."

"He helps my daddy sometime. He showed me how to dig for worms."

"He's good at that, for sure."

They laughed and the swing moved faster, the creaking of the chain loud, proclaiming it was a swing of happiness. And, indeed, it was.

Patty left for home in her daddy's old blue truck, a tightly-wrapped buttered rum pound cake in her hand. She made a half circle in the drive and rolled down the truck's window. "Miss Essie," she shouted, "how many watermelons do I have to load to get to a D cup?"

CHAPTER TWENTY-NINE

After Uncle Wilbur and Aunt Gladys' gospel hour, Jewell and Essie made grilled cheese sandwiches with sharp cheddar from Lon Terry's meat case. It was the same cheese Rana Terry used for her famous macaroni and cheese.

Jewell climbed the stairs for her afternoon nap, humming all the way. Dr. Anderson would be proud that she had put on a pound or two.

On the swing, Essie picked up *Peyton Place* and continued reading about the lonely and repressed Constance MacKenzie and her illegitimate daughter Allison. Scandalous secret after scandalous secret leapt from every page. It seemed ugliness reared its head in every chapter as the small town's social strata became clearly defined.

The engine on the car that pulled down the drive was so quiet that Essie did not know it was there until she heard the car door open. The man who stepped out of the car was unusually tall, a stranger, not from Madison County. He moved slowly, his eyes watching Killer who was taking a dust bath in the lane.

"Hello, there," Essie called. She closed her book and walked to the railing. "The detour will take you over to the Valdosta highway," she said, pointing across the yard. "'bout two miles that way."

The man nodded. He wore a blue suit, its lapels wide, a thin cream stripe running through the garment. His hat was a fedora, but made of straw, like the ones in the tropics. He slowly removed his hat, and she saw his hair was well-oiled, slicked down and coal black, so black it could have been dyed.

Everything about him was mannequin like, his body perhaps infused with a mixture of blood and surely piss from the devil. "Where're you going?" inquired Essie.

The man removed his hat. "I'm—going—right—here." His voice was low, ominous; a slight pause after each word as if he wanted to be absolutely sure Essie understood him.

"Here?" asked Essie.

"You Jewell Donnelly?"

Oddly, Essie wished she had her daddy's gun on the front porch. She looked hard at the man. His eyes were unusual and, at first, she couldn't determine why. Then, when he came a step closer, she saw one pupil was split with two colors—one half blue and one half brown. The opposite eye was blue and perfectly normal.

"No, I'm her sister Essie."

"The accomplice?" he asked with a smirk.

"Accomplice?" Essie raised her eyebrows in question. The man's skin was pale; a city man, no farmer's blood in him, for sure.

"Yes, your sister murdered my little brother and you were her accomplice. Am I right?"

Essie's smile held a sleepy slyness. "I take it you're George Barnwell's brother. From New York? An attorney?"

"All true. Stanley Barnwell." He slowly twirled the hat in his hands. "I'm here to give you a little advice."

Essie raised up, her mouth a firm line. "I don't need any advice from you, Mr. Barnwell."

"Listen here, bitch. Better lock your doors at night."

Barnwell took a few menacing steps to the front porch before the two by four came out of the nearby azalea bushes, a blow to the back and shoulders. DooRay's one arm swung again and caught the man in the back of his legs, sending him and his straw hat into the dirt. Killer flapped his wings and spurred the man while he lay on the ground.

Barnwell rolled over and covered his head. "Get that rooster off me," he screamed, only to be butted by Murphy, whose horns slammed into the man's shoulder. Murphy, Madison County's most courageous guard goat, backed up and came at Barnwell again.

DooRay didn't take his eyes off Barnwell. "Miss Essie, you reckon you ought to get one of your daddy's guns?"

Behind her, Essie felt a poke into her back. It was Jewell and the poke was the barrel of one of their daddy's guns. "Here, Essie."

"Oh, my God, Jewell. Not again." Essie grabbed the gun, raised it and squared off with the lawyer from New York City.

Essie seemed to grow at least a foot, a countenance spreading over her that closely resembled an image of a gunslinger. "I am inclined, Mr. Barnwell, to think you are in a contest with the Donnelly sisters, a one-armed man, one rooster and a billy goat. If that is the case, it is a very unequal contest."

A bold Essie stepped closer. "You see, we find you despicable and far below the standards upon which we stand." It was spoken like the real Scarlett O'Hara, a steady aim, a steady eye. *Get off my farm.*

The gun in Essie's hand never wavered, nor did her resolve. "It would behoove you to leave this property, Mr. Barnwell."

Barnwell backed into his car. His eyes, wide and unbelieving, moved back and forth between Killer, DooRay, Murphy and Essie. "I'll be back." He half stumbled into his car and sped off down the farm lane, fishtailing through the dirt.

Essie lowered the gun by her side and sat down on the brick steps and put her head in her hands. Jewell sat beside her, wringing her hands. Killer strutted up around them, prancing proudly. The tailless rooster had spurred another bad guy. Murphy bleated long and loud—he was a supergoat, all that was missing was his cape.

DooRay leaned against the oak tree, the two by four resting in his hand.

"Jewell," Essie said quietly, "how did you know to bring me daddy's gun?"

Jeweled smiled sweetly at her sister. "Why, Essie, I watched from the upstairs window and when you didn't offer that man any cake, I knew he was no good."

Essie lifted her head and cackled, a mischievous laugh that swirled into the breeze blowing across the Donnelly farm. Giggles shaped in Jewell's throat and came out like hundreds of bubbles. DooRay's shoulders shook like jelly. Caught up in the laughter, he shook his head. "My, oh, my. You Donnelly womens is somethin' else."

CHAPTER THIRTY

Late in the evening, Essie pulled the detour sign across the road and leaned it against the maple tree. Her daddy's gun was tucked in her pocket. Stanley Barnwell said he'd be back, and she was sure he would keep his word.

Tomorrow she would call Sheriff Moore and tell him she had received a visit from the dead man's brother, that he had threatened them.

The moon was up when she walked to the barn. Before she entered the tack room, Murphy gave a soft bleat. He was DooRay's watch goat. Essie saw the dark silhouette of Killer on top of the well house, his head tucked underneath his wing. He had been a brave rooster that day, killed a snake and attacked a man who threatened her. And all without tail feathers.

"DooRay? You asleep?"

"No, mam. Jus' was listenin' to the frogs. Everything all right?"

Essie pulled a bucket off a nail on the wall and sat down. "DooRay, if you don't mind, I'd like you to sleep in the house tonight. I'll make you a bed on mama's couch. Downstairs, where you can hear everything."

"Why sure, Miss Essie."

Essie leaned back against the tack room wall. "I sure was glad to see you with that two by four, DooRay."

DooRay blew out a breath. "That sure was a mean fella."

"I know. I'll call Simmie Moore tomorrow and let him know what's happening." She stood, feeling the small gun in her pocket.

"I'll go make up the couch for you."

"Yes, mam. I'll be right on up to the house." DooRay stood up. "Miss Essie, it okay if I bring Murphy with me?" He stumbled for words. "Not in the house, but maybe on the front porch."

Essie could see his grin in the dark room. "Of course, DooRay. We'll want Murphy nearby for sure."

She left the barn and walked the path to the house. The state attorney would take Jewell's deposition tomorrow at 2:00 o'clock. She hoped Jewell remembered what happened just over a week ago. The butcher knife, the missing ear and the shot through the heart.

She put fresh linens on her mama's blue brocade couch. The living room faced the front porch, its windows tall and narrow. She felt safer with DooRay sleeping downstairs. Then, there was Murphy. He was a good watchgoat.

CHAPTER THIRTY-ONE

Pinetta's sunrise poked through purple gray clouds tinged with pink. The early rays caught the tassels on the high corn across the road, the same field that Jewell incessantly watched for a glimpse of Jimmy Townsend.

Essie walked down the farm lane and moved the detour sign into the middle of the Bellville road and meandered back to the house, hoping the coffee had finished perking. The night before had been quiet, and she had slept well, finally waking when Killer exploded with his first crow of the morning.

DooRay had awakened before she did and had slipped out the back door. He had folded the sheets and blankets, a task probably learned in army boot camp. How he did it one-handed, she didn't know. She took him a cup of coffee just as he was harnessing Murphy.

"I hope you slept well, DooRay." She handed him his coffee and pulled two hoecakes out of her pocket.

"Ah, mighty fine coffee, Miss Essie. Those was the finest sheets I ever slept on. Even better than the army's sheets."

DooRay put his coffee aside and Essie watched the one-armed black man harness his goat. His deft fingers moved quickly and efficiently. "Yes, sir. Ever' thing is gone be all right."

"Where're you going with Murphy?"

"Me and Murphy done found us a patch of beans and squash over at the old house—the one that done burned down. I reckon we can pick those beans and cut that squash and bring them back here

133

and enjoy some good eatin'. Might even find some tomatoes if we's lucky."

"Sounds like some good eatin' to me, DooRay. I'll run down to Terryville after a while, get some good ham slices for supper." Essie hesitated. "DooRay, you be watchful. No telling what that Barnwell fellow will do."

"Yes, mam." Killer jumped on Murphy's back and DooRay eased into the cart, his one hand wrapped tightly around the reins. "Go, you beautiful billy. Go!"

And off they went, Murphy pulling DooRay, Killer and the cart as though they were in a chariot race. DooRay stood broad shouldered in the cart, Murphy digging in his hooves and picking up speed. Killer flapped his wings and dug his feet into Murphy thick hair. Oh, if only he had tail feathers—they'd be flying like a kite in the wind.

Essie poured her coffee and walked out to the porch just as a truck turned down the lane. It was Dr. Davis. The other day he said he'd be back for another piece of cake and here he was.

His faithful dog sat in the truck as Dr. Davis bounded up the steps. "Well, I see there's still a detour through your farm, Essie." He wrung his hands, "Guess I'm gonna have to have another piece of that pound cake." A grin followed.

"How about some coffee, too? Black, right?"

"Oh, how lovely. And where is Jewell this morning?"

"She's still asleep—we had a late night. Be right back."

Essie sliced cake and poured coffee. She heard Dr. Davis sit on the swing. She hoped he didn't see Peyton Place on top of the swing pillow.

"Here you go, Dr. Davis." She placed the cake plate on the nearby table and handed Dr. Davis a coffee mug. She hoped Jewell wouldn't mind her not using their mother's fine china.

"Well, Essie, sad news. Hoot Gibson's bull is still… still unable to… to perform. I reckon he's just out two-thousand dollars. 'course, he could just quarter the bull up into some mighty expensive steaks."

"I'm sorry to hear that, Dr. Davis. Where are you headed to this morning?"

In three bites, the slice of cake was gone, the crumbs but a memory.

"Lewis Hill's mule is sick and that is a tragedy. How can Lewis sell his moonshine if he can't get to town?" Dr. Davis slurped his coffee. "And, oh, how I hate working on that mule."

Don't ask, Essie. Please don't ask. "Why is that, Dr. Davis?"

"Flatulence! Worst case I've ever seen. Sorry, Essie, every time I visit I talk about... inappropriate things." He jumped up. "Got to go. If I don't ever see you again, that mule's done blowed me all the way to Valdosta."

His laughter followed him to his truck. And he was off, his dog hanging out the window, his tongue dragging at least a foot behind.

Jewell stirred in the kitchen. She poured coffee and hummed as she walked through the door onto the porch. "Good morning, Essie. What a lovely morning it is. Who was that you were talking to?"

"Dr. Davis. He's headed over to Lewis Hill's place to doctor his mule.

"What's wrong with his mule?"

Essie fiddled with the buttons on her sleeve. "Upset stomach."

At 1:30 Sam Washington eased down the Donnelly lane. He would sit in on Jewell's deposition with the state attorney, who'd arrive at 2:00 o'clock, along with the court recorder.

Sam had notified the state attorney that Jewell Donnelly was available to give her deposition, but, at Judge Earp's approval, would not do so in court. He provided Jewell's address. The state attorney agreed, with the presiding judge's approval, to interview Jewell Donnelly at her home. John E. Moxley had been appointed the state attorney handling Jewell's deposition.

Sam pulled his briefcase out of his car and bounded up the steps onto the porch. "Yoo, hoo. Anybody home?"

Essie came through the screened door wiping her hands on a dishtowel. "We're here, Sam. Guess you need to talk with Jewell."

"That I do," he said, pulling open his briefcase and pulling out a notepad. "I'd like to talk with you, too. I understand you and DooRay have been subpoenaed and will attend the inquest."

Essie nodded. "We'll be there all right." Essie walked to the swing and sat down. "I don't know how to tell you this, but we had a visitor yesterday. Not a very nice one, either."

Sam closed his briefcase and sat in a chair opposite Essie. "Who?"

"The dead man's brother. From New York City."

"That's not good. What do you mean 'not very nice?'"

A few moments passed while Essie gathered her thoughts. "His language to me was very threatening. He called me an 'accomplice' to his brother's murder. When he started to come up on the porch—uninvited I might add and quite angry—DooRay hit him with a two by four.

"Anyway, I told him to get off the farm. He left, but before he left, he told me we'd better lock our doors—that he'd be back."

Sam said nothing while he stared, unblinking, at Essie. Finally, he rose from his chair and began pacing the porch. "This is upsetting, Essie. Did you call Sheriff Moore?"

"Yes, I called him this morning. He said he'd ride out this afternoon and take my statement."

"Are you filing a formal complaint?"

"Yes. The man is no ordinary man. He has no qualms about coming back and causing trouble. The only reason he left in the first place was because of DooRay and that two by four." She hesitated only a second. "And a gun."

"A gun. You had a gun?" Sam's mouth hung open.

Essie nodded. "He meant business and so did I."

Sam wiped his brow, a nervous gesture, and took in a deep breath. "You and Jewell—and DooRay, for that matter—aren't safe out here. I think the sheriff ought to find Mr. Barnwell and have a chat with him."

"I agree." Essie pulled out a revolver from her pocket. "I've been carrying this around with me." She palmed it and showed it to Sam.

Sam winced. "That will do the job and then some."

"I don't really plan on getting too close to Mr. Barnwell, but he may just try to get close to me."

Sam took the gun from her. "I guess this is your dad's?"

"Yes. It's a Colt M1917—another gun brought back by his brother from the war."

Sam sighed. "Be careful, Essie."

Jewell walked out onto the porch carrying a slice of cake. "Mr.

Washington, you must have a slice of cake."

Her smile was lovely. "I could put some ice cream with it, if you like."

"Oh, no," said Sam. "That cake is perfect just as it is. Thank you so much."

Jewell's eyes searched the field before she sat in her chair. "Looks like rain is headed our way. Look at that big black cloud to the south there. Winds picking up, too."

Sam and Essie both looked south and saw the cloud front moving toward them. Sam stood and walked over to Jewell. "Jewell, you know the state attorney will be here in a few minutes. You've remembered what I told you about your statement?"

"Oh, yes. Just tell the truth, and that's what I'll do." She hesitated. "If the attorney asks me where that man's ear is, I'll tell him I just don't know. 'cause I really don't."

"Well, I don't think he'll ask you about the ear, Jewell."

From the drive, a horn honked. It was the state attorney and court stenographer.

State Attorney John E. Moxley emerged from his car carrying his briefcase, the court stenographer right behind him.

Mr. Moxley was a precise man, known for his meticulousness in the courtroom. He introduced himself to Sam as well as Jewell. He was a Southerner like Sam; his approach in questioning a witness was gentle but to the point. If he thought a witness was lying, he would instantly become on guard, a subtle harshness overtaking his countenance.

As Jewell's attorney, Sam could observe the deposition. He sat on the sidelines when the questioning began.

"Miss Donnelly, do you understand you're under oath?" Mr. Moxley asked.

Jewell nodded.

"Miss Donnelly, in order for your response to be recorded, you'll have to provide a verbal response. The stenographer can't record a nod."

Jewell became flustered. "Yes. I understand I'm under oath."

Mr. Moxley continued. "You understand the stenographer is recording your answers along with the questions?"

"Yes." Jewell smiled tentatively.

"The stenographer," Mr. Moxley gestured to the young woman by his side, "will type up the deposition and you will have an option to review it and make any corrections you deem necessary before you sign it."

The attorney cleared his throat. "Please state your full name, place of birth and date of birth."

Jewell blinked several times before she answered. The porch breeze blew a strand of hair across her cheek and she reached up to push it away. "Jewell Agnes Donnelly. Born in Pinetta, Florida, on August 4, 1921."

"Miss Donnelly, can you tell me what took place on the afternoon of Wednesday, June 27, 1956, when you arrived home from your trip to Tallahassee?"

Jewell's eyes flitted around the porch, a slight smile played along her lips as she hesitated. "Oh, yes. There was a man in prison clothes standing in the middle of mama's kitchen and he was eating from a jar of peanut butter. When I saw him, I screamed. Mama's favorite butcher knife was on the counter. It was her favorite knife, you know." A frown creased her brow as she thought of her mother's favorite knife.

Mr. Moxley nodded to the stenographer. "Please make a note that the prisoner's name was George Barnwell." He turned to Jewell. "Go on."

"And he picked up that butcher knife and swung it through the air when Essie ran into the house." Jewell became breathless and touched her hand to her chest.

"Your sister, Essie?"

"Yes, my sister, Essie."

Mr. Moxley asked the stenographer to record Esther Elizabeth Donnelly's name.

"Well, he didn't talk very nice to Essie when she told him to leave. He said he wasn't going to leave—that he might sleep in our house." Jewell looked out into the yard, thinking, and the frown returned. Red splotches ran across her neck in the shape of geranium leaves.

The attorney nodded as he wrote. He found himself visualizing the scene. The butcher knife. Essie Donnelly, her sister, confronting the inmate.

"Well, Essie took that big ole ax and—"

"Wait a minute. Your sister had an ax?"

Jewell's smile was radiant. "She surely did. And when she raised it up into the air, that man swung the butcher knife at my sister. That's when I shot off his ear."

Jewell sat back in her chair and began shaking her head from side to side. "He wasn't real happy about that. Said he was going to slit my throat. That's when I shot him again." She cocked her head. "The trigger on daddy's pistol was real easy to pull."

Mr. Moxley remained quiet for a long minute. "So, when did you get your daddy's pistol?"

"When that man was waving the butcher knife at Essie, and she was circling him with the ax, I ran upstairs and got it out of daddy's gun cabinet."

"It was loaded, or did you load it?"

"Oh, no. I don't know how to load a gun. It was already loaded."

"Did you know how to release the safety?"

"The safety?" Wide-eyed, Jewell stared at Mr. Moxley. She picked up a glass of water and sipped it, her long thin fingers holding the glass delicately.

Mr. Moxley spoke slowly. "Yes, the safety. Guns have a safety that has to be released in order to fire the gun."

"Well, I just pulled the trigger and the bullet came out, and that man's ear just came off and flew across the kitchen." Jewell slapped her lap with her hands as if punctuating the simplicity of the incident.

"What did George Barnwell do after you shot off his ear?" Mr. Moxley leaned over in rapt attention. Even the stenographer sat on the edge of her seat, her pen posed and ready to catch every word.

Jewell lifted her chin and became thoughtful. "Oh, now I remember. He called me a very ugly name and—"

"Miss Donnelly, can you tell me exactly what he called you, so our records may be complete and definitive?"

Jewell looked at Sam, then Essie, her eyes wide and questioning. She stammered, "Well, I... I think it was... was bitch." She bit her lip and grimaced. "Yes, that was it."

"What else did he say?"

"He called me that very ugly name and then said he was going to slit my throat. He swiped the air with mama's butcher knife and then came toward me."

THE FRONT PORCH SISTERS

"What did you do?" Mr. Moxley stilled because he knew what she did next."

"Why, I shot him again. Right through the heart."

"What happened next?"

"He fell on the floor and didn't say another word. Not one."

Mr. Moxley rubbed his chin. "What did you do after he fell to the floor?"

Jewell glanced at Essie. "Essie rushed over and took the gun from me."

Mr. Moxley nodded. "What happened next?"

"Essie called the sheriff and we went outside in the yard and waited for him."

"You didn't go back into the house?"

"No, we stayed out in the yard."

"Did you know the prison escapee was dead?"

Jewell lingered in thought, fiddling with her hands. "Not really. We just waited for the sheriff."

"Is there anything you'd like to say, Miss Donnelly?"

Jewell looked at Sam. "Mr. Washington just told me to tell the truth and I did." She smiled at Mr. Moxley.

"I see." Mr. Moxley nodded at Sam. "Mr. Washington, that completes Miss Donnelly's deposition. I'll have a copy sent to you for any changes. Then, we'll prepare it for the inquest." He then turned to Essie. "Miss Donnelly, I'll see you and DooRay Aikens at the courthouse tomorrow to process your deposition. I believe the time is 2:00 for you and 3:00 for Mr. Aikens."

"We'll be there, Mr. Moxley."

The state attorney gathered his papers and placed them in his briefcase. "Thank you for your time," said Mr. Moxley as he and the court stenographer stepped off the porch and into the yard. Sam and Essie watched the car turn onto the Bellville road and head for Madison. "Jewell did very well," said Essie.

"Let's hope her testimony will carry the inquest," said Sam as he turned to Essie. "We've got to be cautious with Stanley Barnwell in town.

Chapter Thirty-Two

Murphy trotted up the lane pulling DooRay in the cart. Killer hung on for dear life as Murphy picked up speed and sprinted for the barn. "Slow down, you old goat," DooRay called. "You gone kill us all."

The cart jerked to a stop under the oak tree next to the porch. "Hey, Miss Essie," he yelled. "Got us some fine beans and squash."

Essie and Sam left the porch and walked out into the yard. DooRay lifted a bucket filled with green beans. Then, a second bucket filled with squash. "Yes, sir. They's even some tomatoes and cucumbers in here."

"Oh, my, DooRay. Let's get those beans snapped." DooRay sat the buckets on the ground and snapped the reins. "Get along, Murphy." And off he went, Killer flapping his wings. They were home.

Essie and Sam took the buckets onto the porch. "If you'll start these beans, I'll run to Terryville and get some pork chops for us from Lon Terry."

"Yes, mam. I'd be glad to cut up that squash, too." Sam sat in a rocker and pulled the bucket next to him. "I need a big pan for these beans."

Essie went into the kitchen and brought out two large enamel pans. "Here you go." She went back inside and called for Jewell. "Jewell, there're beans to snap."

"I'll be right down, Essie." Jewell's sweet voice drifted down the stairs like a melody, a song that stayed in your head and played over and over again.

Essie walked to the shed and hollered toward the barn. "Beans to snap on the front porch, DooRay." She hesitated. *How could DooRay snap beans with one hand?*

She fired up the Buick and eased down the lane to the Bellville road. She hadn't even asked Sam to stay for dinner—it was though it was a natural thing to have him sit on the porch and snap beans and then sit down at their dining room table.

Even after his belligerent entry into their lives, she had slowly softened. Perhaps she was waiting to see if he could tolerate what Uncle Lester had called a hard woman. She admitted there was nothing genteel about her. How could there be? She hadn't been the one to go to finishing school in Switzerland. Instead, she had loaded watermelons and cropped tobacco in hot sun, sweat soaking her head beneath her straw hat.

She pulled into the shade at Lon Terry's store where chickens roamed the yard. Across the road, hogs grunted and rooted, trying to stay cool. A water hose hung over the fence, its water spraying out over the hogs, a big sow and her nine piglets clamoring to stay cool. The odor of wet mud and swine filled the air, pungent and bitter, and swept across Essie's nose. She was a hard woman—the smell of hogs didn't bother her a bit.

Lon sat in his big chair, several watermelons nearby that had been split. Lon was known for scooping out the heart of the watermelon for himself and throwing the remainder to his precious hogs. Someone was in the chair across from him, their back to Essie.

"Rana inside the store?" she called.

"Yes, mam. She is."

"Got any good pork chops today?" Essie hesitated and studied the back of the chair across from Lon. The back of a head, the shoulders.

"Had some delivered this mornin'. Beautiful cuts."

When Essie took a few steps toward the back door of the store, she glanced at the profile of the person sitting in the chair. Familiar, but who?

Then, her heart stopped. A face she hadn't seen in fifteen years: Autrey Browning. The star basketball player, of course. Most Likely to Succeed, of course. Most Handsome, of course. Most Likely to

142

Break Your Heart… yes, definitely that. At that moment, he turned and looked over his shoulder—looked directly into her eyes while a slow smile eased across the lips she had kissed so many times.

He stood and turned to face her. "Essie Donnelly," he said slowly. "Been a long time."

Essie felt a rushing sound in her ears as she gasped for breath. Her body seemed to levitate; her feet leave the ground as her head swam, followed by a ringing that shut out all noise. Autrey was talking to her, but she couldn't hear him.

In her vision, Essie saw him fade in and out. The tall, handsome man smiled. Waiting. His brooding eyes held hers. Waiting. "Autrey," she said. "Yes, it's been a long time."

Autrey took a few steps toward her. Essie held up her hand. "No." Haltingly, she turned and went into the store.

Inside the store, Rana Terry sliced cheese, her hand moving quickly across the cheese with a long-bladed knife. "Hey, there, Essie. What can I get for you?"

Essie stuttered. "Ah… I… you can… how about some pork chops—four if you have them."

"Got some good thick ones. I'll weigh them out." Rana reached into the meat case and pulled out four chops, slapping them onto the scale. "Two pounds, 6 ounces, Essie. At fifty-five cents a pound, that's $2.48." Rana began wrapping the chops in butcher paper, then tied it with a string. "You okay, honey? You look a little pale."

"Fine. Just fine. Please add those chops to my account, Miss Rana."

Essie turned away quickly, pushing open the front door and calling 'thank you' over her shoulder. She slid into the Buick, yanked it in gear and pulled onto the Bellville road. Her heart clamored for calm. *Fifteen years. Hello, Essie. Been a long time. Oh, yes. Fifteen years is a long time to carry a broken heart.*

The Buick plowed down the dirt road, swerving back and forth over the ruts and slowing only to turn into the Donnelly drive. Essie gulped down tears as she gripped the steering wheel and slammed on the brakes. *Why? Why did he come back?*

DooRay and Sam, along with Jewell, had moved to the picnic table, the bucket of beans piled on top of the table. Jewell looked up and waved at Essie, who walked across the yard. "Hello, Essie!"

Essie waved back and entered the kitchen from the back porch. She hardly knew what she was doing, a buzz in her head, shaking hands that could not untie the twine that wrapped the pork chops. She slung the pork chops aside and ran up the stairs, a silent curse with every step. *Autrey Browning was back.*

In her room, she fell to her knees beside her bed and lifted the edge of the bedspread and there it was—the small leather suitcase containing her most precious belongings. Her fingertips wiped across the dust, a sprinkle of rust had corroded the metal locks. Angrily, she dug at the locks and flipped open the bag. *Flipped open memories from fifteen years ago.*

A picture of Autrey Browning holding a basketball stared up at her—a clipping from the Pinetta page in the *Enterprise-Recorder: Pinetta Indians Scalp Perry—Autrey Browning MVP.*

Essie pulled the clipping closer. A self-important grin stretched across the sports star's face, a front tooth a little crooked, one dimple on his right cheek. His eyes said it all: dark and serious, despite the grin. They seemed to stare far beyond the camera, far away to a place that was not Madison County. Essie tilted the clipping to read the faded date: February 1940.

A lifetime ago. It wasn't long after the picture was taken that Autrey had disappeared. Essie had visited his mother and asked about him. "I don't know, honey. He didn't say too much to me and his daddy. Just packed a suitcase and left." His mother had been unresponsive to Essie's questions, uninterested in her heartbreak.

Dried flowers. The yellow corsage on her wrist. Essie picked it up and crumbles of memories fell away. They had gone to the prom together—the sweetheart couple—in love forever. Only it wasn't forever.

Essie felt her chest tighten, a sob building. Her throat ached as she tried to swallow it back, back fifteen years. She lifted the lid of a small box, a ring box. And there it was—a promise ring. Sterling silver with double heart gemstones, two hearts proclaiming true love. A promise ring, the promises thrown away and forgotten.

Essie heard footsteps on the stairs, not Jewell's. Heavier and slower. She watched the doorway to her room and saw the tall, lawyer from Madison County smiling at her. Sam said nothing, just leaned against the doorframe and set his blue eyes on hers.

Her breathing quieted as she looked at him, looked at the questions in his eyes. She found herself wanting to smile but couldn't. She had seen his backside and her sexual being had awakened, maybe for only a moment, but it was there. Hiding and untouched, but it was there.

"Guess you found out he was back?" Sam moved closer into the room and looked down at the pretty watermelon queen of Madison County.

"How did you know?" Essie said, her words trickling out, hardly words at all, merely tears that choked into words.

"I've known it a few days." He sighed heavily as he looked around the room, then back to Essie. "When I saw your face a minute ago, I knew you had somehow discovered the same thing. I saw him at the Yellow Pine truck stop, drinking coffee with M. C. Herring a few days ago.

"Did you talk to him?"

"No. But everyone who saw him wondered about you and if he'd come to see you." Sam sat on the edge of the bed. "You two were the love story of Madison County at one time."

Essie looked down at the small suitcase. A few clothes, her bus ticket. Mementos from high school. When she looked back at Sam, she gave him a knowing smile. "I saw him at Terryville talking with Lon Terry."

Sam nodded and at the same time reached out and lifted her chin. His thumb rubbed across her cheek. She could feel the warmth of his hands, smell the sharp fragrance of green beans on his fingers. He spoke softly, almost a whisper. "I kinda look at it this way. Life is like a movie and you're the director, the producer and the star, all rolled into one. So, Essie Donnelly, you write the script for your movie, for your life. And when you're done, let's talk about us."

When Sam left her bedroom, Essie gently closed the small suitcase and pushed it back under the bed, out of sight but not out of mind. Yes, her life was like a movie, and she was its star. The only problem was her movie was shown only in Madison County, on a clay road, and her only audience was the watermelons on her 300-acre farm.

CHAPTER THIRTY-THREE

S am did not stay for dinner. The beans he snapped remained in the white enamel pan on the picnic table until Essie took them into the house for cooking. It was near dark when he left the house and drove down the lane, pulled onto the Bellville road and into the clay ruts toward the Madison/Valdosta highway. He rolled down his window, anxious to breath the calm of a Pinetta evening. The sun had slipped behind the trees and left the horizon dark, while stars began to show themselves in the evening sky.

He passed Terryville, where Lon Terry's hogs lay quiet in their mudholes with only an occasional grunt or flick of their ears.

The small store was dark, even the Shell gas sign was out for the night. The walls of the gristmill seemed ominous, a ghost in the night that rose high into the dark sky. His love of Madison County hovered everywhere, on the rolling hills planted in rows so straight you knew a ruler had been used to straighten the rows.

The dirt roads took him through country where cows grazed, cattle egrets sitting on their backs, and creeks ran lazily to the Withlacoochee River. He had almost left this place—if he had, he would not have become the man he was. His strength lay in his family, his community, and the people who tended their farms, went to church and ran to help if your tobacco barn caught fire. There was no doubt about it: Madison County was home and always would be.

Sam's thoughts drifted to Essie Donnelly. He was at a point in his life he wanted to settle down, have children, maybe a small farm and a wife who adored him. His memories of Essie Donnelly had been pressed into his heart and remained there, unable to dissolve into another place.

He had known her all his life, watched her from afar, even when Autrey Browning squired her around Madison County, cloaked as the "it" couple. He was always on the sidelines, in the shadows—an under classman who was invisible. But, that didn't keep him from thinking about her—the older woman.

Now, he was at a place where school was behind him, and his career was on the move. In life's plan, marriage was next. He looked no further than Essie Donnelly. She was like a magnet that drew him to her. He simply melded to her as if he had no resistance at all. He was smitten at the homecoming parade years ago and he was smitten now.

He felt a little surge of anxiety as he passed through Pinetta to the Madison highway. The return of Autrey Browning had caused a misstep in his quest to woo Essie Donnelly. He knew it and the whole county knew it—Autrey Browning and Essie Donnelly had been inseparable—inseparable until he vanished for fifteen years.

When Sam turned right on the Madison highway, his thoughts spiraled, and all of them of Essie. He didn't notice the car parked at J. T. Woodward's grocery store, its lights out, its motor running. Nor did he notice the car eased forward and turned onto the highway behind him.

Sam lumbered along and turned left onto the Washington loop, past the barbed wire fences, the planted pines, the cows and the old house, a house his granddaddy had built. When he parked outside the barn where his room lay high in the rafters, he didn't notice the car had parked a quarter of a mile away in the road, lights out, and its motor turned off.

Lights blazed in the main house, a radio played while voices came from the screened side porch. He hollered over the music—a country song *Your Cheatin' Heart* twanged across the yard—"Mama, you got any left-overs from dinner?"

He heard laughter, then his mother stepped out onto the porch steps. Night had fallen, and only her silhouette was visible. "Hello, son. Yes, I do. But you'd better hurry or your brothers will wipe them out."

"Be there in a minute." Sam pulled his briefcase from the car and walked inside the barn. He climbed the ladder to his small loft and heard Hank Williams' twang rise up through his opened windows. *Your cheating heart will make you blue. Your cheating heart will tell on you...*

Inside the house, Julia Washington had filled a plate and placed it on a small table on the porch. Nearby, Sam's brothers drank iced tea and listened to Hank strum his guitar and sing of tears and lost love.

"Sammy boy," said Bill. "You sure have been spending a lot of time down at the Donnelly's—every time I drive by, your car is there. And what's the deal with the detour sign? I just go around it. Didn't see a darn thing."

Bill, the oldest brother, tossed a grin at Sam. Bill, thirty-three, helped his father farm. His muscle was much needed since Paul Washington's arthritis had set in.

"All business," said Sam. "Jewell is my client."

Mike, the youngest brother, laughed. "All business? Who could make it all business with Essie Donnelly around?" Mike, twenty-six years old, was home from college, an agricultural major at ABAC in Georgia.

All three of the Washington boys were tall like their dad, dark hair and dark eyes. Handsome men, Hollywood material that made the ladies swoon. Each of them had learned manners from their mother, learned to occasionally spit tobacco from their father. Their mother gave them an easy-going personality, a demeanor that allowed each of them to acclimate socially. Like their father, each had a rough side that came and went like summertime clouds.

Each one born and raised in Madison County, the Washington's were an old family. Will and Cora, grandparents of Paul and his older brother, Tillman, farmed hundreds of acres on land that backed up to the Withlacoochee River.

"What's goin' on with the inquest? Jewell Donnelly goin' to jail for murder?" Bill, the most serious of the three siblings, propped his feet on a nearby stool. "Everybody's wondering if she pulled the trigger or if it was Essie. Jewell wouldn't hurt a fly, but her sister Essie could tame a bull."

Sam rolled his eyes. "It's plain and simple, Bill. Self-defense, no matter how you cut it." He gave Bill a harsh glance. "Can't talk about the case."

Sam stood, pulling the plate his mother had fixed him from the table. "Hey, there's one thing for sure. The facts of the case are not complicated. Judge Earp is fair and square, and he won't take nonsense from anybody. He and he alone runs his court. And runs it his way. And that's by the rule of law."

Mike cut in. "Well, gossip has it that some big New York lawyer is comin' into Madison County with his gun loaded."

"Look! Let's keep this thing in the right perspective. The facts are on our side. I'm not worried in the least."

The room quieted. The radio turned off, Mike strummed his guitar while Bill stepped into the yard to smoke. In a moment, Bill tapped the screen. "Maybe you should be worried, Sam. There's a car sittin' down the road to the house, about a quarter mile away. I can see it through the pines. Never seen it before."

Mike reached up and turned out the porch light. He leaned his guitar against the wall and peered out into the night. "Interesting. Can't see too much detail, but that looks like the shape of the car that drove back and forth down the highway all day. I noticed it when I mowed the southeast field. It parked by the fence for a while. Thought it was broke down but maybe not."

"Oh, come on, guys. Your imagination is working overtime," said Sam, tired and irritated. "I've got some work to do. See you later." He took one last bite of his mama's meatloaf and poured another glass of tea. His walk to the barn was slow, a thinking walk, where things bunched up into one place, and he was determined to sort them out.

In the barn, Sam climbed the ladder, his shoulders slumped. He was tired, mentally and physically. He hadn't slept well for a week. Too many things on his mind.

He smiled when he entered his room. His mama had tidied things, put clean sheets on his bed and fresh towels for when he walked back to the house to shower. He was sure he smelled Ivory soap as he flopped down on the bed. How in the world she climbed the ladder to his loft, he didn't know. A good night's sleep was all he needed. If only thoughts of Essie Donnelly would ease up, flow out of his mind like the waters of the Withlacoochee.

The return of Autrey Browning was disconcerting, to say the least. Sam knew nothing of the man other than his absence for fifteen years. Autrey's family farmed on the west side of Madison County, a small farm, only twenty or so acres of tobacco and they kept to themselves for the most part. The family was small, only Autrey and a younger sister. The sister had moved away long ago, leaving elderly parents. At least, that's what Rana Terry had told him when he inquired about the family a few days back, the day after he'd seen Autrey at the Yellow Pine truck stop.

He didn't know why he did it, but Sam left the bed and pulled the ladder up into his room. He looked down into the barn. Hay bales lay stacked high to the ceiling alongside farm tools, the Ford tractor and a healthy pile of dried manure that his mama used for her flower beds.

Before he closed his eyes, Sam looked at his watch. It was 11:30. The Washington farm lay quiet, only the bawl of a lonesome cow in a distant pasture. The clear July night harbored a full moon and, if it was able to talk, would declare Madison County one of the most beautiful places on earth. The moon's reflection moved along with the Withlacoochee, pulled night owls from their hiding places and touched hundreds of barns whose tin roofs glowed like fireflies in the night.

Sam thought he was dreaming. Someone was touching his shoulder, then a hand clamped down on his mouth. "Shush, brother. Some fellas are walking down the lane toward the house. Me and Bill stayed up and kept an eye on them while you slept your ass away."

Sam nodded and pulled Mike's hand away from his mouth. "You're kidding, right?" he whispered.

"Hell, no. There're three of them. Come on down into the barn."

"How'd you get up here?" Sam pulled on a pair of jeans.

"Climbed up."

"How? The ladder's up here with me." Sam zipped his jeans and looked out the east window. The three men walked cautiously, stopping among their mother's crepe myrtles.

"Jumped on top of the tractor and pulled myself up. Be quiet.

Let's go."

"Go where?" Sam rubbed the sleep from his eyes. For the first time, he realized his heart rate had increased and his hands shook.

"With me and Bill. We're gonna jump these guys."

"Jump them? What if they have guns?" Sam pulled on Mike's arm. "Let's think about this for a minute."

"We don't have a minute. Besides that, we have guns. Come on." Mike shoved Sam aside and slid the ladder to the barn floor. He took the rungs two at a time. Hesitant, Sam came down behind him.

"Where's Bill?" Sam grimaced when Mike squeezed his arm and placed a finger over his lips. Mike pointed to the back of the barn where an open door led out into the barnyard.

Sam dutifully followed Mike. Bill leaned against a fence post holding a shotgun. "Oh, shit," breathed Sam. "Hold on. Let's get the sheriff out here."

"No time for that. Let's see who these fellows are." Bill handed Mike a .38. "It's loaded. Sam, you don't need a gun. We've got all we need right here." He lovingly patted the shotgun.

Bill leaned toward Sam. "Sam, when those guys get within about twenty yards of the barn, you switch on the farm lights.

Sam watched as Mike and Bill eased back into the barn and hunkered down. He moved to the main switch and hid behind a large corn hopper. His eyes on the lane, he grasped the main switch to the yard lights. Sweat poured from the back of his neck and down his back. *There goes my career*, he thought, as his hand squeezed the switch and his eyes narrowed, all the while wanting to run as fast as he could in the opposite direction.

The three men walked slowly, their bodies silhouetted by moonlight. They were average size, moving a few feet at a time, stopping to listen and to get their bearings. They wore dark suits. Not farm boys, for sure. City boys who had probably never been near a farm.

At thirty yards from the barn, they stopped once more. Obviously in charge, the man in the middle motioned for the man on his left to go to the side of the barn. The man on the right stepped off to the right side of the barn. At that moment, Sam pulled the switch on the blinding farm lights.

"Hold it right where you are," yelled Bill, who stepped out with the shotgun in front of him. The men fumbled, surprised they were caught in glaring lights, a man holding a shotgun pointed at them. They pulled in together once again and stood motionless.

Bill took a few steps forward; Mike came out of the barn, the .38 in his hand. Sam moved out from behind the hopper and stood alongside Mike. The three Washington boys, seemingly unafraid, stared at the three men in dark suits, whose hands hung by their sides.

Bill was the first to speak. "You fellas lost?" He stepped closer and raised the shotgun a few inches. His finger was not on the trigger, but it was close enough.

The man in the center gestured at Sam. "Need to talk with him."

Bill ambled a few steps closer. Unfortunately for the three city men, Bill was the Washington brother who gave little leeway when it came to negotiating an issue. He would not be kind; he would not mince words.

"In our neck of the woods, we have manners. We talk in daylight. We make appointments. We don't show up in the middle of the night, unannounced. We don't like strangers who don't have manners."

The three men fidgeted, never taking their eyes off Bill nor the shotgun he held. Finally, the man in charge jerked his head toward Sam. "You got a problem talking?"

Bill raised the shotgun. "You have a hearing problem? I said you have bad manners. Folks who have bad manners are not welcome on this farm."

The man's eyes fell to Bill's trigger finger, to the shotgun, to Bill's burning eyes. "You're messing with the wrong people."

Bill laughed. "That's what I've been trying to tell you. You're the wrong people to be standing here in the middle of the night, without an invitation. It would behoove you to back off and get in that fancy car of yours. Maybe turn on the motor and the headlights. Maybe get outta here with all your limbs."

Bill moved even closer. Then, in a voice deep with anger, he looked at all three men. "You're trespassing. Turn around and walk away. Now."

Mike moved up to Bill's side, his .38 in clear view. Sam eased beside Mike. "Tell Mr. Barnwell I'll see him at the courthouse at noon tomorrow. We'll chat then and, if he's lucky, Sheriff Moore will not put him in jail for interfering with Judge Earp's courtroom."

"Damn, Sam," said Bill, "I was hoping to use this new shotgun."

There was no smile on his face.

The three men backed up a step before turning around and walking down the road to their parked car. The man in the middle called over his shoulder. "Watch your back, Mr. Washington. You don't own Madison County and neither does the judge."

Bill Washington raised the shotgun in the air and pulled the trigger. The loud boom that followed kicked the three men into a sprint to their car, where they backed up and sped down the highway toward Madison.

From the front porch, Julia Washington hollered into the night. "What is going on out here? Your daddy's gonna whip every one of you. Go to bed right now!"

CHAPTER THIRTY-FOUR

T he next day loomed cloudy, a gray day without a breeze. Sam had tossed and turned after the ominous visit by the three strangers, and at daylight he dressed and drove to the Madison courthouse. There was trouble brewing. A menacing Stanley Barnwell had visited Essie, and Sam had been visited by three of Barnwell's henchmen.

Sam Washington was a reasonable man, a man of common sense despite his relative youth. One fact jumped out at him that he could not ignore: Madison County was not safe. His first call of the morning was to Sheriff Simmie Moore.

"Simmie, this is Sam Washington," he said into the telephone. "Got a few minutes to come to the courthouse. Talk a little bit about some things going on."

"I'll be right there, Sam. Do I need to bring a deputy?"

"No. Just you and me for now. I'm in the small conference room on the first floor." Sam hung up and opened his briefcase. Two things were at stake here—the inquest regarding Jewell Donnelly's self-defense motion in the death of George Barnwell. Secondly, DooRay Aikens personal injury claim against the deceased's estate. Both claims related to a New York attorney named Stanley Barnwell, the older brother of the deceased.

Barnwell was no ordinary attorney. From Sam's conversations with Sidney Davis, Barnwell was tied to many not-so-legal activities in the State of New York. It was clear that Barnwell had no intention of allowing the Third Circuit Court of Florida to file a claim against his dead brother's estate. In Barnwell's mind, the only way to win on either of these counts was to strongarm the witnesses as well as the attorney. And, most likely, the judge.

Barnwell was the kind of man who used his power, money and connections to sway everything in his favor. When his three strongarms told him they had no success in intimidating attorney Sam Washington, Barnwell laughed at them.

"Surely, you jest. You goons against a skinny farm boy? I'm not believing this." Barnwell clucked his tongue. "Did any of you bother to pull a gun?"

The three men, all crowded into the small motel room, looked across the room at Barnwell. Their faces were haggard from no sleep, bloodshot eyes that darted around the room, afraid to look at Barnwell. They seemed nervous, not willing to say too much. The man's name was Leo—the one who had commented to Sam the previous evening. Leo garnered enough courage to tell Barnwell what had happened.

"It wasn't just Washington. His two brothers were there… carrying guns. A shotgun, too. Nobody to mess with, the way I see it."

Barnwell stared at Leo. A long stare that made Leo squirm in his chair. "How did they get the jump on you? Why didn't you just go in there with guns drawn and get the job done?"

Leo looked at his partners and shrugged. "Thought they were asleep."

Barnwell shook his head. "You know what I think? I think you all are sissies. These people are farmers. They drive tractors, for Pete's sake. Tractors!" Barnwell screamed across the room. "Tell you what. You guys go on back to New York. They know your faces around here. I'm sure their sheriff has been advised. I'll get somebody down here who can handle this job."

Leo leaned forward, a pitiful twist in his face, "These aren't ordinary farmers."

Barnwell's face turned crimson, his jaw tightened. "I don't give a shit who they are. They're not going to push me around." He slammed his fist into his palm. "Get the hell out of here."

The men stampeded out of the motel room and left Stan Barnwell pacing the room, a thing he did when deep in thought. After a while, Barnwell picked up the phone and called New York.

"Farmers," he said to himself, as he heard 'hello' from the other end of the line.

Chapter Thirty-Five

While Sam waited for Sheriff Moore, he called Judge Earp's secretary and made an appointment for 2:00 to meet with the judge and discuss the Barnwell inquest. At that time, he would also apprise the judge of the intimidating tactics of George Barnwell's brother, the slipshod attorney from New York. He also mentioned Essie Donnelly and DooRay Aiken's deposition had been rescheduled for Monday July 9th by the state attorney's office.

Sam continued to simmer in the small courthouse conference room. It was a blatant attempt on Barnwell's part to skew the inquest into his brother's death, to thwart the personal injury claim on behalf of DooRay Aikens and, most importantly, negatively impact the lives and well being of the people involved; namely Essie and Jewell Donnelly, DooRay Aikens, himself and, he also believed, Judge Earp.

Perhaps Madison County was naïve to think laws would be obeyed, and the innocents would be protected. It seemed Stanley Barnwell had his own method of enforcement that did not follow the rule of law. Hence, Barnwell's visit to the Donnelly's and his goons' visit to the Washington farm in the middle of the night.

In Sam, there was a tad of renegade that enticed him to carry a gun like his brothers and intimidate the bad guys. His personal code of ethics, however, did not allow him to do so. He would file a formal harassment complaint with the sheriff and let the sheriff handle the characters from New York.

A soft knock on the door, followed by Sheriff Moore's entry into the conference room, interrupted Sam's thoughts. He stood and shook Simmie Moore's hand. "Thanks for coming, Simmie. Been a rough night."

Simmie sat across from Sam, concern on his face. "That so?"

Sam let out a breath and shook his head. "You're not going to believe this, but three fellows—whom I believe are in the employ of Barnwell—showed up at the farm around 1:30 this morning. They probably would have done some damage had Bill and Mike not been on their toes. My brothers confronted these men, and I gotta tell you, Simmie, my brothers each carried a gun. Bill, a shotgun and Mike, a .38."

Sam took a deep breath. "These were bad guys. No doubt about it."

Simmie nodded, becoming thoughtful. "How do you know they belonged to Barnwell?"

"Who else would send them out to the farm? We didn't see any guns, but I'm certain they would have pulled them had Bill and Mike not been armed."

"Did they say what they wanted?"

"They said they wanted to talk to me."

"At 1:30 in the morning?"

"Yeah, that's what we thought. Didn't look too good to us at all. Bill didn't give them an inch, though. Had them get off the farm. Before they left, the one in charge said neither Judge Earp nor I owned Madison County. Looks like these folks plan to strongarm their way around Madison."

Sam looked hard at the Madison County sheriff. "That's where you come in, Simmie." He gave the table a loud slap. "Get those fellows in line. Let 'em know we can't be pushed around."

Sheriff Moore gave Sam an affirmative nod, as well as a broad grin at Sam's enthusiasm. "That's for sure. I'll get with my deputies, and we'll have a chat with Mr. Barnwell."

"Looks like I'll be having a chat with him, too. I told his henchmen I'd meet him here at the courthouse at noon. Probably won't show.

"Oh, and by the way. This Barnwell fellow paid a visit to the Donnelly place. Said some threatening words to Essie. When Barnwell got a little too menacing, DooRay hit him with a two by four. Essie pulled a gun." Sam grinned. "God forbid one of those sisters gets hold of a gun."

"Yes, she called me this morning. I'm riding out to Pinetta later today to take her statement. I'll have that to present to Mr. Barnwell. Looks like we'll have to get tough on the man."

Sam looked at his notes. "Okay. I'll file the complaint on the three men trespassing and making threats at the farm. Essie will most certainly file her complaint also. That's pretty good ammunition, if you ask me."

Simmie Moore stood and cornered Sam with a hard stare. "Sam, we don't know what these people are going to do. I'm thinking all of us need to be extra cautious. I may call in reinforcements if they don't back off."

"Reinforcements?" Sam closed his briefcase and stood.

"That's right. Possibilities for corruption, bribery, contempt of court, intimidation. No telling what they're thinking. This Stanley Barnwell won't back off from little ole Madison County."

"FBI?

"Could be. Especially if this Barnwell is connected to the New York mob as you indicated earlier."

When Sheriff Moore left the conference room, Sam grabbed his briefcase and headed to his small office on Base Street. He'd call Essie, then another call to Sidney Davis. Just who was this Stanley Barnwell?

Essie answered the telephone after four short rings. She was on a party line with J. T. Woodward's grocery store and a telephone in the Hanson post office. "Essie. Everything okay?"

"Hello, Sam." Essie pulled a bowl of eggs from the refrigerator. "Why are you asking me if everything is okay?"

"Just a little nervous. Thought I'd ride out for an hour or so. Got to be back into Madison by Noon. Seems that Barnwell fella wants to talk to me."

"Whatever for?"

"A bribe probably. Who knows?"

"Come on out. We're baking cakes."

Sam's call to Sidney Davis was short. "Sid, it's me. Sam."

"What's up?" Sidney was eating a sandwich, and his smacking was followed by a loud burp.

"Barnwell is in Madison County stirring things up. Other than the fact he's not very nice, what more can you tell me about him?"

"Oh, I knew this was coming. Don't mess with him, Sam. He's as crooked as they come. Not only that, he's dangerous. He might not be the one to chop off your fingers, but, trust me, he's very capable of having someone do it for him."

"Yeah. I've already been subjected to that. He sent three of his boys out to the farm. Wasn't very pretty."

"Sam," Sidney's voice raised an octave, "I told you all this in our earlier conversation. I know you're going by the book, but I guarantee you, he isn't."

"Okay. Okay. I'm proceeding with the personal injury claim despite Barnwell's underhanded objections. Let me know if you think of anything else."

"You can count on that." Sidney hung up.

CHAPTER THIRTY-SIX

S am left his office and took 145 past Hanson and then to Pinetta. His drive was slow and thoughtful. He passed Tom Morse' farm, saw Hoot Gibson out on his tractor, his wife Lora working in her flowers, and then slowed at the Bellville road.

A Valdosta Southern Railway train eased up past the depot, the nearby cucumber market bustling with trucks unloading baskets of cucumbers. Charles Buchanan, the depot agent, leaned against a post and talked with Rab Law, Pinetta's resident philosopher, a man who had imparted his infinite wisdom on anyone who was willing to listen, his bottle of spirits giving him any inspiration he may need. Or perhaps his brain had been dusted by DDT.

Sam eased past the school and waved to W. H. Pierce, the principal. Johnny Hollingsworth stood beside him and waved back, a half-eaten apple in his hand. Elizabeth Hinton hurried toward Mr. Pierce, a long wooden ruler in her hand. It was certain someone was going to get a paddling.

He drove slowly on the dirt road, flushed doves eating dropped corn on the side of the road and barely missed an indecisive squirrel that skittered back and forth in front of the car.

Sam admitted he was quite vulnerable, vulnerable enough to carry a firearm. His adversaries were not playing fair, but there was nothing he could do about that. He would depend on Sheriff Moore to rein in the lawyer from New York and his three henchmen. He laughed. For some reason, if Simmie Moore failed, then Bill and Mike could most assuredly handle the job.

In Terryville, he waved to Lon Terry who stood at the fence feeding his hogs. Pony, his nine-hundred-pound Tamworth, nudged the fence with his snout, begging for more watermelon. The ruts in the Bellville road seemed deeper; his Pontiac's tires caught the clay and slid back and forth across the road. He slowed considerably past Grassy Pond, rounded the curve and turned left down the lane to the Donnelly farm.

An unfamiliar car was parked under the oak tree by the porch. A newer car, the chrome shiny against its blue color. Sam glanced around and saw no one. Even the porch was empty. He looked at his watch: 10:30 on the dot.

Murphy nibbled on the bushes that lined the drive, Killer pecking the ground nearby, his lack of glorious tail feathers seeming to be a non-issue. Sam pulled his car near the shed where Essie kept her Buick. He heard DooRay whistling somewhere from inside the barn. "DooRay," he called.

DooRay stuck his head around the corner of the barn. "Hey, Mr. Sam."

"Hello, DooRay. I guess everybody's in the house."

"Yes, sir. They is. They is eatin' an early lunch. Miss Essie fried chicken, and it sure was good."

"Fried chicken? Nice." Sam walked across the yard and entered the back-porch door. Through the kitchen, he saw the dining room and the back of Jewell's head, then heard her laugh softly. A man's voice rose above her laughter. Sam knew immediately it was Autrey Browning.

At that moment, Essie entered the kitchen from the dining room. "Sam! You're just in time for some early lunch. Please find a chair at the dining table."

Sam hesitated. "Sorry. Didn't know you were having company, or I would have come another time."

"Actually, I hadn't planned on company. Autrey sort of dropped in."

"Dropped in for fried chicken?" Sam felt his heart skip a beat.

Essie sent a smile across the kitchen. "It's DooRay's birthday. He's already eaten. We had cake and now we're serving left-overs to Autrey. I'll fix you a plate." Her eyes beckoned him, soft and soothing, like dew on a rose petal.

Sam found himself wanting to touch her. A soft touch—one that said 'hey, we've got something going on between us. Let's keep it that way.' Instead, he smiled and nodded, a feeling of anxiety creeping in his chest. "I'll fix my plate. Is there iced tea on the table?"

"Yes. I'll bring you a glass." She turned away, and he noticed the back of her smooth neck, where wisps of her auburn hair had escaped the clasp and fluttered as she walked. He wanted to make love to her, tell her how much he loved her, but it was too soon. Essie Donnelly wasn't ready for his kind of love.

He walked into the dining room where Autrey Browning sat chatting with Jewell. When Autrey looked up and saw Sam, there was a slight hesitation, a nervousness that was subtle but, nonetheless, present. Perhaps he had heard Essie and he were an item. Good, Sam wanted it that way. There was one thing he was sure of—he would fight for Essie Donnelly.

"Well, I'll be danged. Sam Washington. I'd heard you finished college and moved to New York City." Autrey's smile was genuine. His eyes seemed tired, weathered like he'd been in a few storms in his life.

"Hello, Autrey." Sam put out his hand and the two men clasped tightly. "Heard you were back." Sam sat down opposite Essie's old flame.

Sam reached over and brushed Jewell's arm. "Hello, Jewell."

Jewell, her hair pulled back with a ribbon, smiled and picked up her napkin and patted her lips. She was an extraordinary beauty, a beauty whose mind floated here and there, never stopping in one place except maybe when she read her bible.

Autrey leaned back in his chair and seemed to study Sam. His eyes roamed the room, to Jewell, to Essie who stood at the doorway and then back to Sam. "Yes," he said quietly. "Back. For a while, anyway."

"Where you been all these years?" It was an awkward question. Sam noticed a twitch at the corner of Autrey's mouth. The man fiddled with his napkin, glanced at Essie and then down at his plate. His face was thin; a shock of brown hair was neatly combed to the side, the part a straight line down his scalp. He'd always appeared somber, brooding, as though his mind was troubled and was looking for answers.

"I've been several places. Never anywhere very long." He half-laughed. "It's a big world out there. It was time to come back to Madison County."

"Fifteen years? That right?" Sam cocked his head and seemed to be in a lawyering mode. Questions. Cross-examination. Essie placed a glass of tea in front of Sam and sat down beside him. Her face was a mask, her hands still. She, too, was a beauty. A beauty different than Jewell's. There was nothing delicate about her, her strength evident in her eyes. She seemed aware of everything going on around her and at all times.

"Yes. A good number of years." replied Autrey. "Missed the war. Something about a heart murmur. Just stayed on the sidelines. Worked at the FPO in New York the entire four years of the war. How about you?"

Sam gathered his thoughts. "I remained stateside with the signal corps in Washington. Dad had a distant cousin in Washington who pulled strings. I didn't argue with Dad. It was important to him that I contributed to the war effort. The signal corps was a nothing job, but I learned a lot. War ended, and I started school."

Autrey seemed to drift away, then back again where his eyes fell on Essie. It appeared as though he was measuring the distance between Essie and Sam, counting the inches between them, between their importance to one another.

Essie sat at Sam's left. Her hand rested around her glass of tea. Then, in an extraordinary moment, she slowly placed her hand over Sam's, left it there as if proclaiming that he was, indeed, important to her. Sam casually pulled her fingers into his and rubbed his thumb along her wrist, all the while keeping his eyes on the man across from him.

"Excuse me," Jewell said, as she left the table and walked to the large dining room window. She peered longingly through the glass. "I do wish Jimmy were here." She left the room and went through the front door to the porch.

"Jimmy?" asked Autrey.

"Jimmy Townsend. Do you remember him?"

Autrey nodded slowly. "I heard." He became uncomfortable and shifted in his chair. Clearing his throat, he looked up at Essie. "Jewell okay?"

Essie shook her head. "She's really never recovered. Her mind comes and goes. She thinks he's still alive. Still at the farm with his family." A slight tremble eased into Essie's words. "She waits for him everyday. Watches the hill across the road thinking at any moment he'll come running through the fields and... and into her arms."

They chatted a while about people they knew, crops that failed, the '48 flood, the burning of the school in Pinetta, about marriages, divorces, children born and parents who died.

Sam looked at his watch. "11:30. Got to get back to Madison." He squeezed Essie's shoulder. "Thank you for lunch."

Autrey pushed back his chair. "Thank you for feeding me, too. Your fried chicken tasted like your mama's."

Essie laughed. "Oh, my. Mama would love to hear you say that, Autrey. Thanks for stopping by. I hope things go well for you." Was it a cutting of the string; a send-off to another life. Had Autrey Browning been dismissed from Essie's thoughts? Was she moving forward, away from the memories that had bound her to him for so many years?

"Sam." Autrey reached out and shook Sam's hand. "Good to see you."

"Same here, Autrey."

Autrey carried his plate into the kitchen and set it on the kitchen counter. He was out the back door and down the steps and sliding into his car when Sam turned to Essie. He wanted to see her face, her eyes. He saw nothing to indicate Autrey had again pierced her Donnelly armor. "It's a funny thing," he said.

"What's that?" Essie seemed casual, maybe too casual.

"Why he came back." Sam ducked his head, his eyes sweeping the kitchen and found himself perplexed.

"What do you mean?"

"I'm certain he came back for you," he said with a half-smile, his eyes slyly glancing at her. Then he sobered. "Yet, there's something else there."

"Something else?" Essie frowned. "I don't understand."

"I'm not sure, but Autrey Browning is not who we think he is. I saw it in his eyes."

Essie and Sam quickly washed and dried dishes, put the food away and swept the kitchen floor. Sam looked at his watch again. "Whoa. Got to head to Madison. Thanks again for the fried chicken."

They walked together to the front porch. Essie stepped out first and looked around. "Where's Jewell?" She turned back into the house and called out. "Jewell? You upstairs?" They heard nothing. "Jewell," she called a second time, walking back out on the porch.

"Let me check the back yard." Sam hurried down the brick steps and walked through the back yard and toward the barn. "Jewell," he called.

DooRay came out of the tack room carrying a rake. "Miss Jewell ain't out here, Mr. Sam."

Essie rushed upstairs and went through every room, calling "Jewell." She half-stumbled down the stairs and flew out the front door. "Sam!"

Sam turned the corner of the house in time to see Essie running across the yard. "She's gone across the road. Up the hill to the Townsend farm. I don't want her near their pond," yelled Essie.

Sam caught up with her and they ran together across the Bellville road, slipped under the barbed wire fence, and into the cornfield that ran to the steep hill on the edge of the Townsend farm. They both knew the pond was on the far side of the hill, a deep pond filled with fish and a few alligators. Panting and out of breath, they climbed the hill, all the while calling "Jewell!"

As they topped the hill, they saw Jewell skirting the far side of the swampy pond, her hair blowing in the summer wind, her skirt wrapped around her legs as she plunged forward. Her head was tilted toward the sky, her hands waving. She was going to see Jimmy. "Jewell!" Essie's voice was shrill and pleading. "Stay away from the pond."

Essie picked up speed, only to tumble forward, rolling like tumbleweed down the hill and toward the pond. Sam slithered down the grade behind her, digging his hands into clumps of earth to break his fall. He watched helplessly as Essie catapulted into the pond headfirst. No longer able to hold onto the slick grass, Sam relaxed his body and let himself roll down into the pond, only a few feet from Essie.

The water was waist high, muddy but warm. Sam felt as though his legs were in quicksand as he pushed his body toward Essie. She struggled to stand up, her arms slapping the water. The water level rose to her chin as she clamored for balance. He could see the fright in her eyes as she reached out for him.

"Here you go," he said, while he grabbed her arm and pulled her to him. "Hold on, Essie. I've got you."

"Jewell. We've got to get Jewell." Essie gulped for breath and struggled free. She splashed and crawled through the dark water to the edge of the pond. Sam, right behind her, pulled her onto the bank.

"Take it easy, Essie." He pointed across the pond. "We'll go around to the other side; then cut through that field of corn. She's on the other side of it—not too far away."

"Jewell," Essie screamed again. "I'm coming!" Essie sloshed through the mud on the edge of the pond, her shoes lost in the muck. On her somersault down the hill and into the pond, a limb had caught her cheek and blood streamed down her face.

They covered a hundred yards as they ran around the edge of the pond and up another slight grade that led to a massive stand of corn. "Jewell," Essie screamed again. The stiff breeze snapped her words away and tossed them in every direction. Not only could Jewell not see them, she could not hear them.

Essie stumbled through the corn, the stiff leaves slapping her face. They had lost their bearings; lost in a thousand tall stalks, all looking the same. A symmetrical crisscross of identical plants, the field was one big blur.

"This way!" Sam curved left through the rows and followed the sound of a tractor. "I think that tractor is the same one I saw mowing the south field earlier." He was out of breath and labored to talk.

Essie stayed a few feet behind Sam and followed him to the noise of the tractor's motor. They came closer and closer, smelling diesel and hearing the whir of the mower blades. They broke free of the cornstalks and stumbled out into a smooth field.

The tractor, about fifty yards away, slowed and turned toward them. Sitting atop one of the tractor's fenders, Jewell Donnelly sat like a queen. She waved and, though they could not hear her, Sam and Essie saw laughter in her face, an animated expression of delight as she chatted away with Mr. Townsend. Jim Al Townsend steered the tractor to the edge of the field where Sam and Essie stood, muddied, bleeding and gasping for breath.

"I take it you're looking for Jewell." Mr. Townsend turned off the tractor and stared down at Sam and Essie. "Looks like you folks been in a fight."

Essie looked down at herself, then at Sam. "Yes," she said weakly. "We've been in a fight, all right. That steep hill of yours about whipped us."

Jim Al gave a sad smile as he looked around the field. "Reckon Jewell here is lookin' for Jimmy. That right?" Jim Al gazed out over the field, his eyes searching. Searching just like Jewell. His son was gone, but sometimes in the early mist of morning, he could almost see him walking across the field from the pond, a string of fish trailing behind him. He cleared his throat and straightened his hat.

Essie moved closer to the tractor. She reached out and held up her hand. "Come on, Jewell. Let's go home."

Obediently, Jewell took Essie's hand and slid off the tractor. "Thank you, Jim Al. I'll bring over some buttered rum pound cake later this afternoon, if that's all right."

Jim Al Townsend nodded. His words were a mere whisper. "I dearly loved your mama's buttered rum pound cake."

"I know," replied Essie, her eyes misting over. The two sisters walked through the field to the Bellville road, Sam a few steps behind. Jewell hummed and stopped several times to pick wild flowers. Sam caught up with Essie and grasped her hand. Essie's hair lay matted to her head, pond grass and mud hanging from the auburn locks. The blood on her cheek had smeared across her nose, giving the impression she had fought with an alligator instead of a tree limb.

Her shirt clung to her body, wet and caked with mud. Blue jeans, heavy with pond water, drooped down her hips. When they reached the Bellville road, Essie gently squeezed Sam's hand and fainted dead away.

CHAPTER THIRTY-SEVEN

ooRay!" Sam yelled as he crossed the road with Essie in his arms. DooRay, raking around the azalea bushes that lined the front porch, looked up with wide eyes. Alongside him, Murphy bleated loudly, a mournful bleat that caused Killer to squawk and flap his wings.

"Mr. Sam, I'm comin'. I'm comin'." DooRay threw the rake on the ground and began running down the lane, his sapling legs and bare feet beating the dirt and kicking up dust.

At the end of the lane, Sam lay Essie on the grass. "DooRay, go to the well and get some cool water."

"Yes, sir. DooRay can do that." He sprinted away, Murphy and Killer following.

Jewell hovered nearby, her hands clasped together. "Oh, my. Mr. Washington. What's happened to my sister?" She leaned over and brushed Essie's forehead with her hand.

"I think she's fainted from exhaustion, Jewell. She'll be okay." Sam wished color would come back into Essie's face. He smoothed her hair. "Essie. Essie, can you open your eyes?"

DooRay rushed up with a quart jar of water. Sam took off his shirt and doused his shirttails with water and pressed Essie's cheeks and her neck. "Come on, girl. Let's wake up."

Essie moaned. "Wha... what happened," she whispered, opening her eyes. "Where's Jewell?"

"Here I am, Essie. Right here beside you." Jewell knelt and leaned over her sister. "We're all here together," she said, with a childlike voice. "You, me, Sam, DooRay, Murphy and Killer."

Essie closed her eyes and smiled. "Sister," she said, "before you go see Jimmy, please let me know you're going."

"I will. I will," said Jewell, kissing her sister's forehead. "I'm sorry if I caused you any worry."

Essie opened her eyes. "No worry at all." She turned, and her eyes found Sam. "I'd like to go to the porch."

Sam handed DooRay the quart jar of water. "Whatever the lady wants." Relieved, he laughed and scooped her up and carried her down the lane. At the top of his voice, he began singing. "*Oh, she'll be coming 'round the mountain, when she comes. Yee haw! She'll be coming 'round the mountain when she comes. Yee haw!*" The tune lifted into the July sky, bounced among the limbs of the oak trees and, certainly, awakened the sleeping in the Mt. Horeb cemetery.

At the porch, Sam sat Essie in the swing. "I'm thinking I'll go fill a bathtub with some warm water. You look awful."

Essie laughed softly. "I'd love a warm bath."

Sam left the porch, stopped in the kitchen and put on the tea kettle. He decided a cup of hot tea would do wonders for someone who had rolled down a hill and fallen in a pond. He bounded up the stairs and found the main bathroom, next to the bedrooms.

The room was large, a clawfoot tub and a cabinet nearby with towels and soaps. He placed the stopper in the bottom of the tub and began filling it with warm water. He saw a bottle of pink bubble bath and poured it into the running water. It smelled like roses. The water rose, a soft cloud of bubbles rising like meringue on a pie.

Downstairs, he made a hot cup of tea with sugar and carried it to the front porch. A little of Essie's color had come back. DooRay sat nearby and guarded Essie as if she were a member of royalty. Jewell had eased into her chair and watched the hill across the road.

"Essie, drink this tea. It will perk you up for sure. Lots of sugar. Then, let's get you into a tub of warm water." Sam fussed over Essie, pulled the twigs out of her hair, brushed mud from her shirt and dungarees as she drank the sugared tea.

DooRay lingered nearby, his face full of concern. "Mr. Sam, you need me to get anything for Miss Essie? Murphy and I could hurry up to Mr. Lon's store and get her some kind of liniment. I hear Watkin's can sure make a body feel better."

Sam laughed. "Maybe what she needs is some of Mr. Donnelly's rum. You know, the rum Mrs. Donnelly used for her buttered rum cakes."

Essie laughed. Pink had returned to her cheeks. She would survive the run up the steep hill and the dunk in the pond. "Sam," she said, a glint of mischief in her eyes, "I wouldn't mind a little dab of daddy's rum in my tea."

Sam looked at Essie, then DooRay. "A dab of rum in your tea?"

"Is something wrong with your hearing? A dab of rum is exactly what I said." Essie dipped her chin and studied Sam. "You have a problem with that?"

"Problem? Oh, no. The lady wants rum; the lady gets rum."

Sam hurried down the porch and into the house. One end of the dining room buffet held remnants of Hubert Donnelly's whiskey and there in front was a huge bottle of dark rum, a rum Edith Donnelly used for her famous cake. He poured a few ounces in a shot glass and returned to the porch.

"Here you go, Essie."

Essie held up her teacup. "Just a dab will do, Sam." She smiled. "For medicinal purposes, of course."

"Of course," Sam said, as he glanced at a shocked DooRay. "I'm certain Dr. Bush would have ordered a toddy for you." He rolled his eyes and shook his head when Essie asked for more. Essie was a Donnelly woman. Donnelly women did not imbibe liquor for any reason whatsoever. "More," she said, her cheeks flushed.

Sam obliged. "I… I'm glad you're… feeling better." He took her teacup. "Time to go upstairs." He pulled her gently from the swing and guided her into the house. Essie walked slowly up the stairs, one foot in front of the other, humming a nameless tune. She giggled at the top of the stairs. "Where's the bathroom."

Sam inched her toward the bathroom. The bottom of her bluejeans dragged the floor. "I'll leave you in here to undress, Essie. You slip into the tub and I'll be back to check on you." Essie nodded sheepishly.

"Are you going to shampoo your hair?" Sam pulled a leaf out of her hair.

"Do you think I should?" Essie burped, and alcohol fumes filled the hallway.

"Yes, I do. Or just rinse it in the tub. You have lots of mud on you."

Essie sighed and entered the bathroom, pulling off her shirt before Sam had time to close the door. He closed the door quickly. "I'll be back in a few minutes to check on you."

Sam rushed downstairs and checked on Jewell. She sat on the porch talking with DooRay. "DooRay, please keep an eye on Jewell. I've got a phone call to make."

"Yes, sir, Mr. Sam. I gone sit right here."

Sam quickly rang the courthouse and asked for Judge Earp's chambers. His secretary, Rose, answered the phone. "Rose, this is Sam Washington. Listen, I missed my 2:00 appointment with Judge Earp and—"

"Yes, you did, Sam. And the Judge is not happy. He said if you called to have you go by his house after dinner tonight—say around 8:00 p.m."

"The judge's house? Okay, I'll be there. By the way, Rose, did a fellow show up around noon looking for me?"

"Nobody looking for you around here, Sam. Just be at the Judge's house at 8:00."

Sam was quiet for a moment. Barnwell had not come looking for him at the courthouse. *No, he'd rather wait until the middle of the night, with a gun in his hand,* he thought. "Thank you, Rose." He hung up and ran back upstairs. He tapped on the bathroom door. "Everything okay, Essie?"

No answer. "Essie," he called again. Still no answer. He tapped the door again, louder. No response. He pushed open the door and almost tripped over a pile of muddy clothes. "Essie—"

Essie was asleep in the warm water, her head resting on the edge of the tub. Bubbles floated around her, wet tendrils of hair falling on her shoulder. Sam moved to the side of the tub and picked up a bar of Ivory soap. He lathered his hands and smoothed the soap on her muddy face, her neck and shoulders. She stirred and mumbled something about frying eggs. At the end of the tub, Sam lifted one slim foot and scrubbed away the mud, rinsed it and picked up her other foot. There was a small cut on her big toe. He cleaned it well and then leaned over and gently kissed her foot.

"Essie," he whispered. She stirred and opened her eyes.

"Yes, Sam."

"Let's wash your hair. Can you turn around and lean your head back?"

Essie obeyed. She turned around and he washed her back; he saw a few scrapes spread across her shoulders. "Lean your head back," he said softly. He lifted a bottle of shampoo and poured a small amount onto her hair. He added a little water and massaged her scalp and then the long auburn hair.

"Feels good," she murmured.

"Let's rinse," he said. "Turn around and lean your head under the faucet." Essie dipped her body down into the water, below the bubbles, and tilted her head under the running faucet.

Sam smoothed her hair under the water and watched as the suds disappeared. "Perfect." He stood and reached for a towel. "Here's a towel. Do you think you can stand up?"

Essie looked up at him through dreamy eyes. "Maybe need a little help."

Sam reached out with one hand and pulled her up, wrapping the towel around her with the other hand. "You're doing fine. Now, let's step out of the tub. The edge is kinda high, so be careful."

Essie dutifully lifted her leg and stepped over the edge of the tub. Sam held her and pulled her completely out. "There you go. Now, let's get you into a gown or something and into bed." He shuffled Essie across the hall to her bedroom, the fragrance of shampoo like a soft cloud that smothered him and made him smile. "I'll leave you here and you can dress. I'll be downstairs if you need me."

"You're leaving?" she asked, an ache in her words, her eyes pleading. For the first time, he saw a vulnerable woman, not the farm girl who brandished an ax at an escaped prisoner or one who pointed a pistol at a fancy New York lawyer.

"No, no, I'm not leaving," he said, his words gentle and soothing. "I'll be downstairs with Jewell. You get into bed for a while and rest, and I'll check on you in a little while."

Essie nodded and pulled back the bedspread. He saw the towel drop just before she slipped into bed. He stilled a moment; the gentlemen in him turned away, but he would not forget the smooth backside of Essie Donnelly. He left the room and walked down the hall to the stairs. He looked at his watch. It was 4:00 o'clock.

In the kitchen, he made Jewell a cup of tea and walked out onto the porch. "Here you go, Jewell. Let's get you fixed up here with a nice cup of hot tea."

"My goodness, Sam. What a nice thing to do." She reached out and took the teacup and saucer. Sam noticed her hands were shaking. "Maybe you should get a warm bath, Jewell." Her ordeal had been harrowing, but not like Essie's tumbling down the hill and ending up in the pond.

Sam moved to the swing and, after resting a moment to catch his breath, realized what a mess he was. He was shirtless and as wet and muddy as Essie had been. How could he go see Judge Earp at 8:00 o'clock looking like a reprobate?

He heard a car turn down the lane and watched as Sheriff Simmie Moore drove slowly toward the house, drove as though he were weary and contemplating the woes of the world. He parked under the large oak at the end of the porch, looking for the comfort of shade, much like a mule and wagon in the old days. Simmie's demeanor was calm; he was the John Wayne of Madison County. A big man, he lumbered across the yard. Though it could not be seen, his pistol rested in the right front pocket of his pants. His easy-going manner should not be mistaken for weakness; he had handled many a bad guy.

"Afternoon, folks." He nodded across the porch and walked up the steps.

Sam left the swing, his wet pants leaving an imprint on the cypress wood. "Simmie. How are you?"

Simmie hesitated when he saw the man who looked like he had fought with a bear. "I'm well. But the question begs to be asked, Sam. What in the world happened to you?"

Sam laughed and reached out to shake Simmie's hand. "Oh, I fell in the pond over at Jim Al's.

"I'll say you did from the looks of you." Simmie sat in a rocker and waved at Jewell and DooRay. "Hello, Jewell. DooRay."

Jewell smiled. DooRay grinned, his missing front tooth leaving a dark gap wide enough to hold a pork chop bone.

"You're here to take Essie's statement, I suppose?" asked Sam, returning to the swing.

"That's right. Got to get her comments on what exactly transpired when Stanley Barnwell paid her a not-so-nice visit."

Sam flicked some mud off his pants. "Essie's napping right now, but should be up in an hour or so."

"No problem. I've got to run over to Durward Sapp's place. Seems like somebody went in there and stole some of his cows."

"Sorry to hear that. Do you suspect who the culprit is?" The lawyer in Sam was evident. He'd ask questions and then cross-examine.

"Naw. Durward's son Wayne said he saw some fellow in the south pasture. 'course, Wayne's only ten years old so who knows what he thought he saw."

"How many cows are missing?" Sam studied the sheriff. He seemed tired, his forehead lined with worry.

"Don't know yet. Durward thinks whoever took them will probably brand 'em and take them over to San Pedro and turn 'em out."

Sam nodded. "Knowing Durward, he's not going to let this go. He say anything about going over to San Pedro and checking it out?"

"Well, when I saw him earlier, he was not sure about anything. I'm headed back over there to iron things out—paperwork and all. Then, I might run over to San Pedro to ask a few questions. Some shifty folks over there."

Sheriff Moore left the Donnelly farm, his John Wayne body sliding into his '56 Ford and heading back down the lane.

He'd be back to talk with Essie, hopefully tightening the noose around Barnwell's neck.

Chapter Thirty-Eight

DooRay, do you know how to cook?" Sam slowly rocked and felt his pocket for a cigar. There was none; probably at the bottom on the pond. "I'm thinking about supper."

DooRay, his long legs stretched out before him, yanked at his shirtsleeve, the one with no arm in it, and nodded. "You asking me if DooRay can cook?" He laughed and slapped his knee. "Oh, Mr. Sam. I can make biscuits that could float up in the air like angels they is so light."

Sam chuckled. "I'd like to see you do just that, DooRay."

DooRay closed his eyes and leaned his head back on the rocker. "It's a wonder what a one-armed man can do, Mr. Sam." He leaned forward and eyed Sam. "You make biscuits?"

"Me? Heck, no. But, I'll sure help you make them."

The two men left the porch, Jewell behind them. "I'll go bathe while you cook dinner, Sam." Jewell sang as she sauntered up the stairs. It was a lilting melody, something about a broken heart and the longing for a lost love. *Some letters tied in blue, a photograph or two, I see a rose from you, among my souvenirs.*

Outside, the wind had picked up and pine needles swept through the air likes missiles. Murphy bleated from the back yard; Killer squawked. DooRay looked out the window and saw them running to the barn. They were the farm's weather forecasters; neither of them liked rain, and rain was on the way.

"Now, see here, Mr. Sam," said DooRay. "Take some flour, add baking powder and salt." Sam observed the finesse in which DooRay

176

began making biscuits. He smiled to himself as the black man focused on his work, serious and diligent. "Drop in some cold lard and cross over it with a fork. Like this." The fork slashed across the lard and into the flour, making the dough grainy like cornmeal.

DooRay practically danced as he dumped buttermilk into a well of flour and lard. "Now, Mr. Sam, I wants you to take over. You squeeze this together just a little bit, then dump it out on the counter. You gone knead this dough a little bit."

"Knead the dough? You've got to show me, DooRay."

"DooRay'll show you. DooRay know everythin'."

Behind them, a shuffle of feet. Essie stood at the kitchen door, her hair askew, a sleep wrinkle on the side of her cheek. "Am I dreaming? Two men in my kitchen making biscuits?"

And there in the Donnelly kitchen, DooRay Aikens found a home, his one hand stuck in biscuit dough while he hummed *Beulah Land*. Rocking back and forth, the sleeve for his missing arm dredged itself in flour when he flopped the dough over, a cloud of white puffing in the air.

And Sam Washington? The farm boy who had graduated summa cum laude from Florida State University began to knead the pile of biscuit dough. His fingers worked as efficiently as though he were a heart surgeon. He pulled and tugged on the dough and finally patted it into a one-half inch high round. He stepped back and grinned. "Okay, DooRay. What do we do now?"

Jewell finished her bath and floated into the kitchen smelling of honeysuckle, her cheeks pink. She stood by Essie and put her arm around her waist, completing the circle of friends and family. The slice of ham DooRay slapped into the iron skillet sizzled, coffee perked in the tall aluminum pot and, outside, an evening of quiet drizzle swept softly across the Donnelly farm.

Sam looked at Essie. He couldn't help it—the image of her backside flashed into his mind, only a fleeting second, but it was long enough. All was well on the Donnelly farm.

Around 7:00, Sheriff Moore drove up the Donnelly lane and parked his car near the shed. Between raindrops, he hurried across the yard. He stepped up to the back porch and called through the

screen. "I smell hot biscuits."

Essie pushed open the screen door. "Yes, you do smell biscuits. And there's a piece of ham left in the skillet. Come have some supper."

Simmie grinned. "I'll never turn down ham and biscuits." He sat at the kitchen table while Essie filled a plate and Jewell poured iced tea. In minutes, Sam, DooRay, Jewell, Essie and Simmie were chatting, a buttered rum pound cake in the middle of the table.

"Well, did Durward find his cows?" Sam brushed cake crumbs around in his plate, eyeing the middle of the table and the still-warm pound cake.

"No, 'fraid not. We're both thinking they're probably over at San Pedro. Come Tuesday at the auction at the Madison stockyard, they just might be over there. I'll be there bright and early and so will Durward."

"Yeah. I'll be there, too. Lon Terry and I are taking some of his feeder pigs over there."

The sheriff looked over at Essie. "So, what about this Barnwell fella coming to the farm, Essie?"

Essie sliced another piece of cake for Sam and placed it on his plate. "Oh, he's trouble, Simmie. Thought he was going to intimidate Jewell and me. Maybe keep us from testifying at the inquest. Who knows? It seems he thinks his big city methods will work here in Madison County."

Simmie nodded. "Believe I'll have a talk with him. I understand he's staying at a motel in Tallahassee until the inquest. I'll pay him a visit and make sure he's clear on some things."

Simmie pulled out a small notepad and made a few notes. He was thoughtful as he leaned back in his chair and looked up at the ceiling. He stared a long time without speaking. "Well, I'll be danged," he said, a smile creeping into his tired face.

Essie looked his way, as did Sam. "What?" asked Essie.

"I think we've solved a little mystery."

"What mystery?" Essie and Sam asked in unison.

"The ear. The missing ear," said Simmie. His eyes gleamed with laughter. He pointed to the ceiling, to the light fixture that hung from the ceiling in the center of the kitchen. And, there it was—just as if someone had intentionally placed it across the small glass globe. George Barnwell's ear.

CHAPTER THIRTY-NINE

S heriff Simmie Moore obtained Essie's formal statement on Stanley Barnwell's threatening comments and left the farm with a slice of pound cake. He also questioned DooRay and Jewell. Their statements aligned with Essie's, and Simmie was satisfied Barnwell had, indeed, threatened the three of them.

After showering and changing clothes at the Washington farm, Sam drove to Judge Earp's house in Greenville, arriving at 8:00, just like Rose, his secretary, said to do. From the sound of his secretary's voice, Judge Earp was quite perturbed. Hopefully, the judge would understand Sam's fall into a pond and the rescue of Essie and Jewell.

Curtis D. Earp had a reputation: Don't show up in his courtroom without wearing a suit coat. His clerks suffered greatly during the heat of a Madison County summer in a courthouse that had no air conditioning. If you passed by his house on U. S. 90 in Greenville, you'd see the judge mowing his lawn or riding his horse wearing a long-sleeved white shirt, his dark hair slicked back with Vitalis.

The Judge was an extraordinary man in many ways. Born and raised in Greenville, just fourteen miles west of Madison, the small-town boy played minor league baseball in Tallahassee in the 1930's, boxed in a small boxing circuit in Florida and had the privilege of hosting The Lone Ranger at his humble home in Greenville. He entered the Navy in World War II and survived to come home to the place he loved: Madison County, Florida.

The judge's house sat at the corner of U. S. 90 and 221 North, a white frame house built in the '30's. The house had a welcoming front porch, a porch fostering a feeling of community—a good family lived here.

Sam knocked on the front door only once when it opened wide, and Judge Earp swept his arm into the foyer. A dog yelped at Sam's feet. "Hello, Judge Earp. Thanks for your time tonight."

"Quite alright, Sam. We have lots to talk about—the sooner the better." The dog followed the judge into a small sitting room. Sam followed the dog.

"And what happened to our appointment this afternoon, I dare ask?" There was a hint of humorous sarcasm in his question.

"I apologize, Judge Earp. There was a little... little mayhem at the Donnelly farm. But, all's well." He smiled but wasn't sure Judge Earp, who sat in the chair opposite him, heard him over the barking dog.

The dog yelped again and the judge shushed him. "Yes, well, I'm sure you have good reasons not to show up for an appointment on my busy calendar." Again, a hint of sarcasm. The judge wore a suit, his trademark white shirt stiffly collared. He looked scholarly in the wing-backed chair Sam was sure Mrs. Earp had chosen for the small, but formal, room.

The Judge's eyes came at Sam like bullets. "Now, Sam. We've got to clarify some things going on. First of all, everything we talk about tonight is off the record. Understood?"

Sam snapped to attention. "I have no problem with that, Judge." Sam readied himself for an onslaught by the county's firm but fair judge.

"I hear Stanley Barnwell has threatened Essie and Jewell Donnelly at their farm. Also, Sheriff Moore has told me that three hooligans visited your farm in the early hours of this morning. All that true?"

He leaned back in his chair and, at the same time, the dog jumped in his lap and circled twice before he curled up and closed his eyes. "This here's Ted, for Teddy Bear. It's my son's dog, but he likes me enough to want to sit in my lap."

Sam felt himself relax. He was comfortable having a casual

conversation with a judge who was known for his stringent discipline in court. This was the judge's parlor; surely, Sam could loosen his tie and breathe a little easier.

"That's correct. 'bout 1:30 a.m., three men parked their car in our farm lane, about a quarter mile from the house, and walked to our barn."

"What did you do then?" The judge squinted his eyes in rapt attention.

"Well, I turned on the farm lights just as they were about to enter the barn. Then, Bill and Mike asked them what was going on."

"Were these men armed?"

"Not that we could see."

"Were Bill and Mike armed?"

Sam hesitated only a fraction of a second. "Yes, they were. Bill had a shotgun and Mike had a .38."

"How about you? You have a gun?"

"No, sir. I did not."

"Why not?"

"I don't own a gun."

"What did the men do when the lights came on, and they saw you and your brothers standing there? Especially with Bill holding a shotgun?" Sam wasn't sure, but he thought he saw a slight smile play around the edges of the judge's lips.

"They didn't say too much after they saw Bill's shotgun. Bill told them to get off the property. All they said was they wanted to talk to me. Bill told them to make an appointment and to make it in the daytime, not at 1:30 in the morning."

The judge laughed. "I'm certain the shotgun carried a lot of weight when those words were spoken."

Sam nodded and noticed the dog was snoring, its wet nose wrinkling up and down. "I'll say this—they didn't like being told what to do."

"Hmmmm. What about Essie and Jewell? What happened out there at the farm?"

"Stanley Barnwell drove out to the farm and harassed Essie. Threatened her, saying she'd better not turn her back on him. When he lunged at her, DooRay hit him with a two by four. Then Jewell handed Essie a pistol and they chased the fellow off their farm."

Judge Earp didn't move. Stunned, he stared at Sam, his dark eyes serious. "Two women and a black man chased a New York lawyer off their place?"

"That's about it."

"Well, now. I'm thinking this—all of what you've told me is subject to investigation. Once all the facts are gathered by Simmie and it's warranted, Mr. Barnwell will be served an arrest warrant for aggravated assault and go to the county jail. He may be a big New York attorney, but he and his henchmen can't go around this county threatening people, now can they?"

Sam nodded vigorously. "I'm with you, Judge Earp."

The Judge leaned back and grinned. "See that table over there, Sam?" His arm shot out, and he pointed to the nearby dining room. "That chair on the end?"

"Yes, sir."

"A while back, The Lone Ranger came to the Greenville movie theatre and signed autographs and put on a show for the kids. Gwyndolyn and I invited him to the house for dinner, and he sat right there in that chair."

The judge pushed Ted out of his lap and brushed the dog hair off his pant leg. "Our son—we call him Little Judge—was twelve years old and sat at the table waiting for The Long Ranger to take off his mask. Well, we sat there for two hours eating and talking, and that man never took off his mask." The Judge slapped his knee. "Can you believe that?"

Sam shook his head, grinning. "What a story. That was Clayton Moore, right?"

"That's right." Judge Earp became wistful, his eyes roaming around the room. "I love the Lone Ranger. He has a strict moral code that all folks should have. He believed all things change but truth and that truth alone lives on forever." The judge's eyes found Sam's. "I believe that, don't you?"

Sam found himself seeped in the judge's words. "That's why I became a lawyer, Judge."

The two men walked to the door, Ted, the black chow, following. "We've got to keep these people in line. The inquest will be here before we know it, and I'll not have any witnesses being harassed or threatened." He hesitated and placed his hand on Sam's shoulder.

"The Madison County jail is probably the best place for him."

"Yes, sir," said Sam.

When Judge Earp opened the door, he appeared thoughtful, a frown pushing the skin on his forehead into furrows deep enough to plant okra seeds. "Sam, I've got to tell you. We're going to have to be careful around these folks. They don't go by our rules. And you know us—we're rule followers. We obey the law. We do what the laws tell us. These people may be tough and threatening, but that doesn't exempt them from following the law."

Sam said goodnight to the judge and walked down the steps, then suddenly stopped. "Say, Judge, any chance you are related to Wyatt Earp, the gunslinger?"

Judge Earp shook his head. "I don't think so, Sam. However, sometimes I wish he was in my courtroom with me."

Sam meandered to his car thinking that every word the judge had said was true. Unethical men, men who were used to winning, had raided Madison County. Stanley Barnwell was their leader and Sam was certain he carried a big sword.

CHAPTER FORTY

Essie asked DooRay to sleep on her mother's brocade couch another night, on the ironed cotton sheets and the down feather pillows, down feathers from the geese Edith Donnelly had raised especially to provide stuffing for their bed pillows.

Murphy, Pinetta's most handsome goat, slept beneath a nearby oak tree on a pile of moss, while Killer roosted on the porch rail, evidence of his newly grown tail feathers proudly displayed. The two were not far from the man who cared for them as well as loved them.

Essie had not forgotten Stanley Barnwell and his threat to return to the Donnelly farm to take care of some unfinished business. With DooRay, Murphy and Killer keeping watch, the chances of the New York thug sneaking up on them would be slim.

The smells of the supper Sam and DooRay had prepared lingered in the farm kitchen and had wafted upstairs to the bedroom where Essie lay. Restless, she kicked off the covers and stared at the ceiling. Sleep would not come. Her roll down Jim Al's hill and into his pond had unleashed in her a realization that she was not as capable of caring for Jewell as she had thought.

She wondered what would have happened had Sam not pulled her out of the water and onto the muddy bank. And Jewell. In just moments, she had left the safety of the front porch and wandered across the Bellville road looking for Jimmy. Essie could not let that happen again.

At daylight, after a fretful night, Essie left the bedroom for the kitchen and filled the percolator with cold water. She'd heard DooRay leave through the back door only moments before. While the coffee perked, she walked out onto the front porch and squinted into the rising sun, its rays sweeping the trees like a yellow broom.

Killer scratched in the dirt nearby, making little rumbling sounds in his throat, his wattles seeming to dance in like rhythm. He sounded like he was talking to himself, his left eye tilting up to the sky, a farsighted eye that could easily see a predator hawk. From off in the distance, Murphy emitted a soft bleat; he was looking for Killer. Killer's head popped up, and his bowlegs scurried him toward the barn.

On the lane, Essie walked slowly to the mailbox. She had walked down this path her entire lifetime, and she supposed she would die on this three-hundred-acre farm. Maybe she would be buried on the farm and not in the Mt. Horeb cemetery. *Why not*—everything she had ever known was here, here in the acres of corn and tobacco, not in Paris or New York or any place where she could breathe a life unrelated to a life in Madison County.

It had been almost eight weeks since she had sent her manuscript to New York. *Watermelon Queen of Madison County.* It was apparent to her that no one was interested in a lonely farm girl from Madison County. The novel, however, was more than a story about a young girl who had worn a sparkling crown and sat on top of a flatbed trailer filled with watermelons. It was about a young heart, a young mind stifled by life on a farm, her dreams trampled when her family responsibilities became the priority in her life—not her career, not her dreams.

For one slender moment in time, she almost got away.

The mailbox was empty except for an advertisement from Sears Roebuck. Disappointment washed over her as she reached over to the gnarled maple tree at the end of the lane and pulled the detour sign out to the road. She and Jewell would have to make two more cakes before the onslaught of the day's visitors.

Jewell relished the flurry of people coming and going and flitted around the dining room setting up cake plates, silverware and her mother's lovely linen napkins. The porch conversations, gossip really, were always the same: lively chatter about worms in the tobacco, washing Mason jars, and how handsome Lum Townsend was.

There was also much interest in the condition of Hoot Gibson's bull. No one wanted to see the $2000 bull cut up for steaks. Dr. Davis had done his best, but things were looking quite bleak. It was becoming apparent to everyone that a broken pecker was not fixable. At some point, farmer Gibson would have to make a decision, and everyone waited breathlessly to hear what that decision would be.

Many suggestions had been given to Dr. Davis and Hoot on how to remedy the bull's lack of breeding skill, the least of which a recipe from an old Miccosukee Indian woman who went by the name of Tayki and lived in a shack by the Withlacoochee River, near Negro Town. Her toothless gums had glistened when she grinned at Hoot and handed him a small paper bag of gray powder. "Give to bull," she said. "Him kick 'round real good after while." She walked a few steps away and turned around. "You no take powder. Only for bull." Her grin was as wide as the Suwannee River.

Another topic of interest was the return of Autrey Browning. Where had he been for fifteen years and why was he back in Madison County? News of his visit to the Donnelly farm had spread like boll weevils in the cotton fields.

"Oh, my, Essie. Your coffee is exceptionally delicious this morning. Whatever did you do to it?" Jewell said as she sat in her porch chair.

Essie read another paragraph in *Peyton Place* before she spoke. "It's that coffee pot. You know how old that coffee pot is?"

"No, I surely do not." Jewell sipped daintily.

"It's older than you are, Jewell. Mama got that pot at her wedding shower."

It wasn't even 9:00 o'clock when a car turned onto the lane. Essie looked up when she heard the motor and stared at the large black car, a front grill of heavy chrome seeming to plough its way down the lane like a John Deere tractor. "There any cake left, Jewell?" The car stopped in the middle of the lane and sat a moment, rays of the morning sun dappling the top.

"Yes, most assuredly there're a few slices left." Jewell left her chair and hurried to the kitchen. Her hostess skills had been refined not only from the finishing school in Switzerland but also from her mama.

The car started up again and continued its way to the edge of the yard. The sun glinted off the windows and, at that moment, a car door opened and Eloise Grimes, the preacher's wife, unfurled herself from the car. She was a big woman, buxom, her top half far outweighing her bottom half. Upon seeing her, there was a sense that her long spindly legs could not hold up under such top-heavy breasts. As Essie looked at her, she was sure Eloise had at some time or another toppled forward and landed flat on her face.

Essie didn't move from the swing nor did she tuck away *Peyton Place* under the swing cushion. There was nothing she wanted to hide from Eloise Grimes. The preacher's wife had been an enigma from the first time she appeared at the church, alongside her husband, as the church's new spiritual leaders.

An uneasy feeling crept into the morning air, leaving a fine mist of perspiration along Essie's upper lip. It was if she were preparing for battle with the woman with the spindly legs and enormous breasts and who also carried a black bible in her hands.

Eloise stood almost six feet tall, but that did not prevent her from wearing shoes that lifted her at least another three inches. When she walked, from the waist up, her body was unmoving, while her legs moved like sticks, almost without a bending at the knee. She walked the few yards from the car to the brick steps at the edge of the porch.

As if preparing for a gun duel, the women stared at each other. Essie didn't bother to leave the swing nor extend a word of welcome to Eloise. Eloise lifted her eyebrows and glared across the porch. Without a gesture of Christian warmth or greeting of any kind, the tall woman lifted her defiant chin. "My husband tells me you're not happy with the way I conduct my Sunday school class." There was no inflection in her words; they came out colder than a beaver's tit.

Essie wanted to jump up from the swing and holler, "Hell, yes." But, she didn't. She stayed in the swing and gently shoved her foot along the boards of the porch, pushing the swing into a slow motion. "That is correct," she said, holding her eyes steady.

For an instant, the massive woman hesitated, then recovered. "The decisions I make and the actions I take are all guided by our Almighty Father."

Essie kept pushing the swing. Blue jays fussed in the woods behind the house, sending arrogant chatter across the yard. The fragrance of blooming jasmine caught in the morning breeze and swept across the long porch, softening the moment.

Essie's thoughts wandered as she dissected the words Eloise had spoken—'guided by the Almighty Father.' It confused her that there were those who could, at times, be so cruel, yet were supposedly guided by the Almighty Father. Eloise Grimes was guided by her own agenda, a self-serving façade. She could hide behind her spiritual, holy façade all she wanted to—it was a lie.

"That's good to know, Eloise. So, you're telling me God told you to move Jewell from her class?"

Eloise's haughty eyes blinked slowly, impatient eyes that burned with irritation. Her demeanor seemed to change slightly, a fake humbleness appeared in her expression. "After fervent prayer, I was led to make that decision."

"How interesting. Exactly what did you pray for, Eloise? Pray that Jewell would get smarter? Pray that Jewell would not keep your class from winning the monthly bible verse contest?"

Essie stood and walked to the porch railing, only a few feet from Eloise, a woman whose virginal white collar pressed against her neck and proclaimed she was, indeed, a child of God. She leaned closer. "Eloise, I'm dying to know what you told God for him to guide you like He did? To tell you to move a sweet girl like Jewell into a class of ninety-year-old women."

A fluster. A sharp intake of breath in the broad chest. "Are you trying to come between me and my God, Essie Donnelly?"

Essie laughed out loud, a deep laugh that skipped across the yard. "Oh, no, Eloise. I'd never do that." She dipped her chin and stared at Eloise for a long moment. Her voice lowered. "How could I do that? Not to someone who has a direct line to God—not a party line, not a tin can with a string on it that reaches all the way to heaven—but a bona fide, certified direct line to God. Oh, the power you have, Eloise. You talked God into agreeing with you, agree to move a spiritual being, a bible reading Christian like Jewell Donnelly to another class, so you could be a… a star!"

Eloise's mouth grew into a thin line, her eyes slitted. Her breathing heaved her chest up and down while a red flush crawled up her neck, to her cheeks and ears. Then, a slight smile. A devil's smile. "Essie, my dear, when all is said and done, the facts remain the same: Jewell is as slow as a freight train."

The big woman turned on her three-inch heels and strutted to the car. Behind her, squawking as he ran, Killer flew across the yard and kicked his body sideways, his spurs finding Eloise Grimes' spindly legs. Her scream could be heard as far as the Mt. Horeb cemetery. So could Essie's laughter.

Jewell returned to the porch holding a fine China plate with sliced buttered rum cake arranged in a wheel, a sprig of mint in the center. "Oh, my, where's Sister Eloise?"

Essie plopped in the swing and let out a sigh. "I'm afraid she's run away, the devil right behind her."

"The devil?" Jewell glanced down the drive, perhaps looking for the devil chasing Sister Grimes. She placed the cake plate on the small table beside her chair and sat down. "I don't understand, Essie. How could she run away with the devil?"

"Oh, it's easy, Jewell. You see, when your heart is black, it's no problem to do things that are not exactly loving and kind. You ever notice how nice Eloise dresses, those expensive shoes, the make-up. She tries to hide who she really is on the inside by prettying up the outside." Essie glanced at Jewell. "Eloise's heart needs a... a tune-up. Maybe, some day, her heart will become the Christian heart it needs to be. Maybe. Maybe not."

"How did her heart become black," asked Jewell, wide-eyed, her brow wrinkling into a question.

"Who knows." Essie started laughing. "Maybe she came on a space ship or something. Maybe she's an alien."

"Oh, Essie. Mama doesn't like to hear you talk like that."

Essie felt the heat of the afternoon seep through her skin, dampen her scalp. "Jewell, why don't we go back to church?"

Jewell picked up her bible and grasped it to her chest. "I'd love that, Essie."

CHAPTER FORTY-ONE

S am met Lon Terry at his hog pen just when the sun topped the tall flat-topped cypress that flanked Grassy Pond. Misty purple clouds, shaped like big turnips, tumbled across the horizon and made one wonder what was chasing them. The heavy smell of hogs filled the morning air along with the sounds of grunting, groinking and an occasional he-hon, he-hon, he-hon.

Pony, Lon's prize Tamworth hog, stood by the fence emitting a sharp bark, indicating he was unsure what was happening to his sounder of pigs. About a dozen one-hundred-thirty-pound boars were loaded up in the back of Lon's trailer, the gate snapped shut, and the loud, grunting porkers headed off to the Madison stockyards.

On the Bellville road, Lon eased in behind Lum Townsend, whose pick-up hauled his horse trailer with his cow pony. Lum was considered the best cowpuncher around despite his stiff leg from polio as a kid. He was handsome, a thin man whose face resembled the Marlboro man, weathered like an old saddle. The two trucks and trailers caravanned through Pinetta and past Hanson where Hoot Gibson's cornfields spread far and wide. Tom Morse' watermelon sign out hung by the roadside: watermelons $1.

There was a funeral at 10:00 a.m. at the United Methodist Church for Mrs. Crews, a Madison County native whose trademark blueberry jelly was sure to get her into heaven. Along the way, pear trees hung heavy with pears and, hopefully, would make pear chutney to sell at the Down Home Days, a festival that had lured generations of Madison's citizens to watch parades, hear down-home music and, of course, eat funnel cakes and fried apples.

They passed Audrey and Clifford Leslie's farm where cows grazed on grass wet with morning dew. Fields of peanuts and corn marched in row after row along the highway and, in the distance, a farmhand cleaned out the rows with a tractor, a straw hat shading his head.

"Sam," said Lon, a hint of nostalgia in his voice, "I reckon it's been a good life for me. My ancestors came from Ireland in 1730 and settled in Savannah. I haven't wandered very far. Born in Pinetta in1892, got most all my brothers here. My sister Gladys is over in Dowling Park. Lots of good friends and neighbors. What more could I ask for?" He lit a cigarette and let the smoke trail out the truck window. "I never want this place to change. I like it just the way it is."

They rode along in silence for a while, every now and then a pig squealed from the back of the truck. "This place will change, though. Just give it time. Wasn't too long ago we got electricity. Only two telephones to be had." Lon puffed his cigarette to the end and threw it out the window.

Sam rested his arm on the open truck window and felt the winds of Madison County sweep by him, remembering the history of the '48 flood, the boll weevils devastating the cotton crops, the year-long drought of '52, the peanut boils, cane grindings and the Pinetta Indians beating Perry in basketball.

"Lon, do you remember how the school principal, Mr. Black, read this little ditty before every basketball game: *When the One Great Scorer comes to write against your name, he writes not whether you won or lost, but how you played the game.*"

Sam swallowed hard. "That's why I came back, Lon," he said quietly. "It's how we live our lives that matters the most."

"Glad to hear that, Sam," said Lon, his voice as rough as 50 grit sandpaper. "Got a letter from John, my oldest grandson. Said he'll be out of the navy soon and is coming to Madison County to live. Gonna bring his family here. Guess he thinks this is home, too. He's got a fine wife; Mary's her name. Two fine boys, little Johnny and Jimmy."

"Do I know your grandson?"

"No, don't think so. But, you might know his mama Erma. She's about ten years older than you. Could be your mama and daddy know her. She comes to visit now and then. Drives an old 1939 Ford truck over here from Jacksonville, loaded up with younguns.

"She married Jack Chamblin. I met Jack over in Gainesville when I had a little furniture store over there about 1930.

Sam rubbed his chin. "You know, I think I do know your daughter. Saw her at your store one time. Pretty red-headed woman?"

"Yep. That's her. Got freckles and red hair just like me." Lon laughed his rumbling laugh and lit another cigarette. "She's a daddy's girl."

"Rana's not her mama, is she?"

"No. Her mama is Nettie Terry, used to be a Platt. Nettie's over at the Advent Christian Children's Home at Dowling Park. A house mother for a bunch of children. Cooks and cares for them." He paused and seemed to drift away. "Nettie's a fine woman. Sorry things didn't work out for us."

The truck eased into Madison on Washington Street. "Phewee, hogs," someone yelled. Lon laughed and waved his freckled Irish arm out the window.

Before Sam and Lon arrived at the stockyards, they heard calves bawling, cows mooing and hogs squealing. It was Tuesday and everybody who lived in and around Madison County knew at 1:30 the auction bell would ring and the pandemonium of a livestock auction would begin.

The dipping and tagging of cows had begun at daylight, readied for the auction ring and the mayhem of a day at the stockyards. Cattle buyers from far and wide crowded on the edge of the ring and watched as cows ran helter-skelter around the ring, sometimes slinging their manure into the crowd.

Some of the cattle were wild, coming from San Pedro Bay. They were branded but that was as close as they got to being domesticated. Hoot Gibson pulled his old KB International truck and trailer near the ring, next to Lum Townsend pulling his cow pony, a pony trained to catch and rope cows—some thought he was the best cow pony in Madison County.

Old man Stegall, the auctioneer, rattled on for hours until almost all the livestock had been sold. Daisy Townsend and Audrey Leslie would work into the wee hours of the morning billing buyers and writing checks to the farmers.

After a long day, Lon Terry grinned at Sam. "Well, now. Them twelve feeder pigs did alright." He showed Sam a check Avanell Townsend had written for the sale of his pigs. "Guess Rana will get all this money." He smiled. "She deserves it. She's a good woman."

Across the ring, Sam saw Sheriff Moore leaning against a post on the side of the pen, the shadows of late evening touching his tall body, his hand resting on his hip. His eyes were shaded, but Sam knew the sheriff didn't miss a thing. He walked out through the exit gate and around the back of the stockyard and came up behind Simmie. "Well, did you see Durward Sapp's stolen cows?"

"Not sure. Durward had to go over to the mill early this morning. I can't tell one cow from the other."

Sam laughed. "Me, neither." He pointed to Lon Terry. "Lon's taught me everything I need to know about hogs, though."

"That right?"

Sam chuckled. "Lon said Miss Rana is going to get all his hog money."

Simmie shifted from one foot to the other. "How good are you at details, Sam?" The smell of roasted peanuts drifted across the yard.

"Details? You mean like in accounting or something?"

"No. More like noticing things—especially when they're out of sorts."

"Where're you headin' with that question, Simmie?"

"Look around the yard, Sam. See anything that doesn't belong here?" Simmie pulled a toothpick out of his pocket and stuck it in his mouth.

At least fifty people milled around the arena. Pot Grandy maneuvered his cart through the crowd selling peanuts, his goat stopping and starting on command. The stockyard lights were bright, and moths swirled around them in all directions. George Townsend and Clifford Leslie sat on a wooden bench and studied paperwork, munching peanuts and talking at the same time. Thelma Young hurried through the crowd chasing some young boys who were teasing the calves and throwing rocks at the hogs.

Across the ring, Sam's eyes lingered on Lon Terry. He didn't realize he was such a tall man. His shoulders were hunched over slightly; his big farmer's hat pulled down on his forehead. He was a proud hog farmer, and he was probably discussing Tamworth hogs with Paul Washington. From there, Sam's eyes scanned the people milling around the yard, all of them talking and gesturing with their large farmer hands.

"Heck, Simmie. I guess I'm not a detail man." Sam, frustrated, pulled off his hat with the words *Purina Feeds* stamped on the front and wiped his forehead. He licked his lips and thought about getting peanuts from Pot.

"Okay, I'll give you a clue." Simmie had a half-grin on his tanned face. "Shoes," he said.

Sam jerked back. "Shoes?" He glanced quickly around the yard. "What shoes?"

Simmie crossed his arms over his chest. He wasn't going to make it easy for Sam. "Most every farmer here has on Brogans or some work boots." He took a deep breath. "I'm thinking if somebody wore a pair of shined up, fancy tasseled shoes, they'd be out of place here in the stockyard with all these farmers, cows and hogs, wouldn't you?"

Sam raised his eyebrows while a slow smile spread across his face. "Somebody here that shouldn't be—am I right?"

"You got it. Can you find him for me?" Sam wasn't sure, but he thought he saw Simmie's fingers twitch at the top of his right pocket where his gun rested.

Simmie had never met Barnwell, but a dossier on him had arrived from the NYPD, where his mug shot had revealed a slick, dark haired man whose eyes penetrated the camera like a hot poker. Barnwell had had many brushes with the law in New York, had almost been disbarred and, now, it seemed he was spreading his discontent in Madison County.

Sam, with hyped curiosity, walked out into the crowd. He flitted along casually, whistling as he walked. Nodded at Calvin Gaston. Waved at Murray Johnson. He skirted Pot's goat and cart and eased up along the wall of the sale barn. He leaned back and pulled a cigar out of his pocket.

Then, he saw them: the slick black loafers with tassels. His eyes slowly traveled from the shoes to the man who wore them. Had to be Stanley Barnwell. He wore a long-sleeved cotton shirt, bluejeans and a bandana stuffed in his pocket, trying to look like a farmer. The man looked crisp, like he had just bought everything he wore. It was obvious he was trying to blend in with the crowd but stood out like a fox in a hen house.

Sam saddled up beside him. "Mr. Barnwell, you lookin' for me?"

Barnwell narrowed his eyes, sweeping a devilish look across Sam's face. "Sam Washington. At long last."

Sam barely nodded. Barnwell's jaws showed a fresh shave, but a shadow of black lay like a charcoal smudge. He noticed the half blue, half brown eye immediately. "That right? All you had to do was go to the courthouse and ask anybody about me." Sam gave a slight smile. "Coulda shown up at noon like I told your assistants."

Sam clamped down his jaw. "You afraid to go near the courthouse? Near Judge Earp? Near Sheriff Moore?"

Barnwell glanced over at Simmie Moore. "I'm not afraid of you farmers."

"No? Then why did you send three of your thugs out to my farm?"

Barnwell's eyes shifted over to Simmie once again, then back to Sam. "Let me make myself clear, you hick of a lawyer. That personal injury suit you filed against my brother's estate is not going to fly. My brother was murdered. No small town, crow-black, one-armed cotton-picker is going to benefit from his death. Got that?" He stepped closer, his menacing breath only inches away.

Sam didn't move. From his left, Sheriff Simmie Moore worked through the crowd and quietly reached out and touched Barnwell's arm. His voice was low and even, a slow drawl that meant business. "I'd like to have a chat with you, Mr. Barnwell."

Chapter Forty-Two

"Miss Essie, you up?" DooRay's hoarse whisper slipped through the screen at the back door, Murphy and Killer close behind. He tapped gently on the screen. "Miss Essie, I needs to talk to you."

The dim gray of early morning settled across the farm, the dew heavy and dripping from the eaves of the house. DooRay shuffled down the steps and peeked around the edge of the house, then hurried back to the porch. "Miss Essie, you gots to come," he called softly, anxiety puffing up every word.

"DooRay. You calling me?" Essie pushed open the screened door, a cup of coffee in her hand. She wore work pants and shirt, gloves were stuffed in her pocket. "Come in and get some coffee. I'm getting ready to work in my flower beds."

DooRay stepped inside the kitchen, his one hand flitting nervously in front of him, pointing. "They's a car at the end of the drive. Been there since 'fore daylight. I heard it 'fore Killer even crowed."

"A car? Who is it?" Essie rushed through the dining room and to the front windows. She saw the outline of a car in the soft mist on the Bellville road. "I see it. How long has it been there?"

"'round an hour or so. Been sitting still like that all the time."

"Well, we'll just have to see about this, DooRay." Essie pulled open a small drawer in the buffet, the buffet where all of Jewell's beautiful cake plates were arranged in neat stacks. In the drawer, her daddy's Colt .45 revolver gleamed a steel blue, its grip a polished walnut. It had been loaded weeks ago and kept on the main floor of the house.

After prisoner #458 had invaded their farm, had cut off Murphy's ear and beat DooRay with a two by four board, she would take no chances. Her daddy taught her to shoot when she was twelve years old, and she still remembered exactly how to pull the trigger.

She tucked the gun in her pants pocket. "I'll walk down the drive, DooRay. You stay here." She pointed to the hall closet. "You hear me holler, you get that shotgun out of the closet and come running."

DooRay yelped. "Oh, Miss Essie, don't make me shoot nobody."

"Don't worry, DooRay. Anybody sees you with that shotgun, they'll run."

Essie eased out the front door onto the porch. A slight sliver of sun had eased up in the east over the Withlachoochee and cast soft yellow light on the tops of the cypress trees. She watched the silent car for a few moments before she left the porch and began walking down the long drive. To her left, two squirrels skittered up a tree, bark flying out in the air. On her right, she stayed half hidden by the crepe myrtles that lined the drive, all the while keeping her eyes on the car and her hand on the .45.

At the end of the drive, she stood behind the maple tree and the detour sign and watched. No movement. Then, a realization: it was Autrey Browning's car. Slowly, Essie walked across the Bellville road. Inside the car, Autrey looked at her through the window before he rolled down the glass. "Essie."

"Autrey, what are you doing here? Why are you parked on the road so early in the morning? I thought you were somebody here to cause trouble."

"Oh, no. Nothing like that. I just came to say goodbye." His words drifted out into the gray morning, a sadness mixed in.

"Goodbye? You just got here." Essie noticed a weariness in Autrey's eyes, his face unsmiling.

Autrey looked away, south across the Townsend cornfield, then east down the Bellville road. "I know," he said, barely audible. "Just got to go."

"I don't understand, Autrey. This is your home." Essie reached out and brushed his shoulder.

"Nobody here, really. I been gone too long, I guess." He reached over and turned the ignition key. "Just wanted to see you one more time."

"Wait." Essie couldn't breath. "I... I want you to stay. Stay here in Madison County. It's where you belong."

Autrey pushed in the clutch and took the gear out of neutral. From the west, a truck barreled down the road and passed them, blowing up dust. The smell of manure settled around them as Autrey eased forward. "I can't stay, Essie. I just can't."

Essie put her hands on the car door. "Are you coming back?"

A pain shot across Autrey's face and he closed his eyes. When he opened them, Essie could see only darkness. No light. "No, Essie. I won't be back."

The car eased forward and left Essie standing in the middle of the road. The end of waiting. She watched the car until it rounded the curve toward the Withlachoochee. A stillness covered her as though she were floating in the clouds, no sounds at all. She didn't realize she was crying until she heard herself whimper, felt her knees tremble. Slowly her body eased down onto the dirt road.

"Miss Essie," DooRay whispered. "Miss Essie, you got to get up."

Essie opened her eyes to see DooRay standing over her, his one hand reaching out. "Let DooRay help you up. Come on now, Miss Essie. Git out a this here road. Car come along and run you over."

Essie reached out and took DooRay's hand. "I'm sorry, DooRay. I... I just felt... sad."

"It gone be fine, Miss Essie. Let's go to the house and get you some breakfas'." DooRay pulled her along. "Yes, mam. We git you all fed. DooRay'll help you pull weeds in your flowers. It gone be a fine, fine day."

Essie nodded slowly, then stopped. "Wait for a minute, DooRay. Let's put that detour sign out on the road. Jewell needs some company today."

DooRay hurried to the maple tree and lugged the detour sign to the road, seemingly no effort with just one arm. "Yes, mam," he called. "We's has lots of company today for sure. DooRay sure hopes we gots some a that good cake."

Essie nodded and wondered if she had checked the mail yesterday. "Maybe you should check the mailbox, too, DooRay."

"Oh, yes, mam. Might be a letter from President Eisenhower or somethin'." DooRay pulled open the box, a big grin on his face. "Nope. Not a thing in this mailbox, Miss Essie. It's as empty as some a them chicken nests out back."

The two sauntered down the long drive, DooRay humming while Essie watched Murphy and Killer chase each other cross the yard. Murphy's ear had healed, leaving him as a one-eared goat, but he was still the most handsome goat in Madison County.

On the porch, Jewell had poured her coffee and sat in her chair, her hair pulled back and held by a large clasp. Her smile was radiant. "Good morning. Where have you two been?"

Essie climbed up the steps. "Oh, just ambling around." She found the swing and called to DooRay. "DooRay, get that coffee pot and pour you some coffee. I'll cook up some eggs in a little while."

DooRay waved his arm. "That be fine, Miss Essie. Good morning, Miss Jewell. It's a fine mornin'."

"It is that, DooRay." Jewell sipped her coffee, her hands holding the cup and saucer as if she were in a palace, a queen surrounded by her court. "We must bake some cakes today, Essie."

Essie nodded and opened Peyton Place—anything to keep her mind busy. She was down to the last few chapters. Tragedy after tragedy had occurred in the small New England town, while secrets brewed behind every closed door. She didn't look up from her book. "At least two cakes, I think. Maybe three. Depends on how many eggs those chickens have laid."

"Oh, how lovely." Jewell left her chair and, on tip-toes, peered across the road to the cornfields. Her face beamed. "I'm certain Jimmy will visit today."

Essie pushed the swing and felt the beginning of tears. Always hopeful, her sister waited. How could she not know Jimmy would never come over that hill? *He'll never come back, Jewell. He's gone forever.* "I'm certain he'll want some of your wonderful cake, Jewell," she said, a quiver in her voice.

Just as Essie and Jewell took their last buttered rum pound cake out of the oven, The Gospel Hour burst forth from the radio with *Beulah Land* and Brother Wilbur and Sister Gladys's voices boomed out into radio land, their words filled with praise for their Lord and Savior. They read off the scriptures for the day and Jewell obediently opened her bible and followed along.

Upstairs, in her mama and daddy's bedroom, Essie pulled open the top drawer of her daddy's gun case where boxes of cartridges lined up neatly across the front and back. Right where she left it, the tattered one-page letter beckoned her. *Who was L. Who had loved her daddy so much? Had her daddy loved her?* When did he have time to love anyone but her mama? Many women came to the farm over the years, lovely women, women Hubert and Edith Donnelly had known all their lives.

She read the letter for the hundredth time. *Dear Hubert, please forgive me. I know my love for you is wrong, but I can't help loving you. L.*

Did her daddy love '*L*,' whoever '*L*' was? Maybe it was a love note from years ago, long before Hubert married Edith. If only there had been a date on the letter. Essie folded the one sheet of yellowed paper and placed it under a box of shells. She then thought of the many times her daddy had left for days during duck hunting season. Edith didn't seem to mind her husband's hunting expeditions, if that's what they were. *L?* Even after her mother's death, her daddy seemed to be happy. Did *L* make him happy?

Essie grilled cheese sandwiches for lunch. She sliced tomatoes and salt and peppered them along with cucumbers. There was plenty of sweet tea. She fixed DooRay a plate and carried it out to the barn. DooRay was nowhere to be found, but she heard his voice ringing high above the cornstalks. *While the dew is still on the roses* lifted high and Essie felt the joy of his beautiful voice. The man with a goat and a rooster and one arm loved his God.

After lunch and her gospel hour, Jewell left the porch and walked the stairs for her daily nap in her yellow and white bedroom. She hummed to herself and, at the top of the stairs, called down to Essie. "Essie, would you please cover up those cakes, so the flies won't get on them?"

"I'll take care of it, Jewell." Essie pulled two clean soft dishtowels from a kitchen drawer and placed them gently over the three cakes lined up on the buffet. When she looked out the window, a car moved down the drive, stopping and then starting again. Ever so slowly it eased down the lane, then stopped beneath the large oak tree by the porch. The car door opened and Mrs. Bootsey Birthright poked her head out. "Anybody home?" Her shrill voice carried across the yard. "Hello," she called again as she stepped out of the car and into the yard.

"Miss Bootsey! Hello!" Essie stepped through the porch doorway and down the steps. "Oh, my. What are you doing out this way?"

Miss Bootsey, as tiny as a bird, removed a white handkerchief tucked in the end of her sleeve. She patted her mouth and looked hard at Essie. "I'm looking for my husband. Why else would I be out here in these God-forsaken woods?" The skin on her face was as thin as rice paper, no fat to be seen on her cheeks or neck, and there was a wrinkle for every time she cussed.

Essie nodded. "I understand." She held out her hand to the small woman. "Come on up to the porch, Miss Bootsey, and I'll pour you some tea. Jewell baked a cake earlier and I'm thinking you'd like a piece."

Miss Bootsey slapped Essie's hand away. "I can walk, Essie." She hesitated, taking a moment to look around. "I don't see any petunias blooming anywhere, Essie. Your mama wouldn't be very happy 'bout that."

"Oh, there's some around back, Miss Bootsey." Essie waited until the old woman began her walk to the porch. "It's good to see you."

"Well, I won't stay long. I've got to find that husband of mine."

Essie settled the slight woman in a rocker. "Miss Bootsey, you do remember that Mr. Birthright died a while back, don't you?"

"Well, hell, yes, I remember. How could I forget something like that? I'm looking for the Mt. Horeb cemetery. That detour sign is confusing. How do I get to the cemetery from here?" Her blue eyes were sharp as they scrutinized the porch. "When's the last time you swept this porch, Essie? Looks like hogs have been up here rootin'."

Essie laughed. "No hogs, Miss Bootsey. I changed out some flower pots this morning up here on the porch." She pointed to three large pots full of periwinkles.

"I declare, you girls don't know how to keep a house or a yard. If your mama was alive, she'd be after you with a broom."

Miss Bootsey, probably Madison County's oldest citizen and long retired as the headmistress of an all-girls school in Atlanta, Georgia, lived in Pinetta. The woman was one head-strong, cantankerous woman whose most redeeming quality was her propensity to get things done. She weighed eighty-five pounds, but it might as well have been two hundred pounds. The force with which she went through life was greater than any defensive lineman on any football team at any given time.

Her pale blue suit was of high quality and almost the color of her hair; her shoes the same. Where Miss Bootsey got her highfaluting ways still mystified the most intelligent citizens of Pinetta, Hanson, Cherry Lake, Lee, Hickory Grove, Greenville and Madison. Her reputation ran far and wide. And, she had been Edith Donnelly's best friend.

"And where is Jewell, may I ask?" She lifted her tea glass after examining the slice of lemon on top as though it were a large insect.

"Jewell's napping for a short while. She baked three buttered rum pound cakes this morning."

"Your mama's recipe. Three? Why so many cakes?" Condensation formed on the bottom of Miss Bootsey's tea glass and dripped on the skirt of her suit. "Oh, damn," she mumbled.

"Oh, folks stop by here to visit quite often. Jewell likes company."

Miss Bootsey's face softened. "Jewell's mind still gone? Does she remember anything at all?"

"Miss Bootsey," Essie said, her words firm, "Jewell's mind is just fine. You don't need to worry about her at all."

From the field, Murphy bleated. "Is that a good-for-nothing goat, Essie? Lord, have mercy. You know that goat is going to eat your flowers."

"No, no. Murphy doesn't bother the flowers." Essie pushed the swing gently. "Shall I give you directions to the cemetery?"

"Not yet. I want a piece of that cake."

Essie placed a slice of cake on a lovely China plate along with a small fork. "Here you go."

"My, this is wonderful. Just wonderful." Miss Bootsey's thin fingers picked up the fork and lifted a piece of cake to her small, faded pink lips.

Essie noticed Miss Bootsey's fingernails were painted a soft rose. "Yes, Jewell takes pride in all the things she learned at the Alpin Videmanette in Switzerland. Sometimes we even have high teas right here on the porch."

Miss Bootsey almost choked. "Finishing school? What finishing school?"

Essie looked wide-eyed at the tiny woman. "Mama didn't tell you? She sent Jewell to a finishing school—the Alpin Videmanette in Switzerland when she was seventeen years old. I was fifteen and I missed her terribly."

The porch became quiet. Miss Bootsey scraped her plate, a few crumbs landing on her fine suit. "Jewell didn't go to finishing school, Essie."

Essie raised an eyebrow. "Of course, she did. She was gone a year." Essie didn't know why but perspiration popped out on her top lip.

Miss Bootsey looked out over the yard. "I'm surprised Jewell doesn't remember the baby."

Essie stilled, the swing stopping in mid-swing. "The baby? What baby?"

"Jewell's baby." Miss Bootsey's blue eyes held Essie's, an unmoving stare that made Essie shudder inside.

Essie rose from the swing slowly and sat on the edge of a chair next to Miss Bootsey. "Jewell's baby?" she whispered.

The old woman waved her hand through the air. "Oh, I told your mama to tell you the truth, but she just couldn't do it. When Jewell got pregnant, your mama sent her up to me in Atlanta. Not to any finishing school in Switzerland. It was all a lie, Essie."

The ringing in Essie's ears became so loud she closed her eyes. She couldn't get any air. She tried to suck in a breath, but it wouldn't come. Her lungs were frozen; her nostrils stuffed with cotton. Then, the scream came. Essie swiped at the air with her fist and shook her head. When she jumped from her chair, she almost fell down the steps.

"Now, Essie. It's all behind us. There's no need for you to have all this drama."

Peyton Place. I'm in Peyton Place. "I... I'm not sure you've got this straight, Miss Bootsey. Mama... mama would have told me."

"Well, she should have. She should have told Hubert, too, but she didn't. Kept him in the dark and Hubert went around complaining about all the money the finishing school cost him." Miss Bootsey took a quick breath. "Your mama sent that money to me in Atlanta to take care of Jewell. Your daddy would have had a heart attack had he known the truth."

"Where is…"

"Where's the baby?" Bootsey Birthright blotted her lips with Edith Donnelly's linen napkin. "I don't know. Immediately after the birth, it was given up for adoption."

"I don't understand." Essie's eyes welled with tears. "Who's baby? Who would Jewell have…"

"Who got Jewell pregnant? You mean all these years you never knew anything?" Miss Bootsey shook her head. "What a shame. Poor Jewell. She had the baby, came home and then near drowned. And she doesn't even remember anything—not Atlanta, not the birth." She stood and brushed off her skirt.

Essie labored to breathe, her chest heaved. "You can't leave. Who is the father?"

"Oh, I hate to tell you, dear. It doesn't matter after all these years."

"Doesn't matter," Essie screamed. "Of course, it matters." She reached over and grasped Miss Bootsey's thin arm. "You tell me right now, Miss Bootsey. Right now."

Bootsey Birthright rose up to her four-foot, eleven inch height, her face expressionless, a hint of sadness in the clear blue eyes. "Why, Essie, if I told you, it would break your heart in two."

CHAPTER FORTY-THREE

Simmie Moore walked Stanley Barnwell, handcuffed and morose, to his county car, a '56 Ford with no markings, only a small portable siren he hardly used. It was an ominous car, nevertheless. Everyone in Madison County knew Simmie Moore's '56 Ford.

"You can't do this. This is unlawful." Barnwell barked at the calm sheriff. "You have no charges against me."

Simmie opened the car door. "Slide in there, Mr. Barnwell. We'll get things settled down at the jail. I'm thinking you'll be with us at least twenty-four hours."

"Jail? You've got to be kidding. Charged with what?"

"No charges." Moore's stern look shot across to Barnwell. "Yet. Just some questions—one being why you were carrying a small revolver and why you were at the stockyard. And there're more things you'll have to settle with me."

"I don't have to tell you a thing. So, you can give me my gun back." Barnwell, incredulous, peered up at the sheriff. "Why the handcuffs?"

"I'm a cautious man." Simmie slid in behind the steering wheel and started the car. "It'd best suit me if you'd remain quiet and orderly. Madison folks are just farmers, you know. We don't like a bunch of hubbub about things."

The sheriff paused and smiled into the rear-view mirror at Barnwell. "No hubbub unless it's about a treed coon or worms in our tobacco."

Simmie had left Sam at the auction talking with Lon Terry about the stuffed animal head on the wall of his Terryville store. "No, I'm not tellin' you where I got that Dall sheep head. Let's just say it was a gift."

Sam became frustrated. "Mr. Lon, that sheep head with those big ole curved horns has been on that wall since I was a kid. Ever since then, I've been looking for those kinda sheep around here and there are none."

Lon laughed. "That's true, Sam. Those sheep are found in the Northwest territories or Alaska."

"Does Miss Rana know where you got it?"

"No, she doesn't. Let's just say it was a trade. I traded a porker for that sheep's head. I liked it and I wanted it." The Irishman chuckled, a deep raspy sound from the tall man's chest.

Sam grinned. "I'll say this—as a kid, every time I went into your store, that sheep gave me the stink eye and I hid behind my mama's dress."

The men lollygagged to Lon's truck, the check for Lon's pigs safe in his back pocket. Rana would soon be putting it in the bank and Lon would be back out in his old wooden chair underneath the oak tree, smoking his Chesterfields and eating the hearts out of about a dozen watermelons.

It was almost midnight when Sam left Terryville and saddled the lane to the Washington farm. The house was dark, and the only sounds were the occasional yelps of hunting dogs out in the pen and a calf bawling for its mama. The night air was warm and fragrant, the smell of his mama's roses much sweeter than the pungent manure at the stockyards.

Exhausted, Sam climbed the ladder to his barn bedroom, stretched out on his bed and thought about Essie Donnelly. The day before, their roll down the hill and into the Townsend pond had been upsetting. He wondered what she would have done had he not been there. Pulling her from the water had been easy, but looking for a missing Jewell had been terrifying. He shuddered to think what could have happened.

Seeing Autry Browning had been a surprise; never thought he'd see him again after fifteen years. Yet, he had appeared out of nowhere and shown up on Essie's front porch, then at her dining room table. Once a very handsome man, Autrey had seemed weathered, unfocused, like being lost on a desert, thirsty and near death. His eyes had drifted from Jewell to Essie, then to the window, maybe trying to remember something from long ago.

So far, considering the death of George Barnwell, the onslaught of his brother from New York City and the three men who had paid a visit to the Washington farm, summer in Madison County had not, in any way, been ordinary. Had it not been for his brothers, perhaps the thugs would have completed their mission at the Washington farm, whatever it was, and returned to New York. As it turned out, Bill, the oldest of his brothers, was a decisive man; it didn't take him long to determine the car at the end of the Washington lane had been up to no good.

Mike, the youngest of the brothers, had twirled his .38 like a baton. He was also a determined man, but his goal was to shoot first and ask questions later. Bill, carrying a shotgun, had known he had the upper hand, and his hard style had maintained control over the late-night showdown.

Seeing the three men run helter-skelter down the lane after Bill fired the shotgun into the air was worth a million dollars. Had their mama not hollered out for her boys to go to bed, Mike would have fired his .38 as long as it had bullets.

The inquest into the shooting of George Barnwell would be a fairly simple matter. The witnesses were credible, and the circumstances that precipitated the shooting were ironclad, Lester Terry attesting to the escape of prisoner #458. Stanley Barnwell, the deceased's big-time attorney brother, could yell foul all he wanted to, but the facts could not be changed: George Barnwell had beat DooRay Aikens nearly to death and then threatened two women with a butcher knife. And, what about Murphy's ear and Killer's tail feathers? No small matter when you're a handsome goat and a prideful rooster.

DooRay's personal injury claim against George Barnwell's estate was fairly cut and dried. Stanley Barnwell would dig in his heels in every way possible, but, again, the facts were in DooRay's favor. Both Sheriff Moore and Dr. Bush had seen DooRay's massive injuries and had no problem testifying in DooRay's behalf.

Had Murphy and Killer been able, they would have appeared in court and had a word or two to say. Instead, they had found an opportunity to butt and spur Stanley Barnwell as he threatened Essie in the Donnelly front yard.

On the verge of sleep, Sam reminded himself to ask Essie to go with him to The Suwannee River Jamboree in Live Oak on Saturday night, a chance to see little Benny Cox sing—as well as an opportunity to hold the Donnelly sister's hand, maybe even kiss the lips that he found utterly irresistible.

Had Sam not been so exhausted, perhaps he would have heard the footsteps in the barn below, smelled the gasoline that was being poured and then the sound of a match being struck. He rolled over and pulled the pillow over his head and began a deep sleep that would, hopefully, harbor dreams of Essie Donnelly.

A sharp noise jerked Sam straight up. A menacing growl that sounded like his brother Mike. He heard strange noises: a punch, a shove, a .38 revolver blasting its cartridges into the night. Sam jumped up from his bed, laid his body on the floor where the ladder leaned and looked down into the barn. He smelled gasoline. Then, the yard lights came on and the barn lit up. Mike stood over a lump on the barn floor.

"What's going on, Mike?" Sam shimmied down the ladder and looked around the barn, his heart beating a mile a minute. "Who is that?"

"Oh, I'm thinking it's one of Barnwell's men," he said, as he casually reloaded his .38, standing cock-eyed like John Wayne.

Bill rushed up behind them, shirtless and barefooted, and panting. "Mike, if you wake up mama, we're in trouble. What happened?"

"Caught this fella getting ready to burn down the barn. And I'm certain he knew Sam was in it."

"Did you shoot him? Bill squatted down and jabbed the man's shoulder.

"Naw. Didn't shoot him. Should have. He had just struck a match when I tackled him. Match went out before it hit the gasoline."

"He's bleeding on the back of his head pretty bad." Bill leaned closer.

"Yeah. Well, a harrow disc is not exactly the softest thing out there, Bill."

"You hit him with a harrow disc?" Sam looked around wildly, his eyes finding the disc a few feet away."

"Yep. That's what I did, Sam. You gonna tell mama and daddy?"

"Heck, no. But I've got to tell Simmie Moore. As far as I'm concerned, this is just one more nail in Stanley Barnwell's coffin."

Bill stood, thoughtful, and paced slowly around the barn. "Let's load him up in the farm truck and take him to Dr. Bush. Don't want him to bleed to death."

Sam nodded. "Good idea. I reckon if Dr. Bush works on our hound dogs in the middle of the night, he can work on this no-good rascal."

As quietly as they could, the Washington brothers loaded the unconscious man into their farm truck and covered him with a blanket. All three boys cringed when they heard the back screen door open. "What are you boys doing out here? It's after midnight!" The beam of a flashlight swept the truck and the three boys. "I know you're up to no good. I'm going to wake your daddy, for sure."

"No, mama. Don't wake daddy. Everything's okay. We're going to run up to Pinetta for a few minutes. Be right back."

Sam smiled at his mother through the dark. "We'll be in bed in less than an hour. I promise."

Mike sat in the bed of the truck and kept an eye on the man who tried to set fire to their barn. They drove the few miles to Pinetta, and when they got to Dr. Bush's, they banged on his front door. They heard shuffling and the big wooden door opened, a sleepy-eyed Dr. Bush squinted his eyes, reached in his pocket for his glasses and put them on. "Oh, it's you Washington boys. I suppose you're needing my help."

"Yes, sir," said Bill. "Got an injured fella out in the truck. Don't know who it is, Dr. Bush. He was trying to cause some trouble at the farm and Mike hit him over the head with a harrow disc."

"Harrow disc? Is he still alive?" Dr. Bush peered through the dark out to the truck.

Mike stepped up. "Yes, sir. He's alive. Probably just needs some stitches."

"You leave the doctoring to me, Mike. Meet me over at the office and I'll take a look."

Bill slid behind the wheel of the truck, Sam beside him, and pulled out onto the Madison highway, eased across and parked in front of Dr. Bush's medical office, right next to J. T. Woodward's store.

While they waited for Dr. Bush, Sam slipped inside the small telephone house and rang Simmie Moore. It was precisely 1:30 a.m.—anyone in their right mind would be sound asleep, but Simmie picked up the telephone after one short ring. "Sheriff."

"Simmie, this is Sam. Look, hate to bother you, but we got us another varmint trying to do us some harm. He's up here at Dr. Bush's. Mike whacked him on the head, and he's still unconscious. Thought you should know."

"Well, I'll be danged. They never quit, do they, Sam."

"You're about right, Simmie. He was getting ready to set fire to the big barn—the one where I've got a bedroom up in the loft. I'm pretty sure he knew that when he poured gasoline on everything. Hadn't been for Mike, I imagine that barn—and me—would be a big pile of ashes along about now."

The sound of a deep sigh came across the telephone. "I'll get some clothes on and head that way, Sam. All three of you boys need to make a formal statement so stick around Dr. Bush's."

"Yes, sir. We'll be waiting on you."

Sam hung up and walked out on the steps as Bill and Mike lifted the big man and followed Dr. Bush into his office. "Sheriff's on the way," he called, as the once dark office lit up. He noticed a few drops of blood on the ground leading into the medical office. *Bad blood*, he thought, as he settled on a wooden crate outside J. T. Woodward's store and waited.

People who did not honor their way of life had assaulted their peaceful community. The Washington brothers, the sheriff, his deputy, Essie, Jewell, and DooRay had all felt the brunt of violent men whose purpose had been to intimidate and harm those who got in their way. Perhaps they did not expect the courage of two women, a one-armed black man, three farm boys and a calm, but pistol-carrying, sheriff. The courage of a beautiful white goat and a proud rooster should not be ignored.

Stanley Barnwell would get out of jail in just twenty-four hours unless charges were filed. Sam wondered if the man would return to New York or stay in Madison County and continue his menacing ways.

Mike left Bill with Dr. Bush and his unknown patient and sat across from Sam. Sam smiled at his little brother. "You okay, Mike? Guess you're on cloud nine since you were able to fire your .38 until it was empty."

Mike laughed, his dark eyes twinkling. "That was quite a thrill, alright."

"Who the heck were you firing at?"

"Oh, nobody in particular. Just making sure anyone who might be around knew I meant business."

Sam chuckled, then became serious. "How'd you know somebody was in the barn?"

Mike stretched out his long legs and leaned back on a post. "That's easy. I knew those fellas would be back sooner or later. I've been sleeping in the barn every night since those three rascals paid us a visit a week ago. I woke up when you came home after midnight from the stockyards. Wasn't long before I heard someone moving around in the barn." Mike paused and looked up at the night sky where stars blinked in Galileo's Milky Way, each one shining above the fields of beautiful Madison County.

"That fella in there with Dr. Bush is not one of the three thugs who paid us a visit the other night." Mike drummed his fingers on his .38. He jumped from his seat and paced in front of J. T. Woodward's store, all the while muttering to himself. He stopped in front of Sam. "Who are these people anyway? I'll tell you who they are—they're mobsters, and they've dug their heels into Madison County soil and into the lives of the law-abiding people who live here. I say bring 'em on. We'll whip their butts!"

Mike's face reddened. He pulled his .38 and checked the load for the hundredth time. "That's the last time somebody's trespassing on our farm with intent to do harm." His voice broke, his words tumbling out like his .38 bullets. "You realize you could be dead right now? Burned up along with the barn?"

Sam stood up and reached his hand out. "Come here, little brother. Give me that gun. We're going to handle anything that comes our way, but we're not going to do it with a hot head. Simmie will be here any minute, and we'll talk with him about everything that's going on."

Mike glared at Sam, the vein in his neck throbbing. His dark eyes flitted from Sam's hand to his face. "I'll keep my gun, Sam," he said quietly.

Sam nodded. "I understand." They stood in the night, an owl hooting in the distance. Headlights swept across the storefront and Simmie Moore's '56 Ford eased toward them. They could see the outline of his face as he passed them and parked. The two brothers watched as the sheriff left his car and walked toward them, unhurried, a slow walk that said everything would be all right.

"Boys," he sighed. "It them Yankees again?"

CHAPTER FORTY-FOUR

The Donnelly farm lay quiet in the early morning, only a few birds noticed it was near daylight and began their morning ritual of a tweet here, a tweet there. The house was dark, no coffee perking, no heat in the oven. Even Killer had not acknowledged the beginning of a new day.

Essie lay in her bed unmoving, her eyes staring through the dim light at the south window. She wanted to stay in bed and sleep forever. She felt the slow thud of her heart. It was as though winter had come and her body had gone into hibernation. No warmth. No joy. Bootsey Birthright's visit had shattered Essie's soul, picked it up and thrown it into the nearby Grassy Pond, with no chance of recovery. No semblance of hope remained.

A baby. Jewell had had a baby and Edith Donnelly had never told Essie. Everything was a lie and her mama had died with that lie, leaving Essie with untruths and unknowns. There was no turning back—she could not go to the Mt. Horeb cemetery and dig up her mama's body and demand the truth. *Why?* Why did her mama think sending Jewell away was the best thing to do? Jewell could have stayed on the Donnelly farm, had the baby and lived in the cocoon of *family*.

Essie swallowed to prevent a sob from escaping her chest. She heard a noise in the kitchen, then the aroma of coffee. The sound of the oven door opening, then of running water. Her limbs, heavy and hardly moveable, pulled her out of bed and down the dark stairs to the bottom floor.

Before she reached the kitchen, she heard DooRay's soft voice. A humming, then a few words *I come to the garden alone, with the dew still on the roses.* She stopped and held tightly to the stair rail, her breath slow, gritting her teeth to keep back the tears. *He walks with me and He talks with me, and He tells me I am his own.*

She could not return to that day—the day Jewell nearly drowned, the day they found Jimmy's body in Cherry Lake, the day Autrey left, the day her mama died, the day her father died, and the day the Greyhound bus ticket was tucked away forever. She had only this moment, this time in her life with her sister and the life they shared together.

She heard the pop of frying bacon, then the cracking of eggs. She stood a moment, almost levitating, as the joy of life began to slowly fill her. It was suddenly clear that things never are as you plan them, that the inequities of life are just that—bumps in the road that sooner or later smooth out and make you the person you are.

Essie stepped into the kitchen to see one-armed DooRay mixing lard and flour for a pan of biscuits. His back was to her, and she smiled as his one hand deftly mixed lard and flour in a big ceramic bowl. He hummed as he worked, occasionally kicking out one foot in a jive-type movement. He was a happy man.

Essie wanted to giggle when he swiped lard around the bottom of a skillet and quickly squeezed off biscuit-sized pieces of dough, placing them neatly around the pan. How could this moment move her to tears, she didn't know. It was if the small things in life built upon each other into a big wagon-load of happiness—just like watermelons in the summer.

"Well, now, DooRay. I wonder what I have done to deserve your famous angel biscuits?"

DooRay turned and smiled his DooRay smile, the gap in his teeth almost comical, a place where eating corn on the cob would be precarious at best. "Oh, Miss Essie, DooRay thinks you need some of his biscuits this mornin'." He slipped the pan in the oven. "'sides, you is in need of extra happiness today."

Essie cocked her head. "And how do you know that?"

His eyes found hers, dark and knowing. "Oh, DooRay know everythin'."

Essie studied him a long moment. "I'm beginning to think you do." She sat the table. Hopefully, Jewell would approve. There were no place cards, but that was okay—everybody knew who they were and where to sit. She heard Killer crow, a long screeching crow that went all the way to the Mt. Horeb cemetery. Murphy followed with a resounding bleat.

"I'm going to sit on the porch for a minute, DooRay. I'm sure Jewell'll be down in a little bit." She poured coffee in a chipped mug that she was sure her mother would disapprove of and left for the porch.

Outside, she saw Emmett Gaston in the cornfield, his tractor puffing along. The tassels on the stalks seemed to be dancing to music as the breeze lifted them this way and that. She saw a flock of ducks headed to Grassy Pond and wondered if Ran Terry was waiting for them in the high grass at the pond.

The swing was inviting, the closed copy of *Peyton Place* nearby, waiting to be opened. Only a few chapters remained of the inglorious story of people who were trying to find their way in life. She could relate; she was one of them.

The mailman was early today. Waldo Kinsey sat at the end of the drive alongside the Donnelly mailbox sorting mail for rural route one. From the Donnelly's, he would drive to the Rob Crafton's, the Cecil Crafton's, the Charles Sims, the Talmadge Bland's, Louise Ellington, Bernard Cox, Edgar Blair, Felix Hammock, Ivy Wiglesworth and on and on until the entire small community of Pinetta had received its Sears and Roebuck catalog, *Mother Earth News* and *Progressive Farmer*, along with letters from sons and daughters, grandmothers and grandfathers and the occasional postcard from a far away place.

Sam had asked her to go to the Suwannee River Jamboree in Live Oak on Saturday night. She had thought about it for a long time; Sam Washington complicated things. His persistence had been charming, but there was no place for him in her life. Jewell was her priority and always would be.

She had decided to go to the jamboree; a pleasant outing that would be their last together. She would tell Sam, with adamant finality, that they did not have a future together. Uncle Lester was right: she was a hard woman.

CHAPTER FORTY-FIVE

D r. Davis, Pinetta's premier veterinarian, drove up to the Gibson farm well before daylight, a jauntiness in his step as he left his truck and walked to Hoot's barnyard. "Hoot!" he called. "You in there?"

Hoot Gibson stuck his head around the barn door, a cup of coffee in his hand. "Good mornin', Dr. Davis. What's got you out this early?"

Dr. Davis took off his hat and slapped his knee with excitement. "Oh, I been thinking maybe we ought to try some of that gray powder that old Miccosukee woman gave you. You know, to get your bull going in the right direction."

Hoot grinned mischievously. "Well, I never dreamed you'd be willing to try something so unorthodox. What's come over you?"

Dr. Davis joined in Hoot's laughter. "Here's the way I see it, Hoot. That fine bull deserves every chance we can give him, don't you think?"

"I won't argue with that, Dr. Davis. Poor fella has been out in the pasture bawling non-stop for his women."

"Tell you what, I don't think that old woman's magic powder will hurt him, so let's give it a try and then this afternoon around 3:00, I'll be back, and we'll turn him out with his lady friends."

The two men walked to the barn and filled a bucket with sweet grain. They emptied the small sack of gray powder on top and mixed it well. They walked to the edge of the fence and Hoot hammered on the bucket with his pocketknife. The bull swiveled its head in Hoot's direction and went into a fast trot to the fence where he knew a treat waited for him.

The big bull dove into the grain, saliva running along his gums as he slipped his tongue around his lips.

Dr. Davis looked up at Hoot under the rim of his hat. "You haven't been using that gray powder on yourself, have you?"

Hoot hollered and slapped Dr. Davis on the back. "Oh, no, Dr. Davis. Been saving it for my bull. See you at 3:00."

Dr. Davis left the Gibson farm, his dog hanging out the window daring Hoot's dog to follow the truck. Dust swirled up in the lane; behind him clouds had formed out toward Tallahassee. Probably a rainstorm before dark.

In less than an hour, all of Hanson, Pinetta, Hickory Grove and Cherry Lake knew Hoot Gibson's bull would be put to the test. The stampede to the Gibson farm at 3:00 would be history-making.

CHAPTER FORTY-SIX

T his fella's conscious if you want to talk with him." Dr. Bush came out from the back room of his clinic wiping his hands on a towel. "Mike, you sure gave him a wallop. He'll be all right, though. Might have a headache for a while. Twenty-three stitches."

"I'll talk with him for a little while, Dr. Bush." The sheriff had been waiting for an hour, along with the Washington boys. "Won't take long."

"Of course. Go on in. He's groggy, but he can talk."

Simmie nodded at Sam. "Come on in with me, Sam. Let's see what this fella knows." He looked over at Bill and Mike. "Thanks for your statements. I'll get them recorded properly and be in touch. You can go on home, now. I'll drop Sam back by the house."

Bill and Mike, weary, left in the farm truck. Mike was asleep before they pulled onto the Madison highway, his .38 tucked away, a smile on his face.

In the examination room, the sheriff's face was grim as he walked over and leaned against the examining table where Dr. Bush's patient lay. It was a no-nonsense stance that said he was in charge. The injured man's face was as pale as milk, almost cadaver-like. But, he was alive, and as long as he was still breathing, he would answer the Madison County's sheriff's questions.

Simmie had pulled a wallet from the man's pants while Dr. Bush meticulously sewed the wound together, a moan now and then from the patient. Donald Helmly, 1323 145th Street, New York City. Forty-three years old, five foot, eleven inches, 196 pounds. Eyes Brown.

Hair Brown. The driver's license did not mention he was a member of the mob and a rascal who set fires as he pleased.

Sheriff Moore tapped Helmly on the shoulder, not a gentle tap. "Mr. Helmly, I'm Sheriff Moore of Madison County. I'd like to ask you some questions. It would behoove you to answer the questions and answer them truthfully."

Helmly's eyes darted from the sheriff to Sam and then back again. A slight nod. A grimace. He closed his eyes, then opened them again.

"What were you doing out at the Washington farm? In their barn? With gasoline?" Simple questions; no chance of impropriety. Simmie stepped back and waited.

Sam leaned against the far wall and took note of the man's eyes. They were small and set close together in his round face. He could tell the man was considering whether he'd answer the sheriff's questions and if he would answer them truthfully.

Finally, the man lifted his hand and pointed to Sam. "That man over there," his words almost inaudible. He closed his eyes again, weak and certainly in pain. After a moment, his eyes opened, and he looked up at the sheriff through his weak eyes. "Barnwell wanted him dead."

CHAPTER FORTY-SEVEN

I n the early morning, Sheriff Moore and Sam met in Judge Earp's chambers at the Madison County Courthouse. Stanley Barnwell was under arrest as was Donald Helmly—both for attempted murder. Helmly's confession had sealed Barnwell's fate. Both men would face trial in Madison County and, most likely, be tried by a jury of farmers.

The inquest into the shooting of George Barnwell was scheduled for the following Monday, Judge Earp presiding. Essie and Jewell's harrowing afternoon under assault by the escaped prisoner ended in his death, a death followed by the arrival of his mobster brother, who also happened to be as vicious as his dead brother. Stanley Barnwell had no idea of the Donnelly sisters' courage nor of DooRay Aikens' bravery.

Sam left the courthouse and headed home. After a night of no sleep, all he wanted to do was climb up into his loft and stretch out for a few hours.

His thoughts running rampant, he pulled onto the Madison highway and drove north to Pinetta, to the farm that had been in his family for generations. A farm where he'd worked all his life—at six years old he had loaded watermelons into his daddy's farm truck and rode with him to market and thought he was the luckiest boy in the world.

In tobacco season, he'd hand tobacco sticks, his little hands moving quickly, his mind wishing for one of Lon Terry's cold Nehi drinks. It didn't matter how far he got away from home, his heart was always there. His dad Paul, his grandfather Will and all the cousins that ran with him through the hot cornfields playing hide and seek were as important to him as the air he breathed.

The windows were down in his Pontiac, and he listened as the black asphalt of the highway made his tires whine like a swarm of hornets. He slowed at the farm lane and parked under the shade of one of his mother's Bradford pear trees, next to the big barn. His dad was sitting on the tractor and waved at him. "Son, need to talk to you."

Sam jumped up on the wheel of the tractor, the noise of the motor running smooth with only an occasional pop and spurt. His father yelled out over the engine noise. "Dave Davis has broke his foot. All of us need to go over and help get his tobacco cropped first thing in the morning. Your mama is frying up a few chickens and baking a few cakes. I want all you boys to be up and ready to leave here by sunup."

Sam nodded. "Sure thing, Dad. Where're Bill and Mike?"

"Oh, they're snoozing a bit. Seems they were stirring up trouble last night. Your mama isn't very happy this morning at all. She said it was near daylight when they got home. She asked them all kinds of questions, but both of them were tight-lipped." He narrowed his eyes at Sam. "You know anything I should know?"

Sam lifted his eyebrows, wide-eyed. His blue eyes clouded over as he scratched the top of his head. "Not sure, Dad. I'll see what I can find out." He left his father watching him climb the ladder to his bedroom loft, a perplexed look on his face.

Around 2:30 that afternoon, every farmer within a ten-mile radius had converged on Hoot Gibson's farm. They arrived on their tractors, in their farm trucks and even a mule or two. Clifford Leslie leaned against the fence, his eyes on the big bull. He placed his hand on Emmet Gaston's shoulder. "You reckon that old Indian woman's magic powder will work?"

Emmet chuckled. "We'll find out pretty quick like, don't you think. That bull's been in mourning for a month now."

Jim Al Townsend studied the big bull for any signs of anxiety.

The big animal bawled like a freight train. "I'm thinking that fella is gonna go wild here in a minute."

John Bullard and Benton Sale walked along the fence line toward the main gate. "There's going to be a stampede for sure. Look at that bull. He's starting to snort!"

Lum and George Townsend talked quietly under the shade of a large maple. "What in the world was in that powder that Indian woman gave Hoot?" asked Lum.

George shook his head. "No telling. That old woman has been practicing her magic medicine for years."

A breeze kicked up and the bull began running along the fence line, darting in and out, rushing at the fence and the men who lined up against it. He stopped, turned around and ran to the middle of the field, pawing and huffing as his eyes scanned the far fence, the one that separated him from the apples of his eye. A little foam formed around his nostrils and mouth. He had worked himself into a lather; the heat of summer causing him to breathe hard and toss his head in the air. He flicked his tail at the flies that swarmed around him and pranced in a wide circle.

At 3:00 sharp, Dr. Davis arrived. Hoot Gibson's prize bull was to be put to the test, and the entire community would be watching.

"Howdy, folks," Dr. Davis called. "What ya'll doing here?" He grinned as he watched the massive bull for a few minutes. "Looks kinda frisky, if you ask me."

Tillman and Paul Washington eased over to Dr. Davis. "That bull is frothing at the mouth. You reckon he's all right?"

Dr. Davis pulled off his hat and fanned himself. "He's fine. Just the heat." He walked closer to the fence line and peered across the field. "Hoot, get another bucket of grain. Let's get that bull over here a little closer. Let me take a look at him."

Hoot ran to the barn and returned with a bucket of grain, held it over the top of the fence and slapped his pocketknife on the metal bucket. The bull jerked up his head and snorted. He began an immediate trot to the fence.

Hoot held the bucket while the animal ducked his head into the feed, the sound of his rough tongue scraping the sides. Dr. Davis leaned over and looked deeply into the bull's eyes, then spoke softly, a slight smile beginning at the corners of his mouth. "This bull's in love."

Hoot hollered across the yard. "Dr. Davis says this bull's in love!" He kicked up his boots and did a little jig and turned around several times. "Yes, siree! This bull's in love!"

A collective cheer raced across the farmyard. *The bull was in love.*

Hoot raced over to the gate and pushed it open, clanging the metal rail with his pocketknife. Every eye was on the bull; every man pressed tightly against the fence. Hoot pulled off his hat and waved it in the air. "Yeehaaaaaaaaaaaw!"

The bull remained motionless, licking his lips with his long, wet tongue, a few morsels of grain stuck around his nose. Then, as if in slow motion, the powerful legs began to move, a thunder of hooves as he sprinted toward the gate. The muscles in his massive shoulders rolled like the wheels of a locomotive. Dirt flung high in the air as he hammered the ground with his hooves and soared through the gate. *He was in love.*

CHAPTER FORTY-EIGHT

The sun wasn't up yet when Julia Washington hammered a spoon on a large enamel wash pan at 6:30, the sound loud enough to wake her boys. Even in the barn loft, Sam rolled over at the sound. Paul Washington had been stirring since 5:00 a.m., had gassed up the farm truck, packed his wife's fried chicken and deviled eggs in a box in the back of the truck and loaded extra straw hats for the workers at Dave Davis' farm.

It would be a hot day; the tobacco fields without shade of any kind. Everyone hoped for a stiff breeze, anything to cool their bodies from the July heat. At the Davis farm, Miss Lillian and her daughters Becky, Shirley and Francis had cooked the day before: tomatoes, okra, butter beans, potatoes, corn and, of course, a big ham or two.

Miss Lillian sent Shirley into Hanson for more sugar. Mr. Davis liked his tea sweet! Dave sat on a nearby tobacco sled, his crutches nearby. "Bobby, get some more croker sacks and put them on the inside of the sled. That'll keep the leaves from falling off."

Bobby hurried along, his daddy giving orders despite his broken foot. Dave lifted his crutch and pointed it to Queen, the family mule. "You feed up Queen real good?"

"Yes, sir! She's been fed and the tractor's all gassed up."

Frank, Dave's brother, a short, slender man, arrived with his sons Joe and Sheldon, both tall boys, strong and just right for tobacco work. His daughter, Frankie, was just as strong. She'd work alongside them all day long.

A 1940 Chevy sedan pulled in the farmyard. Miss MacMullen and her granddaughter, Patti, piled out, carrying dishes of food.

Bobby hitched up the mule to a sled, while Wally, his ten-year-old brother, hitched up a sled to the tractor. Together, they headed to the field, workers loaded on the sleds.

And the work began. It wasn't long before Queen, who had been trained to stop and start along the rows of tobacco, got tired of waiting and trotted to the end of the row. Dave hollered. "Ho, mule. Dammit, Bobby. Catch that blasted mule."

At noon, the workers piled on the sleds and rode back into the farmyard, the smell of Lillian Davis' ham and beans drifting in the air. Their bodies were wet with sweat, their arms black with tar. After little sleep, Bill and Mike Washington poured cool well water over their heads—quittin' time was a long way off.

Three large farm tables sat under the shade of a big oak tree, laden with steamed okra, fried okra, okra and tomatoes, sliced cucumbers, stewed squash, butter beans, acre peas, green beans, fried pork chops, sliced ham, fried chicken and Julia Washington's deviled eggs.

Three apple pies, pear crisps, two blueberry pies, banana pudding and oatmeal cookies lined a narrow table where buckets of sweet tea waited for the thirsty workers.

Across the farmyard, Sam sat back against a maple tree, his eyes half closed, watching the folks who sat around the tables. They'd worked hard. Together, that morning, they had cropped Dave Davis' tobacco.

After lunch, they'd return to the fields. The Davis', the Gibson's, the Washington's and many others would travel from farm to farm getting everyone's tobacco cropped and into the tobacco houses for curing. It was like life—a growing and then a curing, all the while the mixing of work and families and the joys of friendship.

Sam closed his eyes and slept.

CHAPTER FORTY-NINE

I n late afternoon on Saturday, Lester and Shelly settled on the Donnelly front porch in rockers that had been painted at least a dozen times over the years. The long day had eased into evening like a soft warm blanket, the sun setting gently in the west, only a few thin clouds pressing themselves into the orange glow of a Madison County sunset. Blue-gray shadows stretched across the fields south of the house and drifted along slowly toward the Withlachoochee River, where a quietness found only at dusk wrapped itself around the trees lining the steep bank.

Jewell sat in her chair, her hands folded neatly in her lap. "Aunt Shelly, what a lovely batch of cookies. Thank you for bringing them."

Shelly, her plumpness rather pretty, rolled her eyes. "Jewell, you'll never know how hard it was for me to keep those cookies from Lester. I had to hide them in the oven until we got ready to come over. He's the worst cookie thief there ever was."

Lester shook his head. "That is not true, Shelly, honey. I was looking for some matches, not your cookies."

Jewell laughed and chided her Uncle Lester. "I will most certainly share these cookies with you." Her lovely green eyes fell on the plate of cookies. "There's plenty for everyone."

Upstairs, Essie rummaged around her bedroom, pulled open drawers and poked around inside her closet. Sam Washington had told her he'd pick her up at 6:00. She had only ten minutes to dress, and she still had a wet towel wrapped around her. Her nervousness was apparent; why should she care how she looked when he arrived—they were just going to an ole country music show in a tobacco warehouse in Live Oak. She could wear farm clothes and fit right in with everybody else.

Frustrated, she pulled on a pair of tapered ankle-length pants. Looking in the mirror she noticed they were quite snug; when did she get those curves? She grabbed an aster blue pullover she had ordered last summer from Sears Roebuck and never worn. Its neckline was bateau, with a small button closing at the center and three-quarter length sleeves. A quick slash of make-up, a brush through her hair and a dash down the stairs brought her to the front porch.

Leaning casually against the porch railing, smoking a cigar, Sam Washington smiled at her. His blue eyes seemed riveted on her, like no one else was in the universe. It was as if the watermelon queen who had never left the farm had captured his last breath and he was dying happy, a dreamy smile on his face.

She blushed and turned away and wished she had worn bluejeans and a flannel shirt. "Hello, Uncle Lester. Aunt Shelly. So good to see you."

"Oh, Essie. How beautiful you are!" Shelly stood from her rocker. "Oh, my," she said, pulling a small bottle of perfume from the depths of her huge handbag. "You have absolutely got to have a squirt of this—it's Shalimar by Guerlain. It just came out and I bought me a tiny bottle when Lester and I went to Tallahassee." She puffed some on Essie's neck. "Now, isn't that just lovely." She grabbed Essie's wrist and sprayed away. "Yes, mam. This fabulous perfume came right from Mendelson's Department Store."

Essie took a deep breath. She was perfumed up for a night out with Sam Washington. *What the hell else could go wrong?*

Sam never moved. Just kept slow puffing his cigar and watching her through the smoke, a hint of a smile along his mouth. It would be a dangerous night if he kept watching her like that.

Shelly walked over to Jewell. "Here, honey. Let's put a puff of this stuff on you, too." A cloud of Shalimar drifted across Jewell's décolleté. "Why, now you're the sweetest smellin' thing in all of Madison County, Jewell."

Jewell closed her eyes and sniffed the air. "I can smell it, Aunt Shelly." She opened her eyes, "How lovely."

Lester jumped out of his rocker. "That's enough talk about that ole smelly stuff. How about some of those cookies?"

"Oh, Lester. Let me go make some coffee first." Shelly waddled into the kitchen.

Sam never took his eyes off Essie. "Miss Donnelly, you look ravishing this evening." He flicked his cigar ashes over the rail. "Shall we go?"

The pompous lawyer stepped forward and put out his hand. A gentlemanly gesture, but intimidating all the same. Essie hesitated while her eyes swept the man who had wiggled his way into her life. She was about to put an end to that—enough was enough.

She took his hand and he gently guided her to his car and opened the door. She slid in and he leaned next to her. In a soft whisper, "Miss Donnelly, it appears to me that I am totally at your mercy this evening." She felt his breath on her face.

"Whatever do you mean?" She looked sharply at him and frowned.

He laughed and stepped back. "That perfume, of course. You can have your way with me." He paused. "If you like." His eyes sparked like a blacksmith's hammer as he closed the car door and waved goodbye to the front porch. "See you folks later. Have a good night."

Sam drove slowly down the Bellville road past Grassy Pond where cattle egrets sat on the thin top branches of cypress, their silhouettes like clothespins on a drooping clothesline. Terryville lay quiet. He supposed Lon and Rana had closed the store for the day. He glanced up to the log house behind the store and saw them settled in porch chairs.

There was no movement in the hog pens. He rolled down his window and yelled, "Yeeee, hogs!" He heard a few loud grunts as he pulled away and sped toward Pinetta, chuckling.

"There's just something I like about hogs," he said, matter-of-factly. "Maybe it's because I like thick slices of ham and fresh collards." He looked over at Essie. "You like collards?"

Essie nodded. "I like turnip greens better, a few turnips chopped up with them." She never looked at him, her hands folded in her lap.

Sam studied her profile and saw softness, not the hard jaw line that indicated trouble was brewing. He saw tender, pouty lips that could turn into a smile with a little prodding. He turned back to the road, deciding Essie changed like the leaves, just like the women in *Peyton Place*. Just when he thought he knew her, she took off in another direction—and usually away from him.

"Ever been to the Suwannee River Jamboree?" Sam slowed at the Madison highway in Pinetta. Across the road, J. T. Woodward's store was still open, the lights in the windows beckoning. It looked like Charlie Grave's barbershop was also open, several folks sitting around the outside waiting for haircuts. He saw M. C. Herring walking with his sisters Ernestine and Thelma. Their mother, Minnie, was Lon Terry's oldest sister.

"Once or twice. Went last year with Uncle Lester." Essie unfolded her hands and brushed at a fly inside the car. "Saw Ernest Tubb."

Sam cackled. "Ernest Tubb. Oh, he's my guy! Loved his *Waltz Over Texas*." Sam drove across the highway and parked outside Jack Woodward's garage. "Give me a minute. I've got to talk to Jack about a battery."

Jack Woodward, a somewhat burly man, was washing his hands in a pan of kerosene, his sleeves rolled to his elbows. A bar of Lava soap, already smeared with grease, rested nearby. "Hey, Jack. Finishing up for the day?"

Jack grinned at Sam. "Yep. It's been a long one. Done worked on two tractors. Tillman Washington told me if I didn't get his runnin', he'd take after me with a fence post."

"Can't have that, Jack. You're needed too much around here. I'll talk to Uncle Tillman and simmer him down a little bit."

"You do that. What's got you out running around?"

Sam picked up the bar of Lava and handed it to Jack. "Wanted to ask you about a new battery. I thought I'd come by next week and get one."

Jack wiped his hands on a rag attached to a nail in the door frame. "That'll work. Come on by and I'll fix you up."

"Appreciate it. I'll be around in the middle of the week."

On the way to his car, Sam bumped into his cousin John. "Hey, John."

John reached out his hand. "Hey, cousin. Where are you going so spiffed up like that?"

"Headed over to Live Oak. Ferlin Husky's performing tonight at the Suwannee River Jamboree. Benny Cox will be there, too. Can't miss that phenomenal nine-year-old guitarist."

John ducked his head and looked over at Sam's car. "That Essie Donnelly in your car?"

Sam smiled and squinted his eyes at John. "Yep."

John grinned. "I'd say you got your hands full, Sam."

Sam left Jack's garage and crossed the railroad tracks, past the checkerboard store and the train depot where Clarence Buchanan, the depot agent, was closing up. In his rearview mirror he noticed the cucumber market was closed up for the day, as was V. S. Smith's grocery.

"Ever eat at the Dixie Grill in Live Oak?" He reached over and casually picked up Essie's hand. It was soft and cool, and he found himself easing back into the car seat and delighting in a Saturday night date with Essie Donnelly. He felt her hand twitch in his and he rubbed his thumb along her wrist.

"No."

A ride through the small town of Lee would have carried them to Live Oak easy enough. But, there was just something about a Saturday night drive through Madison that brought back memories of barbecue at Ada's and the endless cruising through town.

They drove slowly. The farms along the highway had hunkered down into a summer evening, a few tractors still in the fields but mostly put away into barns. Cows huddled beneath the sprawling branches of oak trees, their tails flipping contentedly; some stood knee-deep in the farm ponds.

"I feel like a steak. Maybe a good salad. How about you?"

Sam heard her sigh. "They have chicken livers? Fried chicken livers?"

Sam let out a yelp. "Holy cow, Essie. Fried chicken livers? What's got into you?"

She turned and looked at him. He thought he saw a faint smile on her lips. "I love chicken livers."

Sam shook his head. "I'll stick to steak."

They drove slowly through Madison. Pop Grandy, along with his goat, camped near the Greyhound bus station selling roasted peanuts. The Greyhound stopped regularly at the hotel and most everyone wanted some of Pop's peanuts.

Saturday night in Madison bustled with teenagers in their hot-rod cars, their mufflers loud to impress the girls. The smoke from barbecue tempted most everyone with a dollar in their pocket. The Saturday night cruisers drove west about a mile from Madison, looped through Ada's and then back to downtown Madison, their horns and radios blaring.

They passed through Lee, then crossed the Suwannee River into Suwannee County, where the town of Live Oak crawled with people seeking the excitement of a Saturday night off the farm.

The Dixie Grill was crowded. The smells of frying okra, pork chops, hamburgers and steak drifted out into the parking lot, where cars from Greenville, Hanson, Cherry Lake, Madison, Lee and Lake City lined up on Court Street next to the railroad track and down U. S. 90 and Dowling Street. There was no better place to eat on Saturday night than the Dixie Grill.

They got the last table, over in the corner. Sam glanced around and saw Judge Earp and his wife Gwendolyn and their son Little Judge across the room. A few tables over, Ken McLeod and his wife, Jane, leaned over in rapt conversation, Jane's fork held in mid-air. Ken McLeod was Nettie Terry's nephew.

Sam didn't miss the stares that Essie Donnelly received from across the restaurant. Of course, they stared. Her auburn hair glistened, her dark eyes mysterious, her tall, slender body carried with dignity and confidence. And the face. Serene and calm, a soft blush across her cheeks, her lips smooth and pink, she looked at no one. It was if she were all alone, unattached to those who crowded the restaurant and ate the Dixie Grill's fine food. She sat in the chair Sam pulled out for her.

"Well, now, Miss Donnelly. Let's see if they have those chicken livers. Shall we order a couple of dozen?" Sam lifted his eyebrows, a courtroom stare falling across Essie's face, sarcasm tainting his words.

Essie did not flinch. Not Essie Donnelly, the hard woman from Madison County. The hardships in her life had knitted her muscles quite firmly. It was from that hardship that she had developed her power—though some would call it a mean stubbornness. She was like a kite rising against the wind, not with it. By God, she would eat as many damn chicken livers as she wanted.

"That would be fine," she said, lifting her chin and returning Sam's stare.

At the tobacco warehouse, Sam paid their thirty-five cents each admission to the Suwannee River Jamboree and gently pulled Essie through the crowd. Posters along the walls paid homage to renowned celebrities in the country music world: Ernest Tubb, Ferlin Husky, Grandpa Jones, "Jumpin' Bill Carlisle and The Clinch Mountain Boys.

And, of course, little Benny Cox. Ferlin Husky and The Drifting Cowboys had just taken the stage, the sound of instruments being tuned. Ferlin was a handsome man, matinee-idol dark looks, with a guitar slung across his chest. The Drifting Cowboys, Hank William's band, had backed Ferlin since Williams' death and the crowd hushed as the country singer ran his fingers across the strings of his guitar. "Listen, folks. I got somethin' I want to say to you." His voice boomed out over the old warehouse as he pointed over to the edge of the stage. "Come on out here, Benny."

Benny Cox, the twelve-year-old performer from Bellville, Florida, who had been performing since age five, came on stage, hugging his guitar. Ferlin put an arm around his shoulder. "Let me tell you, folks. This here fella asked if my steel guitar player would accompany him on the song *When Hank Williams Died*. I told him I'd do better than that—the whole dang band will back up this little fella." He looked down at Benny. "You ready, boy?"

The crowd went wild as Little Benny Cox played and sang his tribute to the famous country music star Hank Williams.

Near 10:00 o'clock, Sam started up his Pontiac and found the black asphalt of U. S. 90, west to Madison, a sliver of a young moon in the western sky, Jupiter nearby. "Want to go by Yellow Pine truck stop and have some coffee?"

"No. It's late and I know Uncle Lester and Aunt Shelly need to go home."

Sam turned on the radio and kept the volume soft. "I haven't seen Autrey lately."

Essie shifted in her seat and crossed her legs. "He left for... for parts unknown."

"When was that?"

"A few days ago."

"Say where he was going?"

"No."

Sam drove a mile or two. "Do you know why he came back?"

There was a lingering quiet. Only the hum of the engine and the muffled sound of Pat Boone's *I'll Be Home*. "Nothing here for him, I guess."

Sam thought about it for a moment. In the dark, his words came soft. "He came back to tell you something."

Essie felt herself catch her breath. "How do you know that?"

Sam shrugged. "It makes sense. Why else would he come back and then leave again so quickly."

Essie never answered. In her mind, she saw Autrey at Lon Terry's store, looking at her. Then, a step toward her, his mouth open to speak, his eyes almost pleading. Then, her putting up her hand, saying *come no farther.*

His visit to the farm on DooRay's birthday. Lunch in Edith Donnelly's dining room. His car in the early morning at the end of the drive. Just waiting. He said he was waiting to tell her goodbye. Was that all he wanted to tell her? She had watched his car fade away in the early morning light, perhaps taking with him words she would never hear him say.

Madison was dark except for a few streetlights and the lights at the courthouse. The sheriff's deputy Son Stokely sat in his dark, unmarked car at the edge of town. He waited for speeding semi-trucks that did not obey the town's speed limits.

Sam turned north onto 145, driving without hurry, his window down. "Hear that train whistle? Kinda lonely, isn't it?"

"Hmmmm." Essie rolled down her window, and a breeze carried night smells that stirred memories of her childhood; the smell of cut grass and fireflies blinking in the night.

"Want to go by Cherry Lake? Listen to the frogs?"

She turned to him. "Sure. Only for a few minutes. I know Uncle Lester is already asleep in daddy's chair." She would tell him she didn't want to see him anymore. *She was a hard woman.*

They walked down to the lake's edge and stood looking across the water to the other side, where faint lights flickered. Sam leaned his head back. "Look straight up and you'll see the constellation of Lyra." He pointed upward. "See. It sorta forms a lopsided square with a tail to Vega, its brightest star."

Sam put his arm around Essie's shoulder. "Do you know anything about Greek mythology? Orpheus?"

Essie shook her head, stepped back and looked up. "No. Not a thing."

"Well, Orpheus was a great musician and was given a harp by Apollo, and it's said that his music was more beautiful than that of any mortal man. His music could soothe anger and bring joy to weary hearts. After his wife died, he wandered the land in deep depression. He was killed, and his harp was thrown into a river. Zeus sent an eagle to retrieve it and it was then placed in the night sky."

Sam reached out and lifted Essie's chin. "Look up. Straight above you. See the tilted square with the tail and the bright star at the end."

"Oh, I see it."

The air off the lake was cool and smelled of a wild freshness. Sam eased behind Essie and placed his arms around her. "Essie Donnelly," he whispered. He tucked his chin into the crook of her neck and closed his eyes. "Let's work this thing out. You and me." He heard her breathing, felt her chest rise and fall.

She was silent. Around them the water lapped the edge of the lake. A night bird skimmed across the top of the water emitting a soft call. She turned in his arms and looked up at him. "I don't want you in my complicated life, Sam. How can I subject you to the care of my sister?"

Sam leaned his head back and looked into the heavens for a long moment. He then rested his chin on top of Essie's head and held her close. "Let me make that decision, Essie."

"No, Sam. It's mine to make." She pulled away and walked back to the car. She stood and waited for him. "Let's end this now."

CHAPTER FIFTY

Sunday mornings were like no other. A peacefulness that began at daylight and lasted all day.

Jewell hummed as she placed a cup and saucer for Essie on the kitchen table. Coffee perked and already the sounds of Murphy and Killer came from the barn, followed by DooRay's clear voice. *On a hill far away stood an old rugged cross...*

"Essie, coffee's ready." Jewell smoothed her dress and straightened her hat. She called out the screen door. "DooRay, come get your coffee. It's good and hot."

Church. They were going to church. Jewell had studied her scriptures the entire week; had memorized her Sunday school lesson perfectly. Her crisp white gloves and bible were placed near the door.

Behind her, Essie came down the stairs. "Gracious, Jewell, it's only 8:30 and you're all dressed and ready to go, aren't you?"

Jewell wore a yellow dress; an overskirt of white chiffon embroidered with soft green leaves fell softly to her ankles. She looked angelic, her face beaming, a ready smile that captured her love of God. The morning sun came through the dining room window just as Jewell turned toward Essie; an image of pure perfection, the rays of light shining across her face.

Essie smiled at her sister. It was the right thing to do. Go back to church despite Eloise's treatment of Jewell. Despite the preacher's insults.

Jewell wasn't aware of their hatefulness—she was going to church to worship her Lord and Savior. She had also missed her friends, had missed the fellowship, the choir, the Sunday sermon. It would be a new day for her. A beautiful new beginning.

Essie's distaste for the hypocritical lives of some of the church members was no longer important. How could she judge them? Whatever her feelings, they should not prevent Jewell from sitting in the church pew and praying for the redemption of souls.

"I have a wonderful idea, Essie. I'll pick a few roses to take to church. Won't that be lovely? Maybe give them to Louise Ellington."

Essie poured her coffee. "I know Louise would love them, Jewell. The pink ones at the east side of the house are in full bloom; watch out for bees.

Essie climbed the stairs with a troubled mind. Her dismissal of Sam the night before had been her decision, a well-thought-out decision that required the hardness for which she was known.

There was no need for debate. As Jewell's caretaker, Essie had room for just the two of them. And, of course, DooRay. They were just fine as they were. No need to complicate things any further. Let Sam Washington find a woman who was footloose and fancy free, no strings attached, no 300-acre farm to worry about.

She leaned against the wall in the hallway and felt the tears come. Hot, heavy tears that raced down her cheeks. *She loved Sam Washington.* She wanted him near her, wanted him to sit with her on the porch swing, wanted him to tell her about the stars. *Oh, my god. What have I done?*

Her body slid to the floor. And, there in the darkened hallway, it all came apart, all the hardness falling away like the melting of snow. All that remained was a soft woman, a woman whose heart wanted to be whole. *I love you, Sam Washington.*

The noise was a mixture of sounds: a thump, loud voices, DooRay calling. "Miss Essie. Miss Essie. You got to come."

Essie stumbled down the stairs, her hands grabbing for the banister, her heart thudding. "I'm coming, DooRay."

She tore through the front door, onto the porch, gasping for breath. She saw DooRay running down the lane toward the Bellville road. "Oh, Lawd. Oh, Lawd. What done happen to Miss Jewell?"

"Jewell!" Essie's scream tore through the branches of the oak trees, up high to the soft blue sky and into the white clouds that moved softly above Madison. "Jewell!"

The yellow dress. The yellow dress was all Essie saw as she ran down the lane, her bare feet pounding into the dirt, her arms flailing as she pumped her body as hard as it would go. "Jewell," she called. Her lungs burned, and her legs stung with pain as she staggered onto the road. "Oh, Jewell," she whispered as she fell into the soft dirt and leaned over her sister.

"Jewell, baby. I'm here." Essie pressed her cheek against Jewell's face. "I'm here, darling. I've got you. You're gonna be just fine, Jewell."

"Miss Essie, we gots to call an am'blance." DooRay hovered over her, his one hand resting on her shoulder.

"Yes, DooRay. You go on in the house and call." Essie looked up and saw one of the Walker boys sitting on the side of the road watching her, his truck sloped sideways into the ditch.

"Miss Essie, Jewell ran in front of my truck. I couldn't stop. I'm so sorry. So sorry." He put his face in his hands and sobbed.

"Jewell, baby. Can you hear me?" Essie rubbed her fingers lightly across Jewell's cheek.

Jewell stirred, her eyes opening, a smile forming. "Oh, Essie. I saw Jimmy. I saw him at the top of the hill. I wanted to carry him some roses. Some of mama's beautiful pink roses."

Essie watched the color slowly drain from the beautiful face. Saw her sister's eyes turn toward the hill. "Oh, Essie," she whispered. "There he is again. Waving at me. He wants me to come with him to the pond. Maybe swim a while."

Jewell's smile widened, her eyes ever-watching the hill. "I'm coming, Jimmy. I've got some lovely pink roses for you."

Essie held Jewell's body until Dr. Bush gently touched her shoulder. She had rocked her for over an hour and whispered to her about the times they had shared together as sisters. About the hours spent on the front porch, about making their mama's buttered rum pound cake, about the scriptures, about their mama's recipes and their daddy's cigars, about the farm, the watermelons, the corn, the cows, the chickens and the beautiful fields of tobacco that ran clear to the Withlacoochee River.

One last whisper into Jewell's ear. That's all she wanted. One last touch on the beautiful cheek. "Thank you, Jewell, for loving me just the way I am."

CHAPTER FIFTY-ONE

It was a perfect day for a funeral. Cool air from Canada had made its way south and teased Madison County into thinking fall was on the way. The farmers knew better; they knew it was a fleeting coolness that would disappear as quickly as it had come.

Essie had left the Mt. Horeb church quietly by the side door. She would return to the gravesite later in the day, in the quiet of late afternoon. She'd talk to her sister and tell her about Murphy eating DooRay's hat. About Killer finding another snake, a garden snake this time, and carrying it to DooRay for his approval. She'd also tell her about Emmet Gaston's foot slipping off the brakes of his tractor and him running through the fence north of the house.

She'd tell her how lonesome the front porch had been without her. How she'd left everything on the porch just as it was. The big chair with the floral cushion, the table with her bible on it, her prissy teacup, her fragile handkerchief with the tatting on it and her initial J.

She'd tell Jewell she wanted to make some buttered rum pound cakes, but couldn't seem to remember the recipe. *How many eggs, Jewell, should I put in the cake?*

The afternoon faded away and the shadows of a setting sun crept along the fields; Essie had closed and locked the gate at the end of the drive for the first time in years and lay down in the swing. She could not pull her eyes away from Jewell's chair, hoping any moment, somehow her sister would call down the porch to her: *Essie, I do declare, what a beautiful Lord's day it is.*

CHAPTER FIFTY-TWO

The inquest into the death of George Barnwell had proceeded on schedule, despite Jewell's death. Essie and DooRay had appeared in court on the 16th as planned and completed their dispositions on the circumstances surrounding Barnwell's death.

Judge Earp conducted the inquest based on the written testimonies of Jewell, Essie and DooRay. As their attorney, Sam Washington provided all the required information as efficiently as Judge Earp had ever seen in his courtroom. Stanley Barnwell remained in jail awaiting prosecution for the attempted murder of Sam Washington.

Sam Washington's personal injury claim against the estate of George Barnwell on behalf of DooRay Aikens had been elevated to a higher court. Sheriff Simmie Moore, his deputy Son Stokely, Dr. Bush, as well as Essie Donnelly provided substantiated proof of George Barnwell's misdeeds. It would be a drawn-out process, but Sam's tenacity would win out.

Sam had driven by the Donnelly farm numerous times, only to find the gate closed and locked. He leaned against the gate late one evening and talked with DooRay, who had been fishing in Ran Terry's pond.

"Oh, Miss Essie done cried herself to sleep ever' night, Mr. Sam. I's hear her along about midnight. She walkin' the yard, walkin' the porch, layin' out on the swing all night. That girl done lost wit'out her sister."

CHAPTER FIFTY-THREE

Almost two months after the funeral, September eased across the Donnelly farm and found Essie raking oak leaves around the azalea bushes. A breezy day, she had tied her hair back with one of her daddy's big handkerchiefs. Her gloves were his, too.

She looked up when a car horn sounded at the end of the lane. Waldo Kinsey waved, his hand full of mail. "Got a certified letter for you, Essie. You got to sign for it."

"Coming," she hollered and leaned the rake against the side of the porch and look off her gloves. The lane was dusty, no rain for a week. She sifted through the dirt, passed Killer and Murphy, both uninterested in the daily mail delivery.

"Hello, Waldo." She wiped her hands on her pants. "Where do I sign?"

"Right here, Essie. On this line." His bony finger pointed to a heavy black line.

Essie dutifully placed her signature in the proper place and looked up at Waldo. "Thank you. Want some iced tea?"

"Oh, no, Essie. I'm late on my route today. Them dad-blamed magazines done loaded up my delivery. Why, I ought to burn every one of them. 'specially, those seed catalogs. They're so heavy my arm aches ever' night when I go to bed."

Essie nodded and smiled. "You take it easy, Waldo."

The walk back to the house seemed to take forever. Essie stuffed her certified letter in her pants pocket and sorted through the rest of the mail. Just like Waldo said; a seed catalog. Two cards, probably sympathy cards.

A letter from an unknown address in Texas. She knew no one in Texas. She fingered it carefully. The handwriting seemed familiar somehow. She stopped midway down the lane and slowly sat down on the cool dirt. Her hands shook, her fingers not working.

Midland, Texas. So many miles away. She gently tore open the seal and pulled out a two-page letter written on lined paper. Blue ink from a fountain pen filled the page with small, rounded letters, seemingly written hesitantly, slowly. The letters were precise, perfectly spaced. The writer had labored patiently; there were no smears, no crossed-out words.

Dearest Essie,

The words in this letter are words I should have spoken to you on that last morning on the Bellville road. My heart was too sad to say to you the things I needed to say. So, here I am at the end of my life and wanting to make things right with you.

Yes, I'm at the end of my life. I knew I was ill while in Pinetta for that short while. I did not discover the extent of my illness until a few weeks ago. It seems I'm in the last stages of tuberculosis. I've gone untreated and it's too late now. I'm sorry to have to tell you this.

When I came back to Madison County after fifteen years, it was to set things straight with you. To tell you why I left so suddenly so long ago. It is a sad story, but you deserve to know the truth, though I don't want to harm your life in any way.

Jewell had a baby when she was seventeen—my baby. We didn't mean for it to happen. It was a foolish moment in our lives and we both regretted it deeply. When your mother found out, she sent Jewell to Atlanta to have the baby. She banished me from Madison County; said she'd have me whipped and quartered if I ever came back.

Being a young man, I fled and put it all behind me. In looking back, it was an immature thing to do. But, we were so young. It seemed at the time there was no other choice.

I anguished over being unfaithful to you. And, now, after all these years, I must ask your forgiveness.

I don't know what happened to the baby; I choose to believe he or she grew up in a loving, caring home.

I'm not sure Jewell remembers anything about us, about the baby. It seemed when I visited that she was unaware of her past with me.

Be happy, Essie. It looked to me like Sam Washington was smitten with you.

Love forever,
Autrey

Long after Waldo Kinsey delivered the mail, Essie remained sitting in the dirt, silently watching rain clouds approach from the west, tumbling like big herds of buffalo. She heard far-away thunder, then felt cool winds sweep past and scatter oak leaves across the lane.

She clutched Autrey's letter to her chest. *A raindrop will smear the blue ink*, she thought. The words lost forever.

"Miss Essie, Murphy and Killer done run to the barn. You best run, too. Rain done headed our way, for sure."

Essie glanced back to the house. Saw DooRay on the porch, waving at her. "Come on, now, Miss Essie. Let's get you up outta that dirt."

Essie heard him, but could not seem to move. Her limbs were heavy, like wet fence posts. The remnants of seed catalogs blew around her, a flyer from Western Auto. Then, DooRay's one hand under her arm, lifting her. "Come now, Miss Essie. I done made you a hot cup of tea, plenty a sugar in it."

DooRay pushed Essie along, his hand placed gently on her back. *"Oh, I got a home in Dixieland that outshines the sun. I gotta home in Dixieland that outshines the sun, way beyond the blue.* That's it, Miss Essie. Up those steps now."

The black man hummed across the porch, pushing Essie all the way to the swing. 'Now, just sits right here and I's get your hot tea." He covered her with Jewell's soft blanket and tucked a pillow behind her back.

Essie closed her eyes, the letter still in her hand. *Autrey was dying. He was the father of Jewell's baby. Her mother knew and never told her.*

Essie slept through the night on the porch swing. DooRay sat up in a nearby rocker until daylight. He heard Killer crow and then a long mournful wail from Murphy, a sound that carried over the farm like an out-of-tune bugle.

The sun pushed up over the horizon, its rays finding the porch for only a few moments before moving over the top of the oak trees. Essie opened her eyes. She saw Jewell's empty chair and the teacup and saucer. DooRay's song of the morning was *Beulah Land*, his favorite hymn. The words rang out like a mighty choir. Not only was DooRay singing but Murphy and Killer had also joined in.

Essie sat up, stiff and sore. The letter. It was still in her hand. She folded it carefully and placed it inside the cover of *Peyton Place. The summer was ending,* she thought. There would be no end to the seasons, nor the winding Withlacoochee. The leaves would eventually turn, and Emmet Gaston would plow the earth and ready the fields for next year.

In the swing, Essie opened the two sympathy cards Waldo Kinsey had delivered the day before—one from Savannah and one from Thomasville. The return address on the Thomasville postmark was from Rosaleigh Gramling. Rosaleigh had moved to Thomasville eight years ago, right after Hubert Donnelly had died. She was born and raised in Pinetta, went to school with Edith and visited the Donnelly farm often.

Essie brushed her fingers over the front of the envelope. Oddly, she felt a prick of memory. The handwriting was in lovely blue ink, slanted and written with a distinct flourish.

She ran her fingers along the back of the envelope and pulled out the card. Across the front, in embossed letters: *My Deepest Sympathy.* Sweet red roses swept along the edges of the card. Essie opened it and began reading Rosaleigh's note.

> Dearest Essie,
> I am so saddened to hear of the passing of Jewell. I know your heart is broken and I pray that God gives you peace and understanding.
> Fondly,
> Leigh

Leigh? The mysterious *L* in the love note to Hubert Donnelly. The

Donnelly's had always referred to her as Rosaleigh, but now, after all this time, Rosaleigh had become *Leigh*.

Essie was certain the handwriting on the card was the same as the writing on the love note. She tucked the card back into its envelope where it would stay. She'd never know the extent of Leigh's love for her father, nor would she ever know her father's feelings for Leigh.

She left the swing and sat on the porch rail. Her eyes followed the lane to the Bellville road. The gate had been closed since the funeral—almost two months. Perhaps it was time to open it. In wrinkled bluejeans and shirt, dirty bare feet, she walked the lane to the road and unlocked the gate. She pushed it open and felt the slow unleashing of her heart.

The Bellville road was smooth from the previous late afternoon rain. No ruts from cars or trucks. The dried corn stalks in the Townsend field swayed in the breeze, as if waving their last goodbye to the summer.

Essie leaned on the fence and saw the detour sign. She studied it a long moment and then smiled. It had been a glorious summer.

She turned to walk back to the house and felt something in her pocket. The certified envelope. It was from the Thomas H. Fox Literary Agency—most likely a rejection of her manuscript. She sat at the bottom of the big maple tree and opened it.

CERTIFIED LETTER

September 22, 1956

Miss Esther Elizabeth Donnelly
Rural Route 1
Pinetta, Florida

Dear Miss Donnelly:

It is with pleasure that the Thomas H. Fox Literary Agency accepts your manuscript *The Watermelon Queen of Madison County* for publication. Our publisher, The Viking Press, has approved a $10,000 advance for the publication rights.

Our editors, as well as myself, find your work fresh and compelling. We feel your writing skills are superb for a first-time author. We are excited about your writing career and extend to you every encouragement to pursue your writing.

We have enclosed a contract, which we'd like you to read and sign. Upon receipt of the signed contract, we will forward your check for $10,000.

At some future date, after signing the contract, we would like for you to visit our offices in New York to discuss future works as well as provide input on *The Watermelon Queen of Madison County's* cover and other details regarding publication.

Please feel free to contact me should you have questions.

Most sincerely,

Thomas H. Fox, President
Thomas H. Fox Literary Agency
1495 Park Avenue
New York, New York

There it was—the bus ticket out of Madison County—an acceptance letter for her manuscript. She closed her eyes and felt the peace of early morning. If she breathed softly, perhaps she could hear geese over in the Townsend pond. She opened her eyes and saw a pink sky to the east. Then, a flock of wild geese flew south, their honking almost melodic.

She stood from the tree and found the soft dirt of the lane. She lingered a moment in the quiet morning. Her gaze found Jewell's bedroom window and she almost waved, her ears listening for her sister's sweet voice. The smell of wood smoke drifted in the air, hazy furls lifting on the far side of the barn, DooRay cooking his breakfast.

The porch beckoned her, told her there was love waiting there for her. Slip yourself in the swing and sing a little song. *Mammy's little baby loves shortnin', shortnin'; mammy's little baby loves shortnin' bread. Put on the skillet, slip on the lid, mammy's gonna make a little shortnin' bread.*

She climbed the brick steps and settled back into the swing. She heard a soft bleat from Murphy; he was Madison County's most beautiful, one-eared goat. She was sure he was curled up near DooRay, as was Killer. Essie pushed the swing and felt it glide across the porch, a soft creak in the chain.

From the drive, a car eased slowly down the lane. Sam Washington. She watched him park and walk across the yard to the porch. It was a lazy walk, a cigar between his thumb and forefinger. He wore his Panama hat tilted to the side. She had seen no one since the funeral; it had been a healing time.

He said nothing to her as he sat in a rocker and propped his feet on the porch rail. He puffed on his cigar and leaned back. "How many eggs you get outta the hen house yesterday?"

"Fourteen."

"Fourteen," he repeated. "That'll make two buttered rum pound cakes."

Essie said nothing.

"Got plenty of butter?"

"Yes."

Sam pointed to the side yard west of the house. "That pear tree's loaded with pears. You wouldn't happen to have a recipe for canning pears, would you?" He tapped the ash off the end of his cigar into the pot of periwinkles.

"I do."

"Reckon you got enough sugar. Takes a lot of sugar to can fruit."

"Yes."

A sharp wind whipped up and rattled the corn stalks across the road and in the field down from the house. Somehow it spoke of change, perhaps a foretelling of some kind that made one sit up and listen.

"Want to go to church with me Sunday?" Sam turned his head and looked over to the swing at Essie. He was smiling, the silly cigar poking out of his mouth, clenched in his teeth.

"Yes," said Essie.

"You reckon we ought to pull that detour sign out to the road?"

Essie lifted her chin and her eyes found the lane to the road, the road that led to a lifetime of memories in a place called Pinetta. She thought of the Crafton's, the Townsend's, the Ellington's, the Terry's, the Keeling's, the Washington's, the Gaston's and all the families who had settled in Pinetta and the surrounding towns; families who had been linked to each other since Ireland, England and Scotland, who had filled the churches, who had farmed the land and who had found in each other the value of family and friendship and the joy of knowing the simplicity of hard work and its ability to build character.

This was where she wanted to be. Essie turned and looked at Sam. "The detour sign?"

Sam nodded and puffed on his cigar. The porch seemed to wrap itself around the small-town lawyer as he melted into its memories, its history and had, just at this moment, become a part of its future. "I figure I'd help you bake those cakes."

Essie stared at Jewell's empty chair and then looked out to the hill across the Bellville road. The morning sun had set it afire with yellow light and, there in the soft rays, Essie thought she saw Jewell and Jimmy holding hands and laughing as they ran toward the sun. She blinked, and they were gone.

Essie scowled. "What makes you think you know how to bake a cake?"

Sam took the cigar out of his mouth. "I reckon you can teach me."

"That right?" Essie found herself smiling at the Pinetta farm boy. "Why don't you come over here and sit in the swing with me?"

At that moment, DooRay's voice lifted high into the sky above the Donnelly farm. *I got a home in Gloryland that outshines the sun... way beyond the blue.* Murphy's bleat shook the barn rafters while Killer's crow was as melodic as the choir at Pinegrove Baptist.

"Well, now," said Sam as he ambled over to the swing. "I do believe Essie Donnelly has at last succumbed to my charm."

THE END

ABOUT THE AUTHOR

Author Sue Chamblin Frederick. She is known as a sweet Southern belle, a woman whose eyelashes are longer than her fingers, her lips as red as a Georgia sunset. Yet, behind the feminine façade of a Scarlett-like ingénue lies an absolute and utterly calculating mind—a mind that harbors hints of genius—a genius she uses to write books that will leave you spellbound.

A warning! She's dangerous—when she writes spy thrillers, she's only six degrees from a life filled with unimaginable adventures—journeys that will plunge her readers into a world of breath-taking intrigue. Put a Walther PPK pistol in her hand and she will kill you. Her German is so precise, she'd fool Hitler. *Her amorous prowess?* If you have a secret, she will discover it—one way or the other.

When she writes romance, her readers swoon and beg for mercy as they read her seductive stories about luscious characters. Be sure to have a glass of wine nearby as you snuggle up to her books about love.

The author was born in north Florida in the little town of Live Oak, where the nearby Suwannee River flows the color of warm caramel, in a three-room, tin-roofed house named 'poor.' Her Irish mother and English father's voices can be heard even today as they sweep across the hot tobacco fields of Suwannee County. "Susie, child, you must stop telling all those wild stories."

The author lives with her Yankee husband in the piney woods of north Florida, where she is compelled to write about far-away places and people whose hearts require a voice. Her two daughters live their lives hiding from their mother, whose rampant imagination keeps their lives in constant turmoil with stories of apple-rotten characters and plots that cause the devil to smile.

THE DONNELLY SISTERS

BUTTERED RUM POUND CAKE

1 cup butter, softened
2 ½ cups of sugar
4 large eggs
3 ¼ cups all-purpose flour
1 teaspoon baking powder
½ teaspoon baking soda
1 teaspoon salt
1 cup of buttermilk

Butter/Rum Sauce

1 cup of sugar
½ cup of butter
¼ cup of water
¼ or ½ cup of rum

Cake:

Cream butter until light and fluffy. Gradually add sugar and beat at medium speed for five minutes. Add eggs one at a time, beating well after each.

In another bowl, combine flour, baking powder, baking soda and salt. Whisk until blended.

Add dry mix to butter mix, alternating with buttermilk until well blended. Stir in vanilla.

Use a 10-inch tube pan or a 12-cup Bundt pan. Grease and flour well. Poor in batter. Bake 325 for one hour.

Cool in pan on wire rack for 15 minutes, then transfer to cake plate to cool completely. Once cake is cool, return to baking pan and prick holes at 1" intervals with a wooden pick or skewer.

Pour 2/3 of sauce mixture over cake and allow to soak in for about 15 minutes. After 15 minutes, remove cake from pan again and pour remaining butter rum sauce over cake.

Sauce:

Combine sugar, butter and water in a small saucepan and cook over medium heat until sugar melts. Stir constantly. Once thickened, remove from heat and stir in rum.

A Good Year for Roses

A Novel

BY SUE CHAMBLIN FREDERICK

She'd get on that damn train. Catch the Atlantic Coast Line coach at 3:59 p.m. and travel east to Waycross, then northeast to Savannah. At Savannah, she'd say goodbye to Georgia as she boarded the *East Coast Champion* and arrived at New York's Grand Central Station at 11:45 a.m.

The Thomas H. Fox Literary Agency had proclaimed her the fresh, new voice of the South, her novel *The Watermelon Queen of Madison County* slated for release on November 1. She'd never heard of the Hudson Theatre, the same theatre where Elvis had performed the previous July, where Mr. Fox had made elaborate arrangements that would surely propel her to stardom.

Mr. Fox had also made a reservation at The Premier Hotel, just off Times Square, on 44th Street, where she'd stay at least a week promoting her novel. It was true Mr. Fox was enamored by her Southern charm. Said he'd like to see her novel adapted to a Broadway play. *The sky's the limit*, he had said.

And why shouldn't she go to New York? Leave Madison County. No family left, except Uncle Lester. Jewell's grave still fresh. Sam Washington busy putting Stanley Barnwell in prison for attempted murder.

She'd been up since daylight. Packed two fancy dresses, some of her mama's jewelry and Jewell's cashmere sweater. At the top of the stairs, suitcase beside her, she closed her eyes, her breath coming quickly, her heart pounding into the word 'no.' She shoved the suitcase down the stairs and watched it tumble end over end.

Oh, hell. No way I'm going to New York City. Come on, Jewell, let's go find your baby.